JERRY GRAHAM'S

San Francisco

ALSO BY THE GRAHAMS:

Jerry Graham's Bay Area Backroads (Revised Edition)

Jerry Graham's More Bay Area Backroads

Jerry Graham's Bay Area Backroads: Food and Lodging Guide

Jerry Graham's Complete Bay Area Backroads

JERRY GRAHAM'S

San Francisco

BACKROADS AND BACKSTREETS

Jerry & Catherine Graham

HarperPerennial

A Division of HarperCollins*Publishers*

HarperCollins books may be purchased for educational, business, or sales promotional use. For information please write: Special Markets Department, HarperCollins Publishers, Inc., 10 East 53rd Street, New York, NY 10022.

FIRST EDITION

Designed by Irving Perkins Associates

Library of Congress Cataloging-in-Publication Data
Graham, Jerry, 1934–
   Jerry Graham's San Francisco: backroads and backstreets/ Jerry & Catherine Graham.
     p. cm.
   Includes index.
   ISBN 0–06–273406–7
   1. San Francisco (Calif.)—Guidebooks. I. Graham, Catherine, 1955– . II. Title.
F869.S33G73 1997
917.94'61045.3—dc20   96-33298

97 98 99 00 01 ❖/RRD 10 9 8 7 6 5 4 3 2 1

To Lillian

Contents

PART 5

Lodging and Special Occasions 197

Introduction

Welcome to San Francisco! Now get lost!

No offense, but that's the idea of this book. It's all about the simple plea-sure of getting lost and finding new discoveries. Use our destinations as starting points for endless adventures in the city.

There are many reasons San Francisco is called America's favorite city. Whether you're coming from across the continent, the bay, or just across town, you are in for a treat. The city (as you know, you never call it "Frisco") is a wonderland filled with impossible hills, breathtaking views, and colorful, exotic people.

I'm often asked, "So where do you go in San Francisco? What do you like to do?" I'm best known for my travels outside San Francisco, on the Bay Area's back roads, but inquiring minds still want to know some tips on how to spend time in the city that is the hub of the Bay Area. The purpose of this book is to help Bay Area residents and visitors who shun the term "tourist" to enjoy and appreciate the magic of this special place.

This is not a typical tourist guide. First of all, it's highly selective. I include places I enjoy and want you to know about, as if we were sitting around a coffeebar and chatting casually. I make no claim to offer a comprehensive view of every neighborhood and every public attraction. There are many very good guidebooks that do just that. For some, too much information can be overwhelming. So I have tried to weed out places that are overrated, like Fisherman's Wharf; overrun, like much of Haight Street; and overly obvious, like Union Square or Alcatraz. Instead I concentrate on offering personal rec-ommendations. Most of all, I hope to give you some ideas that will set you out on your own explorations.

This book assumes that you are somewhat familiar with San Francisco. If you're from out of town, you've probably been here before. If you are a Bay

Area resident, you probably have taken out-of-town visitors around to places like the Golden Gate Bridge and Union Square. Hopefully, your vistas are about to be broadened.

As for the term "backroads," a bit of explanation is in order. I am referring to a state of mind as much as a specific location. The idea is to explore new territory, which might be way off the beaten path or might be just a floor above or around the corner from a better-known destination. Sometimes it's just a quick discovery that becomes a lasting memory. For example, while heading to a meeting at a remote location on the waterfront, I came upon the Japan Fish Club at Eighteenth Street, just beyond Third Street. My curiosity was piqued enough to stop the car and see what the club was all about. Inside was a friendly man behind a simple fish counter. When I asked him what kind of club it was, he said, "I got fish, you're in the club." The entire exchange took about a minute, but we both laughed, and it was one of those moments that just happen when you allow yourself to roam.

The method in doing this is more important than the actual roads or streets. "Backroads" also refers to a pace of exploring. Don't try to plan much in one day. Save time for just hanging out. This is not for the tourists who I overheard at lunch one day: She: "When are we going to Tahoe?" He: "Friday." She: "Then we better finish the city this afternoon and do the Napa Valley tomorrow." The book is for people who like to linger awhile and get to know a place before moving on to the next stop.

In researching this book, my wife Catherine and I would drive to various parts of the city and then free ourselves of the car as soon as possible. If you work around the hills, San Francisco is an easy walking town. In the act of strolling, you will see things in a new light. Sometimes we'd go alone and wander around, talking to folks about their neighborhoods, or sit in a park or café to watch and listen. If we got lost roaming around town, all the better—it usually led to a new discovery. Fortunately, San Francisco is small enough to allow hopping around from one neighborhood to another in short periods of time, traffic and parking permitting.

We'll give you as many convenience tips as our experience allows, like where to park, when to ditch the car, how to get to know a neighborhood, best times to go, best times to avoid, and so on. We'll also try to save you money. One way is suggesting that you try to plan trips on Wednesdays or Thursdays, when many attractions that normally charge admission offer once-a-month free days.

This is basically a daytime guide. San Francisco has the nightlife and cultural activity that you expect from a world class city. There is quality theater, symphony, opera, and ballet and a movie climate that encourages exhibitors to show almost every film here. Every major rock tour stops in the area, and all major sports are represented. Of course, there are always detractors. One memorable night Catherine and I were at the symphony when it was announced that the program would be changed; the Brahms would precede rather than follow the Bach. The disgruntled patron behind us groused to her half-awake spouse, "Once the Barbary Coast, always the Barbary Coast."

To plan your evening's entertainment beyond dinner, we recommend checking the listings in the local newspapers to see who and what is playing where. The pink sheets of the Sunday *Chronicle* are fairly extensive, but we also suggest picking up the *Bay Guardian* and *SF Weekly* to see some of the more avant-garde attractions. Sometimes, simply reading the listings of various acts is entertainment of itself. For example, one recent listing at the Elbo Room promised Engorged with Blood, Hermaphrodaddy's, Broun Fellinis, DogSlyde, and Mingus Amongus.

A good place to start getting to know the city is where thousands of visitors begin, at the San Francisco Convention and Visitor's Bureau, which is opposite the BART station in Hallidie Plaza below Powell and Market. An average of more than $13 million a day is spent by tourists in San Francisco, so the bureau goes out of its way to make them feel at home. We locals might as well take advantage of this resource, too.

Here you can pick up some valuable free material, such as a good map of the city with bus, trolley, and cable car routes, an updated book of hotels and inns (those who are members of the bureau), and tons of brochures advertising various guided and unguided walks and shopping tours. You can also buy Muni Passports here, giving you unlimited travel on public transportation for one day, three days, or a week. Warning! If it's summertime and therefore the heart of the tourist season, don't go there in the morning.

There are usually lines outside the door. Wait until the afternoon, or better yet, visit during other times of the year.

The politically correct thing to do would be to tell you not to drive into the city. There is a very good public transportation system available, whether it's BART, bus, ferry boat, or rail. And once in the city, there is an extensive network of buses, trolleys, and cable cars available. There are also several taxi services. By all means, use public transportation if you can. But at the same time, we've got to be honest. Just like all those other Bay Area residents who jam the freeways and bridges, we like to have our car available for spontaneous decisions and for the ability to hop around the city when we feel like it. Not exactly a defensible position, considering pollution, traffic, and the occasional assault on the nerves, but hey, we're human.

So, if you are not a saint and are addicted to your car, here are some tips for navigating around with some semblance of ease.

First of all, never travel during rush hour if you can avoid it. That means, don't head into the city until after 9 A.M., and never leave the city between the hours of 4 P.M. and 6 P.M. You could still run into traffic jams during other times, but at least you have a better chance of breezing in and out of the city. If you must travel during the rush hours, find a couple of passengers to carpool, and take advantage of the less-crowded diamond lanes.

Always have a good supply of quarters on hand. You will need them for the meters around town, and there is nothing worse than finding a parking space and then not having the right change for the meter. Actually, there is something worse: having the good fortune to find a broken meter but not having a pen or paper to write a note saying that the meter won't work. That's why we always carry a little sign that reads METER BROKEN, ready to be placed in a visible spot on the windshield.

Be aware that meters are good for various times, depending on the degree of traffic in a given area. Nearest downtown, you will find many fifteen- and thirty-minute meters, while as you move around town, you might be lucky enough to find a two-hour meter. You are supposed to vacate when your time expires rather than feed the meter. If you want to tempt fate, or the meter maids, check to see if your tire has been marked,

In general, avoid driving through the busiest sections of town: the Union

Square area, the financial district, and Chinatown. One major traffic jam on Montgomery Street or Grant can ruin a whole day. It's worth the effort to go out of your way to get around town. Good east-west streets are Bush and Pine, Howard and Folsom, and Oak and Fell. Each is a one-way street with well-synchronized lights. The Embarcadero, despite construction, is usually a good way to skirt traffic.

If you are not familiar with driving San Francisco's hills, they can either be a breathtaking thrill ride or a nightmare. For drivers with stick shifts, there is nothing to test your skill like heading up a steep hill, say Fillmore toward Broadway, and having to stop in the middle of the street behind a line of cars. The best advice is to leave lots of room between you and the car in front of you, and to use your hand brake to hold the car in place. Then, as you start up the hill again, scared to death of rolling back down into the car behind you, let out the clutch and accelerate before you release the brake.

Finally, always have a good map of the city in the car. San Francisco can be both easy and difficult to get around in. Parts of the city are laid out in a logical grid, while other sections twist and curve and take off in confusing directions. Streets with names become streets with numbers. Numbered avenues run from Arguello out to the ocean. In the Sunset district, streets are in alphabetical order, and nearly everywhere you go, there's a sign that announces the "49-mile scenic drive." Only a good street map, such as the one available at the Convention and Visitors Bureau or the one that is free to CSAA members, can sort out the potential confusion.

What to wear? San Francisco is a casual town, much to the chagrin of many old-timers who long for the days when gentlemen wore ties and hats and ladies donned white gloves for a day's shopping at I. Magnin's. There are a few restaurants that enforce dress codes, but generally the concept is to be comfortable. If you can do that with a dash of style, you'll fit right in like a native. The important thing to remember is to be prepared for the city's various microclimates and the fact that the weather can change in an instant. It can be shirtsleeve weather at two in the afternoon, and then the fog rolls in, and you need a jacket or a sweater. Bring layers, and don't expect the weather in the San Francisco to be the same as it is in Oakland or San Mateo or wherever you are coming from.

You should know that there are several walking and bus tours available if you choose to let someone else do the guiding. Most of them charge for the service, but the San Francisco Library has a wonderful service called City Guides, offering free tours to various parts of the city. Phone 557–4266 for a recorded schedule. As for the many phone numbers included in the book, all are in the 415 area code.

Happy Trails!

JERRY GRAHAM
Berkeley, CA

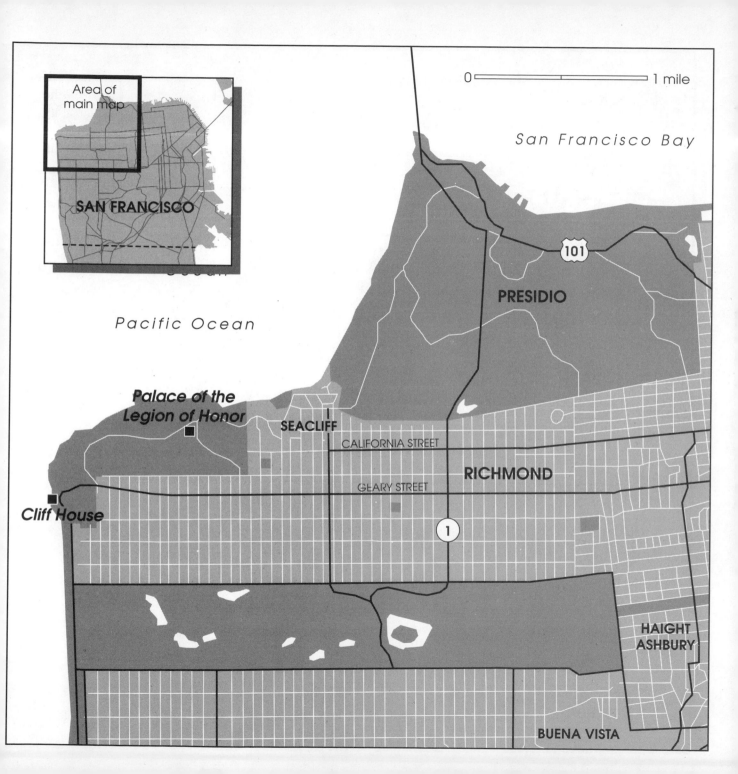

Area of
main map

SAN FRANCISCO

Pacific Ocean

San Francisco Bay

PRESIDIO

101

*Palace of the
Legion of Honor*

SEACLIFF

CALIFORNIA STREET

RICHMOND

GEARY STREET

1

■ *Cliff House*

HAIGHT
ASHBURY

0 ⊢━━━━━━━━━━━━━━━━━┤ 1 mile

BUENA VISTA

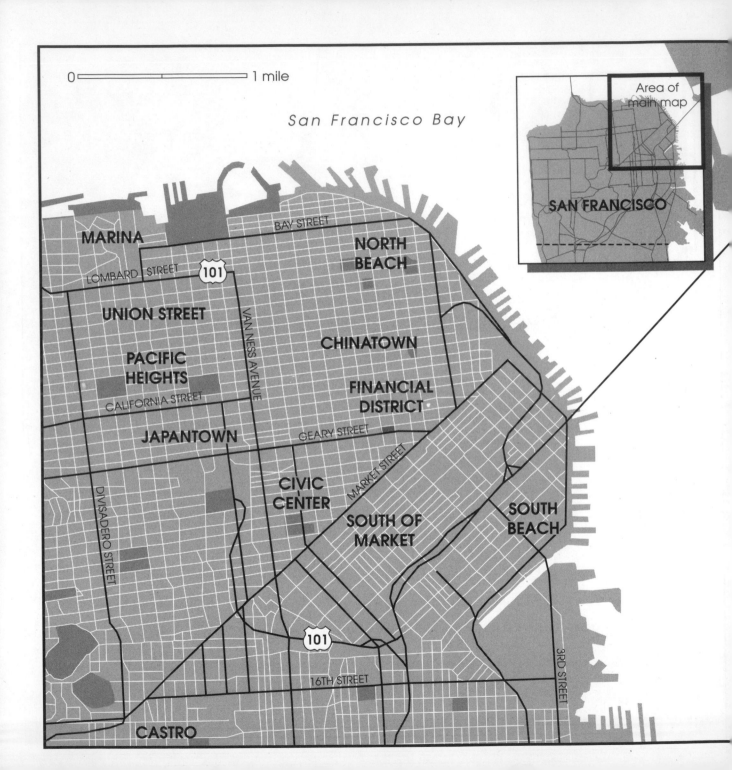

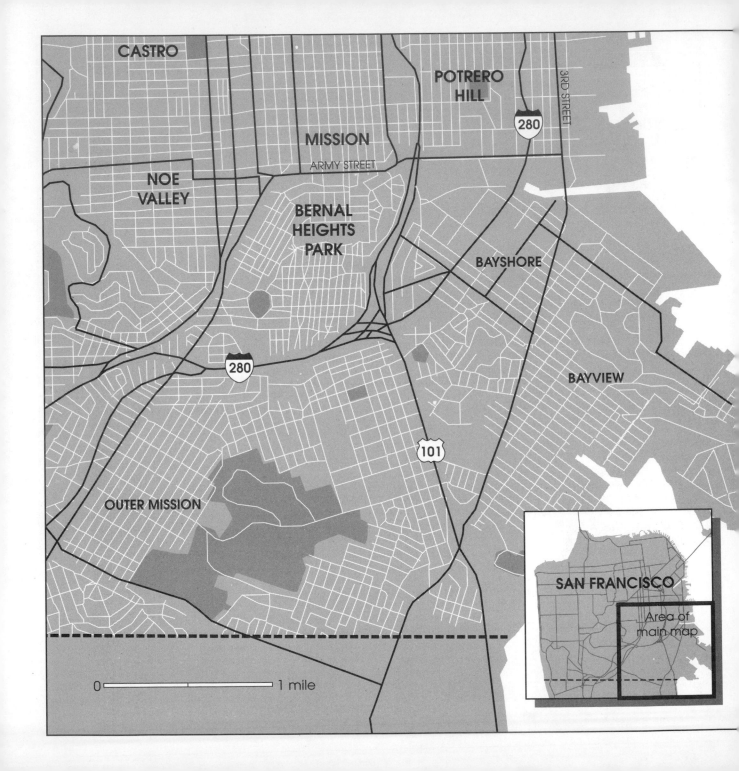

PART I

"Only in San Francisco"

San Francisco is a surprisingly small and compact city. You can drive from one end to the other in less than a half hour—that is, of course, if you are in the right place at the right time. If you are in the wrong place at the wrong time, say the financial district during the afternoon rush hour, it could take you a half hour to go a few blocks. Those blocks are part of a city full of well-defined and unique neighborhoods. We will concentrate on those neighborhoods that combine beauty, historical interest, and other elements that define the quality of life in San Francisco—the good life of cafés, shops, architecture, parks, and an interesting mix of people.

Like other American cities, you will find some of the same businesses cropping up in many neighborhoods. What makes San Francisco different is that the chain operations are not burger and fried chicken franchises but top-quality coffee and bagel shops. Food is the dominant religion of San Francisco, and because of the freshness and abundance of produce and the highly developed tastes of the consumers, there is much to worship here.

1

Believe it or not, San Francisco is a great walking town. One might assume that all those darn hills would get in the way, but no. It's easy to circumnavigate the hills, or at least to minimize them (unless, of course, you'd enjoy the heart-thumping athleticism of climbing halfway to the stars). Anyway, in high traffic areas, walking is the only way to go if you really want to see and experience things.

CHAPTER *1*   # North Beach and Chinatown

There are so many wonderful neighborhoods in San Francisco that it's difficult to decide where to begin. We chose North Beach and Chinatown for several reasons: both illustrate the city's international flavor and are compact and easy to walk, lively, safe, and steeped in history. The list could go on. Suffice it to say that if you have only time to visit one or two places in the city, you have to make it North Beach and Chinatown.

North Beach

North Beach is the quintessential San Francisco neighborhood. Locals, tourists, and newly arrived immigrants intermingle in one of the city's best climates to create an area full of life. Streets and sidewalks are busy, as are the cafés and parks. Not only is there sunshine—a valuable commodity in foggy San Francisco—but also surrounding hills, charming antique buildings, abundant good food, coffee, and conversation. Everyone here has some subtle understanding that this is a very special part of the world. North Beach is the most European-feeling area of San Francisco, with a long Italian tradition mixed with a growing Asian community. The main drag, Columbus Avenue, has both English and Italian street signs ("Corso Cristoforo Colombo"). Small streets, namely Via Ferlinghetti, Jack Kerouac Alley, and William Saroyan Place, bespeak the literary significance of the place; Turk Murphy Way acknowledges the jazz influence.

North Beach is an area to visit often, for an hour or for an entire day, making sure to enjoy the pleasure of a perfect cappuccino, people-watching, and perhaps a little shopping. It's easy to strike up a conversation or simply eavesdrop and watch the world go by.

Parking

One of the first things to consider on a visit to North Beach is where in the heck to park. There are metered spaces on many streets, and patience usually pays off on Columbus or Grant Avenues; however, your meter time might be limited to fifteen minutes to one hour, and your supply of quarters can be depleted quickly. Your best bet is to head immediately for the municipal parking garage next to the police station on Vallejo Street between Stockton and Powell near the border of Chinatown. The rates are as good as anywhere in town, and you will feel liberated from your car on the narrow, crowded streets. Or you can take one of the bus lines that serve the neighborhood, such as the 30 Stockton or 41 Union.

NORTH BEACH MUSEUM

As you wander around this neighborhood crammed with hills, restaurants, coffeehouses, bakeries, nightclubs, shops, and apartment buildings, you may wonder why they call this area a beach. To find out, spend a half hour or so in the North Beach Museum. Few San Franciscans know it even exists, but there it is on the second floor of the Eureka Bank on Stockton Street, just a few steps from the back exit of the Vallejo Street parking garage. Simply walk into the bank's main entrance and up the stairs on the right. If it looks dark up there, don't worry—the lights go on automatically when someone climbs the stairs.

The museum offers a graphic introduction to San Francisco's favorite neighborhood. This is a very low-key but charming operation, consisting of two or three rooms of photos and artifacts that preserve the history of North Beach. Changing displays tell many stories, thanks to the donations from people who have lived in the neighborhood.

As you enter the bank lobby on the main floor and head up the stairs on your right to the museum, you'll see a picture of North Beach in 1851. It looks like a remote beach community, which, at the time, it was, before the bay was filled in from what is now Francisco Street. When North Beach was, indeed, a beach, there were sand dunes, a few frame homes, and the bay . . . period. Another memorable photo in the collection shows Washington Square, just a few blocks north of the museum, right after the 1906 earthquake, a scene of total devastation.

There are scores of other priceless photos and artifacts at the museum: early shots of Joe DiMaggio, Frankie Crosetti, and Tony Lazzeri, three young stars of the New York Yankees who are considered sons of North Beach; a handwritten manuscript of "The Old Italian's Dying," a poem by the beat writer Lawrence Ferlinghetti; photos of the infamous "Meigg's Wharf," built in 1852 by unscrupulous entrepreneur Harry Meigg for his own ships to unload lumber from the forests of Mendocino. You'll also be able to follow the story of the Italians who began arriving around the Civil War, and the history of the Chinese in neighboring Chinatown, whose first major wave of immigration began around ten years earlier.

1435 Stockton. Open Monday through Friday 9 A.M. to 4 P.M. 391–6210. Free.

ITALIAN MAGAZINE AND GIFT STORE

A nice place to soak up the current Italian flavor of the neighborhood is A. Cavalli, a charming Italian store that opened in 1880 and today caters to locals and visitors who want to keep in touch with the old country. Here you'll find the video *La Bella Et La Besta* (Disney's *Beauty and the Beast*) and the children's book *Dové Spot?* (*Where is Spot?*) The shelves are stocked with Italian newspapers and magazines, pasta makers and espresso machines, greeting cards, maps, sweatshirts, CDs, and records—all in Italian.

John Valentini runs the place and spends his day switching his conversation between English and Italian. His family took over the store in the 1920s from the Cavallis. He can tell you about the area and how it's changed over the years. You can even ask, "*Dové il gabinetto*?" (Where is the bathroom?). John switches effortlessly from English to Italian on a moment's notice.

1441 Stockton (near Columbus). Open Monday through Saturday 9 A.M. to 5:30 P.M. 421–4219.

WASHINGTON SQUARE PARK

If there is a community center of North Beach, it is Washington Square Park, which borders Columbus and Stockton, and Union and Filbert Streets. It's a gently sloping expanse of green lawn and trees, with some park benches and walkways. At Columbus there is also a small children's playground. At first glance it doesn't appear to be much. But if you just turn off your internal clock and relax, there is much to see and learn. Here's what I noticed at around five o'clock one sunny weekday afternoon.

From a bench near Stockton Street, I saw a curious cement marker that read, 1869: U.S. COAST GUARD AND GEODESIC SERVICE. The marker lists the latitude as 37°47'57" North and the longitude at 122°24'37" West. Nothing special, but I had been in the park at least twenty times in the last several years, and never noticed it. I also saw five dogs being walked, three of which became instant friends and romped unleashed through the park, entertaining the crowds with their antics. I saw runners with Walkmen, strollers wearing berets, lovers on blankets, tourists snapping pictures, a guitar duo on a bench singing "Hotel California," Italians arguing about women and politics with the flag of Italy on a building behind them on Union Street, Chinese men and women practicing tai chi chuan, mothers pushing baby strollers, a man sleeping under a grocery cart that appeared to carry all his belongings, three street people on a bench, each talking to himself. And in the background were the chimes of the impressive Sts. Peter and Paul's Cathedral (see next item), which overlooks the park.

Sitting on that bench, occasionally reading a newspaper, but most of the time just being there, I started to feel a part of North Beach, which is as much as I can ask from any place I visit.

Generally the benches have their own patterns of occupancy. On the Filbert Street side, the street people and wandering musicians usually take their place in the shade of the trees. On the Stockton Street side, there's a pretty good mix of people who stop for a few minutes while passing through and those who like to read their papers and magazines while facing the afternoon sun. On the Union Street side, the local Italian-Americans usually hold fort and are a great source of stories about North Beach, past and present.

SAINTS PETER AND PAUL CHURCH

Lawrence Ferlinghetti once referred to this impressive cathedral as "the marzipan church." Indeed, the twins towers of this neo-Gothic building testify to the affluence of the Italian community that prospered in the local fishing and market gardening businesses when the church was consecrated in 1924. Each October a procession departs from the church to Fisherman's Wharf for the annual blessing of the fishing fleet. This is where Joe DiMaggio and Marilyn Monroe were photographed following their City Hall wedding (They couldn't be married in the church because of her divorce).

Saints Peter and Paul Church is as quintessentially Italian as any landmark you might visit in the old country. As you enter, across the facade you will see the opening line of Dante's *Paradise*: "The glory of Him who moves everything penetrates and glows throughout the universe." Inside, the first thing that you notice is the aroma of candles, then the crowd of statues and images, including a naive painting of the Madonna and Child; the Madonna is lifting a sinner from out of the pit of the inferno. The altar is an extravaganza of Catholic imagery gone wild—a heavenly city of marble spires and life-size angels. Mass is said in three languages: English, Italian, and Cantonese.

666 Filbert Street. 421–3730.

COFFEE WARS

I will confess that I am abnormally fond of great coffee and have been disappointed too many times by a cappuccino that tastes burned or had too much water run through the grounds or arrives without foam or any of a number of abuses that have followed the fad of gourmet coffee. It's great to see so many places opening up everywhere and so many beautiful espresso machines in every neighborhood, but it's discouraging when the result is an overpriced, tasteless brown liquid drink.

In North Beach, however, I'm rarely disappointed. Many locals, like the Italian bookstore operator John Valentini and the restaurant critic Patricia Unterman, are certain that the best cappuccino in North Beach (or the rest of the city for that matter) is at Caffe Greco, which competes mightily for the honor with its neighbors, Caffe Trieste and Caffe Roma. Perhaps you'd enjoy judging the best for yourself.

CAFFE GRECO

At Caffe Greco, making a coffee drink is an art, practiced as in Italy by a *barista*, who plays the espresso machine like Maurizio Pollini plays the piano. The first matter of importance is the coffee bean. Caffe Greco uses what many connoisseurs believe to be the finest: Illycafe beans imported from Italy. The coffee beans are ground just so, the milk is steamed quickly, and then the bubbles are banged out so the foam is almost the consistency of whipped cream. The machine itself is tuned to produce an espresso topped with a light brown *crema*, which looks like a coating of cream. And when the barista adds the steamed milk, a special flick of the wrist insures that the cappuccino will have a perfect brown ring around the white foam. Man, that's coffee.

423 Columbus Ave. Open Monday through Thursday 7 A.M. to 11 P.M.; Friday through Sunday to midnight. 397–6261.

CAFFE TRIESTE

Located near the fashionable shops on Upper Grant, Caffe Trieste has its faithful followers, including my coauthor and wife, Catherine, who likes the atmosphere that hasn't changed much since the beatniks ruled North Beach and the likes of Jack Kerouac and Allen Ginsberg hung out here. The walls are crammed with photos of friends, family, and the famous who have imbibed espressos and consumed focaccia bread and Italian pastries over the decades here.

Politics, poetry, and art still are discussed at length, while a single person will tie up a table for hours with a single cappuccino and paperback. That is, until Saturday afternoons, when the family and various friends of owner

Gianfranco Giotti sing opera; the place gets so jammed that you're lucky if you can get in the door. The coffee is good and strong; they roast their own beans, which are marketed to local restaurants and consumers. But it's mainly the relaxed if funky atmosphere of the place that keeps people coming back and hanging out.

601 Vallejo Street (at Grant). Open Sunday through Thursday 6:30 A.M. to 11:30 P.M.; Friday and Saturday to midnight. 392–6739.

CAFFE ROMA ROASTING COMPANY

What is now the Café Figaro used to be one of North Beach's favorite hangouts, Caffe Roma, which was famous for its pale blue murals of angels and cherubs. But because of skyrocketing rents, the owner, Sergio Azzolini, moved his entire operation down the street into the Roma Roasting Company space. The burlap bags of coffee beans that used to serve as informal benches for drinkers have been replaced by tables and chairs, and a selection of pastries has been added to go with their terrific coffee.

In the front of the store, the modern roaster is in constant operation, and the unbeatable aroma of freshly roasted coffee wafts throughout the café and into the street. There are a few tables in front on Columbus where you can enjoy your coffee in the sun if the bus and car fumes don't bother you.

This is a family operation where everybody seems to know everybody, and it doesn't take long before you feel like part of the group.

526 Columbus Avenue. Daily 8 A.M. to 11 P.M. 296–7662.

MARIO'S BOHEMIAN CIGAR STORE

Further down Columbus, across from Washington Square Park, is yet another North Beach institution. They don't really sell cigars at Mario's, and there aren't many Bohemians still around, but this tiny café has its loyal followers. The major attraction here is not the coffee, although it's fine, but the giant grilled focaccia sandwiches. Grab a seat at the counter, and you will probably be engaged in a conversation within a few minutes. You can watch the sandwiches being made and then choose the one that looks best to you. House favorites are the meatball, the chicken, and the eggplant. They're all good, and very filling.

566 Columbus Avenue. Lunch and dinner. Open late. No credit cards. There is another branch of Mario's on Upper Polk Street. 362–0536.

CITY LIGHTS BOOKSTORE AND THE BEAT GENERATION

On the TV show *Jeopardy*, the answer would be: First bookstore in nation to sell exclusively paperbacks. The question: What is City Lights Bookstore? This North Beach institution opened at this location in 1953 to publish and sell works of counterculture poets and writers who the mainstream press wouldn't touch with a 10-foot beret. Still thriving despite the onslaught of giant chain operations, it features books of poetry, philosophy, classical and avant-garde literature, and political texts that are hard to find elsewhere. There's also a great magazine section.

The ghosts of the Beat Generation loom large at City Lights. In the 1950s of the uptight Eisenhower administration, a group of free thinkers found their way to San Francisco's North Beach, where the rents, spaghetti, and red wine were relatively cheap. San Francisco *Chronicle* columnist Herb Caen coined the word "beatnik," and it stuck. The movement centered on Jack Kerouac (*On the Road*, 1957), Allen Ginsberg ("Howl," 1956), their mentor William Burroughs, and poet-publisher Lawrence Ferlinghetti, founder and still owner of City Lights, the bookstore and publishing company. City Lights shook up the literary world when it published the text of Ginsberg's revolutionary poem "Howl," and Ferlinghetti was prosecuted for publishing obscenities that are common today on television.

City Lights is browser-friendly, with chairs downstairs and notices announcing what is going on in the neighborhood.

261 Columbus Avenue. Open daily 10 A.M. to midnight. 362–8193.

VESUVIO CAFÉ

Another Beat shrine survives across Kerouac Alley. Vesuvio Café is located in a pressed-tin landmark, built in 1913. Originally an Italian-language bookstore, this café and bar occupies the ground floor and mezzanine and features an alcove reserved, for reasons unknown, "for lady psychiatrists." You can ask the bartender to flick on a slide show that pays homage to James Joyce. One comes here to drink coffee or something stronger and to people-watch, especially if you can get one of the tables that overlooks Columbus Avenue.

255 Columbus Avenue, across the alley from City Lights. Open daily 6 A.M. to 2 A.M. 362–3370.

TOSCA

If you have time for just one evening drink, make it at Tosca's. This beloved seventy-five-year old bar, graced by a huge eagle-topped espresso machine (spiked coffee drinks are the specialty of the house), is a world-class landmark. Anybody who's anybody in the world of art, music, dance, and film-making stops by when he or she is in town. The owner, Jeannette Etheredge, is a local character who regularly makes the society pages. Hidden in back is a room with a pool table where only special friends of the owner are admitted; you may glimpse the likes of Mikhail Baryshnikov, Nicholas Cage, or Robin Williams as they scurry to the security of privacy. Even us nobodies are at ease in the booths amid the noise of conversation, laughter, and the clinking of glasses. The jukebox is stocked with Italian arias, which compete late at night with the thump-thump from a dance club in the same building.

242 Columbus Avenue. Open nightly 5 P.M. to 2 A.M.. No credit cards. 391–1244.

BROADWAY

Probably the most famous street in North Beach, Broadway saw its heyday in the fifties, when jazz and comedy clubs like the Purple Onion and the Hungry I brought cool culture to the West Coast. Comedians such as Lenny Bruce, Jonathan Winters, and Mort Sahl and the top names in jazz played here. With the liberated sixties and seventies came topless and then bottomless; Broadway became synonymous with the sleazy sex shows that dominated the block.

Today, the strip has returned as a scene of restaurants and cafés, with a few "talk to a nude girl" joints and the long-running drag queen revue at Finocchio's to maintain a historic perspective. At the corner of Broadway and Columbus is the remodeled Condor Club, now a café. Gone is the giant sign featuring a nude woman with nipples in neon; nowadays you'll find a respectable-looking historic landmark marker designating this as the site of the first topless nightclub (June 19, 1964) and the site of the first bottomless show (October 3, 1969). Apparently, once they hit bottom, there was nothing else to show and the clubs simply died out.

FIGONI HARDWARE

Most neighborhoods have an old-fashioned hardware store that seems to have missed the changing times. It's a good bet that Figoni Hardware looks a lot like it did in the early days of the Italian community.

In two adjoining store sites you will find everything you need for the home, plus an extensive selection of Italian cookware. Harder to inventory is the nostalgia induced when you enter Figoni's. The wood floors, the high ceilings, and the goods stacked high and hanging from the rafters evoke memories of neighborhood stores that have since been replaced by warehouse-sized chain operations.

1351 Grant Avenue (between Vallejo and Green). Open daily except Wednesday and Sunday 8 A.M. to 5 P.M. 392–4765.

PLACES TO EAT

BUCA GIOVANNI

Surprisingly, for an Italian neighborhood, North Beach doesn't have that many great Italian restaurants. Buca Giovanni is one of the exceptions to the rule. In his intimate cellar Giovanni offers the kind of food you might get in a traditional restaurant in Tuscany. Nothing trendy or "lite" here. The food is substantial and hearty. Let the waiters help guide you through your selection of homemade pastas and roasted meats and fowl.

800 Greenwich Street
776–7766
Open Tuesday through Saturday for dinner
Moderate
Credit cards

CAFÉ JACQUELINE

There is one thing that you get at Café Jacqueline: soufflés. Oh, you can have a salad to go with it, and some French bread, but the entrees and the desserts are all soufflés. They also happen to be the best soufflés you've ever had. When you are ready to forget about cholesterol and fat for a night, this quiet, romantic spot is a treat.

1454 Grant Avenue
981–5565
Open Wednesday through Sunday for dinner
Moderate
Credit cards

ENRICO'S

There is no more beloved institution on Broadway than Enrico's. Once the domain of Enrico Banducci, who brought the likes of Mort Sahl and Bill Cosby to his Hungry I nightclub in the 1950s, his sidewalk café fell on hard times and finally closed in the 1990s. Enter Chef Rick Hackett and his partners. They remodeled the place, put in a contemporary Italian menu, and made it an institution again. There's one menu for lunch and dinner and late into the night, and all the food, which includes hearty pasta dishes, pizza, and seasonal specials, is terrific.

The design of the indoors at Enrico's is also worth special mention. One of my pet peeves is being seated at a table for two when all I can see beyond my dining partner is a wall. Enrico's solves that problem for me by placing mirrors behind all the booths and tables so no matter where you sit, you see the entire room.

504 Broadway
982–6223
Lunch and dinner daily; open late at night
Moderate
Credit cards

HELMAND

You've probably never had Afghan cooking before. I certainly hadn't before I had the pleasure of dining at Helmand. I admit I first tried it with dubious motives. As a practical joke, a friend and I welcomed a new colleague from the Midwest to the city by taking him to what we called a typical San Francisco restaurant. As our guest searched through the menu for something familiar, like a burger, my conspirator and I casually discussed whether we felt like the Kaddo Borawni or the Dwopiaza. Even though none of us really knew what we were ordering, we had a wonderful meal.

The food is best described as a cross between Middle Eastern and Indian. Lamb dishes are a specialty, as are the variations on pasta. It's the seasonings that make the food so exotic and delicious. Although the dining room and the service are elegant, the prices are surprisingly low.

430 Broadway
362–0641
Dinner nightly
Inexpensive
Credit cards

IDEALE

This is one of the newer Italian restaurants in North Beach, a part of the Upper Grant Street renewal. Billed as a Roman-style ristorante, Ideale specializes in pasta dishes that are seasoned with subtlety and grilled and roasted meats. Eating here instead of the older, larger neighborhood restaurants, with their mushy pasta and heavy tomato sauce, is like making a quick trip to Italy.

1315 Grant Avenue
391–4129
Dinner nightly
Moderate
Credit cards

LE COCO'S

In the heart of North Beach, Le Coco's is something of an anomaly: a Sicilian restaurant in a Genovese town. What that means for you is delicious pizzas, salads, and pasta dishes in a friendly, informal setting. The specialty of the house is scallops in a reduced red wine sauce. They also feature calamari sautéed in wine. Dessert is not offered.

510 Union Street
296–9151
Dinner Tuesday through Sunday
Moderate
Credit cards

L'OSTERIA DEL FORNO

This is a tiny storefront restaurant on Columbus Avenue that you will probably recognize by the line waiting outside. The key word here is *forno*, which is Italian for "oven." Everything is cooked in a brick-lined oven, and the result is comfort food at its homiest. There's a daily pasta, pizza, and my favorite, the roast pork in milk.

519 Columbus Avenue
982–1124
Lunch and dinner daily, except Tuesday
Inexpensive
No credit cards

MARIO'S BOHEMIAN CIGAR STORE

You won't really experience North Beach until you eat at least once in Mario's. The tiny café, which overlooks Washington Square Park, packs them in at lunchtime for their huge sandwiches on focaccia. The favorites are the meatball and the grilled chicken, but there are several other choices. Try for a table by an open window, and enjoy a cappuccino or a glass of wine with your sandwich. You won't want to leave.

566 Columbus Avenue
362–0536
Lunch and dinner daily; open late
Inexpensive
No credit cards

MO'S

This place probably has the best burgers in San Francisco. From the outside window you can watch the counterman grill 7-ounce hand-shaped burgers in this North Beach café. It looks like an old-fashioned soda shop with a white tile floor and black and chrome dinette tables and chairs. You will dine under the goofy gaze of a series of Three Stooges posters (inspiration for the name Mo). Choose from a no-frills burger served on regular roll or customize your own with seven choices of cheeses, mushrooms, grilled onions, and the like. These are at least three-napkin burgers.

They also serve vegetarian specials such as grilled eggplant on focaccia. There's a long counter, as well as plenty of tables and booths. If you're not counting calories, you can wash down that burger with a classic milk shake.

1322 Grant Avenue
788–3779
Open daily for lunch and late dinner
Burgers start at $4.95
Credit cards

Overview

It would be quite a journey from Italy to China, but you can move from one culture to the next simply by crossing the street from North Beach to Chinatown. This transition is most dramatic at the intersection of Stockton and Vallejo Streets. On the northeast side of the street, there's the Little City Market, which has been selling meats and poultry to Italian families for generations. On the southeast side of the street, there's the Victoria Pastry Company, famous for its Sacrapantina, which is a fantasy of cake and cream puffs. On the north and southwest sides of the intersection, Chinese produce and fish markets display their wares on the street. And all of this is in the shadow of the skyscrapers of the financial district.

Chinatown appeals to most everyone. It's near the top of every visitor's list. Asian families from the neighborhood and all over the Bay Area shop for food here. Locals delight in roaming the area and discovering new nooks and crannies. And while some sections look like the creation of a modern theme park designer, this is a genuine neighborhood, the most densely populated in the city and possibly the nation, with unmeasured thousands living in a sixteen-square-block area. Second-generation families may move on, but new immigrants continue to arrive from all over Asia.

Part of the mystique of Chinatown is that there is a hidden, almost secret quality to the area, no doubt a holdover from the days when American laws excluded the Chinese from just about every right granted by the Constitution. Those who came to the city called "Gold Mountain" were forced to remain in a tightly confined area to create their own new world.

Parking

If you happen to find a space on the street, grab it, although that may be like saying if you happen to win the lottery, cash in the ticket. Streets are narrow in Chinatown, and it is frustrating to try to drive around, so the best idea is to ditch the car as soon as possible or, better yet, take one of the many buses or cable cars that service the area.

There are several parking lots and garages in the area, three of which are municipally run with reasonable rates.

The Portsmouth Square Garage is in the heart of Chinatown with its entrance on Kearny, just north of Sacramento. There must be some karmic irony involved here, since Kearny Street was named after a transplanted Irishman who led the fight to send the Chinese back home.

The Sutter-Stockton Street Garage is only two blocks from the main entrance to Chinatown, at Bush Street and Grant Avenue. As you exit from the garage onto Sutter Street, turn left to Grant and then left again to the famous entry arch, Dragon's Gate.

Finally, the Vallejo Street garage in North Beach is steps away from the northern section of Chinatown and its main food shopping street, Stockton.

PORTSMOUTH SQUARE

This split-level park atop the parking garage is not only the de facto civic center of Chinatown but also the site of the birthplace of San Francisco. This was the original town plaza laid out for the Mexican port of Yerba Buena. In 1848 Captain John Montgomery raised the American flag here when the United States took over the settlement. The Square was named for Montgomery's ship, the *Portsmouth*. Just one year later, the word resounded through the square that there was gold in "them thar" Sierra foothills, and the rush to the promised land was on.

Today the Square is a beehive of daytime activity and relatively quiet at night. On most days you are likely to see kids chasing pigeons and climbing on the pagoda-style play structure. Their mothers and grandmothers will be sitting on benches, the elderly reading Chinese language newspapers and reminiscing about the "old country." Individuals and groups will be practicing martial arts exercises, and men will be clustered around the chess tables, playing mysterious card games and making like there is no money at stake.

Sit a while and soak up the atmosphere before you wander. It takes only a short time to get into the rhythm of the neighborhood and to convince the often tourist-weary neighbors that you are not on a quick search-and-destroy sightseeing mission.

There are a few notable monuments in the Square. The most recent is a sculpture of the Goddess of Democracy, modeled after the one that hung briefly in Beijing's Tiananmen Square during that one massive demonstration for freedom.

On a more literary note, there's a tribute to Robert Louis Stevenson, who spent many a day writing in the park. The monument is a bronze statue of the ship *Hispaniola* from his novel *Treasure Island*.

There's also a plaque noting that this was the site of the first public school in California.

CHINESE CULTURAL CENTER

If you'd like to get more information about the community, cross the pedestrian bridge that leads from the Square to the Chinatown Holiday Inn. On the third floor is the Chinese Cultural Center, which features changing exhibitions and offers tours of the neighborhood for a fee. The galleries are quite spacious and present contrasting shows. On my last visit there was a collection of beautiful Chinese prints in one gallery, while the other featured a neighborhood project in which people searched their roots and presented their family trees, complete with photos. There's also a gift shop on the premises.

It's worth a visit if just to meet M. J. Lee, who is the receptionist, greeter, and all-around chief cook and bottle washer.

After she showed me around, M. J. told me some of the history of the place and the neighborhood, and then asked my opinion of a story she had just written to submit to *Reader's Digest* for its "Life in these United States" feature. Her story and enthusiastic reading were so memorable, I decided on the spot to include the story in the book, no matter what the editors of *Reader's Digest* decided:

My skin is yellow, my eyes are slanted, and the truth of the matter is I did not have a "Chinaman's chance" of becoming a cheerleader in high school. However, my Mama always said, "If you have a dream, go for it!" At my fiftieth high school class reunion, each student was requested to stand and say something to his or her classmates. The majority of their responses followed the same monotonous pattern: "My name is, I'm married to, we have x number of children, grandchildren, great grandchildren, etc." Those of us who attended the fortieth and forty-fifth reunions have previously heard all these tedious responses. When my name was called, I bolted from my seat in wild anticipation to remind my fellow classmates that in our high school days, all the cheerleaders were blond, blue-eyed, and white. For Mexicans, blacks, and Asians like me to become a cheerleader was emphatically mission impossible!

"I've always had this dream," I said to my classmates. "Will you help me fulfill it tonight?" Edison's class of 1946 were behind me 100 percent as I got into my cheerleading stance and led them into our school yell, "ED . . . ED . . . EDIS . . . IS . . . IS . . . ISON . . . EDISON . . . EDISON . . . EDISON, RAH, RAH!"

The reverberation in the room was exhilarating . . . dreams do come true.

M. J. Lee. When you visit, tell her you read her cheerleading story.

Chinese Cultural Center, Chinatown Holiday Inn. Open Tuesday through Saturday 10 A.M. to 4 P.M.; Sunday noon to 4 P.M. 986–1822.

Back Alleys

If Grant Avenue and Stockton Street, which we will cover later, are the main roads of Chinatown, the backroads are alleys where tourists seldom venture. Safety is not the issue—it's simply a matter of less glitter and action. Still, some of the most interesting places in the neighborhood are off the beaten path.

WAVERLY PLACE

Nicknamed "Fifteen Cents" Street because that's the price barbers used to charge at the turn of the century, Waverly Place is probably the most Chinese of Chinatown's alleys and streets. Its buildings are painted bright colors with red doors and dark green window frames. They are referred to as multiuse layer cakes, with shops on the first floor, business associations on the second floor, and temples or residences on the third floor. Many of the structures have balconies, often decorated with drying laundry.

Just amble along Waverly, and stop in at any place that interests you. You can peek in at garment factories, acupuncture parlors, music stores, and herb shops which are the Eastern equivalent of a Western pharmacy. If you've a taste for the quirky, don't miss the Wonder Food Company at 133 Waverly Place, where they make Mickey Mouse cakes with Chinese writing.

Waverly Place is just two blocks long, running from Sacramento Street to Washington Street, one block east of, and parallel to, Grant Avenue.

ROSS ALLEY

This street is even smaller and narrower than Waverly Place. Only one block long, to the east of Waverly and running from Washington to Jackson, Ross was nicknamed Gambler's Alley, and you can imagine what games might have been played behind closed doors.

That San Francisco invention, the fortune cookie, is produced by the thousands at the Golden Gate Cookie Factory at 54 Ross Alley. You can see the works in the back, and pick up a bag of cookies, including those with X-rated jokes. It might surprise you to know that the fortune cookie was not created by a Chinese-American. The first were produced around the turn of the twentieth century by the gardener at the Japanese Tea Garden in Golden Gate Park.

At 14 Ross Alley is the Sam Bo Trading Company. Behind a lavish Edwardian door, there is a store packed with Chinese religious goods, including more Buddhas than you have ever seen in one place. There are also jewelry counters featuring the real stuff, not the trinkets typical of the tourist shops on Grant

Avenue. The customers here know one shade of jade from another and are willing to pay.

ST. LOUIS PLACE

St. Louis is tinier yet, running from Washington to Jackson, south of Waverly Place. Frankly, there is not much here, but you should know that it was called "Murder Alley" because so many bodies were dumped here during the heyday of the Barbary Coast. From the late 1800s to the early 1900s, every vice imaginable flourished nearby on Pacific Street, which once had more than twenty saloons jammed into one block. Dark, hidden St. Louis Place was a convenient place to dispose of victims of fights and robberies.

The major attraction now is the fact that St. Louis Place is San Francisco's narrowest street at its end, and a person of average height can stand in the middle of the street and touch the buildings on both sides. Hey, fun is fun!

BROOKLYN STREET

You don't have to bother going there: it's just a half block long, running south of Sacramento Street above Stockton. It's just worth knowing for a trivia game that there is indeed a Brooklyn in Chinatown.

STOCKTON STREET

If there is a main street for the daily life of Chinatown, it would be Stockton Street, which is rather plain but filled with life, especially in the late afternoon as the residents are shopping for dinner. Running parallel to Grant Avenue, this is the section to head for if you want to do some serious food shopping. You will see fish markets where the day's catch is still squirming in the display boxes out on the sidewalk. Vegetable hawkers and their exotic wares are side by side with stores selling Asian newspapers and CDs. The action and the noise are at a high level.

Sometimes, the scene approaches chaos. One afternoon, outside the New Ping Yuen Bakery at 1125 Stockton Street, there were crowds of people squeezing in to scoop up pastries that were set on a table near the door. Two tourists couldn't get anyone to explain what everyone was getting, so one said to the other, "It's three for a dollar . . . just give him a dollar and see what you get." They seemed to be satisfied as they bit into their bean paste cookies under the sign of the wonderfully named Sincere Bank.

Lien Hing Supermarket

Just down the street at 1106 Stockton is the Lien Hing Supermarket, where you can browse along with the local residents amid the cases of exotic fruits and vegetables, such as five-pointed star fruit and Chinese long beans. Fresh fish are also on display, and there's a large meat market. This is one of the newer markets in the neighborhood, and like the others, it becomes more crowded in the late afternoon as shoppers search for the freshest ingredients to take home and cook for dinner.

May Wah Shopping Center

Stop in at the May Wah Shopping Center at 1230 Stockton, between Broadway and Pacific. This is like a gallery of exotic food, where you can just wander around the enormous variety of fresh foodstuff and groceries, knowing that some of the city's finest chefs might be there with you. There are tanks of fresh fish; buckets brimming with live clams; produce, walnuts, and pickled greens, all being carefully examined by the serious shoppers.

Mee Mee Fortune Cookies

For something a bit different, check out Mee Mee Fortune Cookies at 1328 Stockton, between Broadway and Vallejo. Here you can have your own custom message created. They also make cookies in different colors and with off-color messages. By the way, we are still looking for the place that made the most unusual fortune we've ever encountered, which read, "Do not think of Charlton Heston today."

Janmae Guey

The sight of barbecued ducks and chickens, browned and glistening as they hang upside down in the store window, brightens many a block in Chinatown. At 1222 Stockton is one of the oldest and most established barbecue houses in the area. You can eat in the tiny dining room where they will cut the duck of your choice into pieces and serve it with soup and noodles, or package your meal to go.

GRANT AVENUE

The least backroads–like of all the places to visit in Chinatown is Grant Avenue, but it, too, is worth a look. First of all, there is the historical significance. This is the oldest street in San Francisco, called *Calle de la Fundacion* when the area was the Mexican village of Yerba Buena. Later it was changed to DuPont Street and became infamous for its brothels and gambling dens. After most of the area was burned to the ground in the fire that followed the 1906 earthquake, the local associations lobbied for respectability and named the street for President Ulysses S. Grant.

The most famous section of Grant is the entrance to Chinatown at the corner of Bush Street. Here you might be asked to take a picture for visitors who want to pose under the great Chinese arch, called Dragon's Gate. Most people will want to cuddle the Mythical Lion Dogs that protect the entrance from evil spirits.

So what do you do there to not feel like the average tourist? Well, first of all, suspend your cynicism and appreciate the effort put into the brightly painted buildings with their ornate second-story balconies and pagoda roofs. To do this, you have to look up, above the merchandise that is on display at street level. Take note of the streetlamps, painted turquoise and red with dragon's tails trailing down the light posts. Appreciate the mix of exotic stores with white ginseng twisting inside jars; the contemporary world, represented by the likes of McDonald's and the Bank of America; and the souvenir shops, with their backscratchers and personalized miniature license plates. Listen to the sounds, which range from heavy metal rock blaring out of a boom box and tape store to the sounds of ancient Chinese instruments playing "Swanee River." This is an only-in-America experience.

Chong Imports

This is a great place to stock up on some inexpensive gifts: pincushions, decorative hair combs, slippers, kid's toys. Catherine saw where her friends had bought a lot of the gifts she's received and enjoyed over the years. It's also a good place to take kids. Many items are in the $1.39-to-$3.00 range. There are also extensive selections of garden pots, Chinese cookware, food items— including Chinese candy and rice wine—and, for the carefree do-it-your-selfer, acupuncture needles.

838 Grant Avenue, in the Chinese Trade Center. Open daily 10 A.M. to 8 P.M.; 9 P.M. on weekends. 982–1431.

Ginn Wall

This is the closest thing to a neighborhood hardware store on Grant. You can replace that lost key here or get some picture hooks and unusual lightbulbs. Cooks know that they can get everything for the kitchen here, including woks of all sizes, steamers, rice makers, knives, and sharpening tools.

1016 Grant. Open daily except Thursday 10 A.M. to 6 P.M. 982–6307.

TEN REN TEA ROOM

Interspersed with all the gift stores you will find some stops like the Ten Ren Tea Company, which offers complimentary tea tastings in a ritual setting. Tea is taken very seriously here, and the selection is extensive.

More than fifty varieties of tea are offered, according to Dr. Ray Lee, the manager and my host for a tasting. Dr. Lee holds that tasting tea is more complicated than tasting wine because three conditions are required: heaven, earth, and humanity. There are special techniques for tasting, too.

First you smell the tea, then you sip it slowly three times to enjoy the fragrance, aroma, and flavor. Ten Ren sells teas in all price ranges, including rare teas for more than a hundred dollars per pound. Several varieties of ginseng are also available, as well as various herbal remedies. The shop is set up to accommodate the both the connoisseur and the neophyte.

949 Grant Avenue. Tastings are offered daily 9:30 A.M. to 9:30 P.M. 362–0656.

OLD CHINESE TELEPHONE EXCHANGE

Now the Bank of Canton, this beautiful pagoda was designed along the lines of a Chinese temple. It's not so much a destination as a curiosity. If you happen to be walking down the street and glance at it, you'll probably do a double take. Here's the story. Originally built in 1909, this was the old Pacific Telephone and Telegraph Company's Chinatown Exchange, probably the only telephone exchange in the country to be operated in a foreign language. The operators were required to be proficient in English and five Chinese dialects. Originally all the operators were male and lived on the building's second floor. Later women were allowed to work here, and the positions were so coveted that they were passed down from mother to daughter. The bank has preserved the building and welcomes gawkers.

743 Washington Street, between Grant and Kearny.

ST. MARY'S SQUARE

There is an abundance of asphalt and cement in Chinatown and not much greenery, which makes St. Mary's Square such a surprise. With stairway entrances on Pine Street and California Street, off Grant, this is one of those small parks that you could pass by a million times without knowing it's there. Much of the park is actually the roof of the parking garage below. Here you'll find a tranquil (although usually shady) oasis from the hustle and bustle. If you're looking for a place to sit for a while, or let the kids run around a bit, this is it.

You'll probably share St. Mary's Square with practitioners of Tai Chi, lunch-hour office workers, and homeless folks with their belongings in supermarket shopping carts.

It's worth noting that there is a Metro Toilet here, one of those French kiosks that is self-cleaning and costs a quarter. The outside of the kiosk has an excellent map of the city if you need to get your bearings.

Also of note in the park is a Benjamin Bufano steel-and-granite statue of Sun Yat-Sen (1866–1925), the Chinese revolutionary leader who lived in San Francisco for many years, spreading his gospel in a local Chinatown newspaper.

RELAX AT THE IMPERIAL TEA COURT

After the hustle, bustle, crowds, and noise of Chinatown, it may be wise to remember what the five thousand years of Chinese culture is all about. The Imperial Tea Court is a good place to end your visit or make this a destination of its own.

Off the beaten track, in a residential section of Chinatown/North Beach, the Imperial Tea Court is set up to be a place to savor tea and relax. The interior—wood panels, tassled hanging lamps, marble floor, even the nails—all came from China. Quiet and relaxing Chinese music floats in the background. A row of Chinese lacquered tables, each with its own pot of steaming water, waits for you to plop yourself down, take a deep breath, and look at the menu of white teas, green teas, black tea, oolong, and scented teas. If you haven't the faintest idea what you'd like, here's your chance to learn. The tea master or mistress will spend lots of time explaining the differences, let you smell various leaves from giant jars, and answer any questions you might have about this ancient tradition of drinking tea. Once your choice is made, a tiny cup and saucer arrive with a small lid. Then your host or hostess will instruct you on the proper way to hold the cup so that the leaves (brewed in the drinking cup) do not touch your lips and your sip is just the right temperature.

Tea-tasting is $3.00 for each selection, and you will walk out calm, refreshed, and ready to face the rest of your day.

Bulk tea is also sold here, and there are plans to add snacks and light lunches to accompany the teas. Classes in tea appreciation are also offered.

1411 Powell Street. Open daily 11 A.M. to 6:30 P.M. Credit cards. 788–6080.

PLACES TO EAT

DPD

This tiny restaurant shares the "best hole in the wall" award with its neighbor, House of Nanking. When you can't get into one, try the other. You'll get huge plates of delicious food at ridiculously cheap prices. The specialty here is Shanghai noodle dishes, but everything is good. There are daily lunch specials for $3.95, but get there early if you want a seat.

901 Kearny
982–0471
Lunch and dinner daily and open late at night
No credit cards

GOLD MOUNTAIN

Every visit to Chinatown should include at least one dim sum lunch. If you've never enjoyed the experience, all you have to do is sit down at a table and then choose as carts or trays of little dishes are brought by for your selection. Try a series of dumplings, soups, noodles, rice dishes, meats, and even desserts until you have had your fill.

It can be rather frantic, so you might want to go to a parlor like this one where you can get an explanation of the various dishes. Gold Mountain manages to satisfy local Chinese customers and non-Chinese with grace despite the crowds.

644 Broadway
296–7733
Open daily for breakfast, lunch, and dinner
Inexpensive
Credit cards

HOUSE OF NANKING

One of two jammed "hole in the wall" restaurants that occupy the block on Kearny between Jackson and Columbus, the House of Nanking is the Chinatown equivalent of "grunge hip." I was always told to eat only in Chinese restaurants where Chinese people were eating, but this is not the case here. The few tables at the House of Nanking are filled with people who are either young actors and models or wish they were. They are drawn not only by the unusual and tasty food, but also by the dirt-cheap prices. It's a scene to eat here, banging elbows with the person at the next table.

The food is chef Peter Yang's Americanized version of Shanghai cuisine, heavy on noodles and dumplings, with lots of sautéed dishes. Everything is cooked right in front of the twelve-seat counter.

919 Kearny Street
421–1429
Lunch and dinner Monday through Saturday; dinner Sunday
Inexpensive
No credit cards

ORIENTAL PEARL

The number of restaurants in Chinatown can be overwhelming, especially since so many of them are geared for either tourists who (1) want bargain basement prices or (2) want lavish decorations fit for an emperor. Oriental Pearl bridges the gap nicely. It's a pleasantly decorated dining room with well-dressed and very helpful waiters, and it's a medium-priced restaurant. Best of all, the food is very good. Here you will eat interesting but accessible Chinese creations using all the finest ingredients. Dishes that you have had in many neighborhood Chinese restaurants somehow rise to a new level here. Your waiter will be glad to guide you through the menu.

760 Clay Street
433–1817
Lunch and dinner daily
Moderate
Credit cards

R AND G LOUNGE

Like many of its neighboring restaurants on Kearny, R and G Lounge offers lunch specials for under $4.00 that are terrific and filling. The main reason for the restaurant's popularity, however, is the seafood, much of it pulled fresh from the tank and served in the original space downstairs and in the newer upstairs dining room. If you are feeling experimental, urge your waiter to suggest dishes, some of which may not be on the menu.

631 Kearny
982–7877
Lunch and dinner daily
Inexpensive to moderate
Credit cards
Entrance to the upstairs dining room is on Commercial Street

CHAPTER 2

Well-Known Neighborhoods

The Castro

The Castro district is nationally known as the center of San Francisco's Gay Community. On Castro and Market Streets the various stores and restaurants draw a mixed crowd of locals and gawkers. You're more likely to see gay and lesbian couples walking arm in arm than to see a heterosexual couple. Sadly, it's also not unusual to see young men pulling oxygen tanks along as they battle the epidemic of AIDS.

The best way to visit is to wander up and down the streets and soak in the atmosphere. Although the Castro is basically a friendly neighborhood, there are some bars and restaurants where straight people are considered intruders. Two businesses on Castro and one on Market will give you an immediate feeling of the neighborhood and its uniqueness.

A Different Light

This is *the* neighborhood bookstore, the place where you will find all the local publications and handbills advertising the various services and performances available in the community. Books and magazines are selected for their interest to the Gay Community. At the counter, they display some items you probably won't find in any other bookstore in town, such as special male lubricants. This is not an overly serious place, as evidenced by the large selection of funny postcards from the gay perspective.

489 Castro. Open daily 10 A.M. to 10 P.M. 431–0891.

CLIFF'S VARIETY

This is a large, high-ceiling store that carries everything from hardware to cookbooks. It's the kind of place that usually has a motto like "If we don't have it, you probably don't need it." The workers and the clientele are a mix of sexual preferences. Rather than being on the cutting edge, as is much of the Castro, at Cliff's you'll be helped by guys in plain shirts with pocket protectors who account for the tax on your purchase by saying, "And a little something for the Governor."

479 Castro Street. Open Monday through Saturday 9:30 A.M. to 8 P.M. 431–5365.

CAFÉ FLORE

This is the unofficial neighborhood coffeehouse for the Castro district. If you want to strike up a conversation and get the feeling of the area, Café Flore is probably your best bet. Go up to the counter and order your beverage or bite to eat, and then try for one of the outdoor tables. You will see a colorful passing parade of customers, both locals and visitors. If you are the type who would rather just sit and listen to your surroundings, you will not be bored.

2298 Market Street at Noe. Open daily from 7:30 A.M. to 11:30 P.M. 621–8579.

AIDS MEMORIAL QUILT/NAMES PROJECT VISITORS CENTER

In contrast to the often lighthearted nature of life on Castro Street, there's a graphic reminder of the toll AIDS has taken and continues to take on the neighborhood, the city, and the world. Once you enter the Names Project Visitors Center, your mood will change as you learn more about AIDS and the Names Project. This small storefront is an educational center where some quilt panels are on display and where new panels are created. The major purpose of the center is to raise consciousness about AIDS and enlist support for the fight against it.

Don't expect a major display or the quilt itself. (It's now so huge that it has to be housed in a giant warehouse.) This is a place to stop and think about your own mortality and about those we have lost.

2362 Market, off Castro. Open Monday through Wednesday and Friday noon to 7 P.M.; Saturday and Sunday noon to 5 P.M. 863–1966.

UNCLE MAME

If you like kitsch, stop in at Uncle Mame, which is an entertaining "shmutz" store run by self-proclaimed master of ceremonies David Sinkler. Emcee Sinker moved from Cleveland a few years ago to pursue his dream of showing and selling collections of memorabilia from the recent past. He calls his emporium an American pop culture store.

On display are snow globes, posters, Pez dispensers, funny hats, gizmos, doodads, and gewgaws. There's that set of Mr. Peanut salt and pepper shakers you were looking for and that Oscar Meyer wiener whistle you always wanted. Some of the items look as though they were made yesterday but designed to look old, while others are genuine collectibles. Either way, something will trigger a fond memory or a laugh.

2193 Market Street. Open daily noon to 7 P.M. 626–1953.

CASTRO THEATER

This is one of the city's few remaining ornate movie palaces that has somehow escaped being divided into several theaters. The programming of films here is often in keeping with neighborhood tastes, and watching a classic like *The Wizard of Oz* or *All About Eve* can be quite a cultural experience. On weekends an organ concert often precedes the movie, usually ending with a rousing rendition of "San Francisco."

Castro at Market. 621–6120.

PLACES TO EAT

CARTA

So what do you feel like eating tonight? Spanish, Brazilian, Russian, Turkish, Indian, Caribbean? You'll find it all at Carta and more. This unusual restaurant features the food of a specific country or region each month, and somehow it manages to pull it off very well. It's a good idea to call and make sure you are interested in the food from the cuisine of the month. Since the menu is small, feel free to inquire about specific dishes.

1772 Market Street, near Gough
863–3516
Lunch and dinner Tuesday through Sunday
Moderate
Credit cards

DAME

If your name was Dame, what would you call your restaurant? (There is nothing like a . . .) The owner/chef, Kelly Dame, took the most direct route for her California-style Italian restaurant on the eastern edge of the Castro district. The Italian influence is evident in the antipasti and pasta courses; the California touches come in with items like gorgonzola french fries and the sumptuous desserts. Decor is not a strong point here; all the money goes into the food.

1815 Market Street
255–8818
Lunch Tuesday through Friday; dinner Tuesday through Sunday; brunch Sunday
Moderate
Credit cards

2223 MARKET

The Castro district was waiting for this place, a stylish, semi-upscale restaurant that serves contemporary California cuisine. Although the clientele is predominately gay, this is one meeting place in the neighborhood where a straight person feels welcome. The menu somehow touches all the bases with offerings of pasta, pizza, salads, grilled and roasted meats and fish, and daily specials. There is also a bar menu, featuring killer cocktails for $6 apiece.

2223 Market Street
431–0692
Lunch and dinner daily
Credit cards

The Mission

Overview

Talk about your melting pot. The residents of the Mission district through the years have included Ohlone Indians, Spanish settlers, Germans, Norwegians, Italians, Irish, and Asians. It is now the center of life for people from Mexico and Central America, with occasional remnants of groups from the past. Lots of artists and young people live here, where rents and food can be cheap and the neighborhood alive and vibrant.

The neighborhood is named for Mission Dolores, which was the sixth in the chain of twenty-one missions that connected Southern and Northern California.

Today's Mission district has several personalities. Highly rated restaurants like the Flying Saucer are cropping up on Guerrero and Valencia Streets, bringing with them a modest form of gentrification. There are probably more coffeehouses around here than anywhere else in the city, ranging from Italian chic to the more prevalent funky bohemian style, like the venerable La Boheme on Twenty-fourth Street near Mission. Each street seems to have its own personality. One example is Sixteenth Street between Mission and Guerrero, one of the most representative of these contrasts: here you will find the arty Roxie Theater, inexpensive coffee shops and doughnut parlors, a high-style shop for designer eyeglasses, a fancy flower shop, and several trendy cafés serving tapas, bagels, espresso, and crepes.

The Mission also boasts one of the prettiest streets in the city, Dolores. If you have time, drive up and down the hills of Dolores Street for a while just to enjoy the attractive palm-tree-lined thoroughfare.

The main east-west road in the Mission is Twenty-fourth Street. For the true Latino flavor of the area, turn left on to Twenty-fourth Street from Dolores, and continue for several blocks until you a try to ditch the car around Bryant Street. There is usually street parking available. Then, take a stroll down Twenty-fourth Street. The street will be crowded with customers at the many markets and shops. Locals often start their mornings with the handmade tortillas at La Palma. Mothers and daughters comb through the girls frilly "fufurufu" dresses on streetside racks. And right in the thick of things the venerable St. Francis Soda Fountain continues to serve up homemade ice cream, candies, and other treats. When you sit at the counter or in one of the old wooden booths, you expect Annette Funicello and Frankie Avalon to hop in any minute with the latest school gossip.

This area of Twenty-fourth Street had its down period when the York Theater closed. It was recently taken over by the group Brava, which celebrates women in the arts and plans programs of film and live theater.

The Mission is the city's most colorful neighborhood, but it's also an area that you should approach with some planning. A great place for walking during the day, the Mission is not a place to wander around at night unless you know the territory.

MISSION DOLORES

A good place to begin a visit to the Mission district is at the beginning, at Mission Dolores. Except for schoolchildren on their obligatory tour of the California missions, most area residents never quite get around to visiting San Francisco's oldest building. Pity.

Most of us think of California as the "new" America, but consider that the first mass at Mission Dolores was five days before the Declaration of Independence, on June 29, 1776. The present site was built with Indian labor sixteen years later, and thanks to its adobe construction with giant beams fastened by leather straps, the basic structure has survived major earthquakes and fires.

The mission is small and welcoming, with a reception area and gift shop and an impressive historic chapel. Don't miss the adjoining cemetery, where you will see the markers for many early settlers whose names became city streets: Noe, Arguello, Bernal, Valencia, Guerrero. This and the veteran's cemetery at the Presidio are the only remaining cemeteries in the city. Because of the shortage of available land, the town of Colma became the home for San Francisco's dearly departed. If you're a film buff, this location will feel familiar to you. This is where Kim Novak was spotted by Jimmy Stewart in Hitchcock's *Vertigo*.

Folks who work at the mission say their visitors are mostly from out of town. They are struck by the fact that rarely do locals take the time to visit even though the mission is in the heart of San Francisco and is a continuing monument to the beginning of life in the city.

3321 Sixteenth Street. Open daily 9 A.M. to 4 P.M. 621–8203.

BALMY ALLEY

Even when much of the city is in fog on a typical summer day, the Mission will be sunny and warm, protected by the hills that block the inflow from the Golden Gate. That heat is heightened by the pulsing sounds of music on the street and by the bright colors that greet you from so many corners. Murals are as much a part of the Mission as burrito shops, and make for a vivid display of "people's" art.

The most concentrated collection of murals is on Balmy Alley, a small street that runs between Capp and Twenty-fourth Street, and is recommended only in the daytime. The artwork is bright and colorful and mostly political. Otherwise, you can get a tour of the art of the Mission or pick up a map of the murals from the Precita Eyes Mural Center at 348 Precita Avenue. Phone: 285–2287. Another good source for information on the murals, and for getting to know the art of the Mission, is the Galeria de la Raza, 2857 Twenty-fourth Street near Bryant Street. Phone: 826–8009.

PLACES TO EAT

ANGKOR BOREI

There was great excitement surrounding the opening of this Cambodian restaurant in the Mission several years ago. Friends in the area insisted that we have dinner there as soon as possible, and we're glad they did. To palates accustomed to Chinese cooking, this Asian cuisine is filled with new taste combinations and new discoveries. The mixtures of hot and cold, spicy and sweet, crunchy and chewy add up to a multitextured dining experience. In other words, whatever you get, it'll be swell.

3471 Mission Street, near Cortland
550–8417
Lunch and dinner daily
Inexpensive
Credit cards

EL TORO

When you are in the mood for a bulging burrito or a taco filled with flavorful and fresh ingredients, get in line at El Toro. There are so many good taquerias in the Mission that choosing one is basically a matter of personal taste. I've never been disappointed at El Toro, and it's somehow easier to find a place to park nearby than at some of the Mission Street places.

598 Valencia
431–3351
Lunch and dinner daily
Inexpensive
No credit cards

FLYING SAUCER

An evening at the Flying Saucer may be the most unusual dining experience you've ever had. Certainly you will eat creations that don't appear in cookbooks but spring only from the imagination of chef/owner Albert Tordjman. On a recent visit I had duck confit in a dark, rich brown sauce served with a potato pecan pie, a hunk of artichoke, sliced zucchini, beets and other vegetables, and leaves and herbs, all artfully arranged on a huge plate. This was preceded by an appetizer of an unusual squid salad with shredded vegetables and squid cooked two different ways. Every plate is a spectacular work of art, piled high with food. You will be stuffed.

All this is in a Mission district setting that resembles what I would describe as artsy thrift shop. The joint is jumping, but the waiters and the cooks seem to handle it all with humor and grace.

1000 Guerrero Street at Twenty-second (there's no sign for the restaurant, just a
    neon flying saucer in the window)
641–9955
Dinner Tuesday through Saturday
Moderate
Credit cards

LA TAQUERIA

In one of the busiest parts of the Mission, you can immerse yourself in the flavor of the neighborhood by joining the throngs that walk through the line choosing their favorite taco or burrito. You can have your food as mild or spicy as you desire, and be assured that the freshest ingredients are being used.

2889 Mission Street
285–7117
Lunch and dinner daily
No credit cards

LE TROU

Long before the area around Twenty-second Street and Guerrero became a dining destination, Le Trou was serving fine country French cuisine. The intimate dining room and the French home cooking makes for an experience far different from eating in a high-presentation restaurant. It's more like being a guest in someone's home. The food is never trendy or showy here. It's based on fresh seasonal ingredients and complementary taste combinations. The menu changes weekly and offers four or five entree selections covering a range of fish, meat, and vegetable dishes. For us this will always be a restaurant for special occasions. Close friends took us here to celebrate our engagement.

1007 Guerrero Street
550–8169
Dinner Tuesday through Saturday
Moderate
Credit cards

MANGIAFUOCO

Across the Street from the popular Flying Saucer and practically next door to Le Trou, this Italian restaurant would look and feel right at home in Firenze. It's modern yet dark and cozy. The huge open grill is filled with roasting meats and fowl. Pasta dishes are also specialties of the house.

1001 Guerrero Street
206–9881
Dinner Tuesday through Sunday
Moderate
No credit cards

TI-COUZ

This is San Francisco's answer to the International House of Pancakes. This comfortable and informal Mission café serves French crepes in a mind-numbing assortment of choices. This is a great place to eat alone, sitting at the counter watching the crepe maker at work on the round steel pans. Salads and a few other items are also available, but it would be a crime to come here and not have at least one of these luscious crepes.

3108 16th Street
252–7373
Lunch and dinner daily; open late
Inexpensive
Credit cards

TISANE

In a hip neighborhood of artists, musicians, and writers, known by the acronym NEMIZ for Northeastern Mission Industrial Zone, you'll find Tisane. The decor is Industrial Modern, which some might find a bit cold with its sharp edges and stainless steel finish. The chef calls herself a "food conceptualist" and offers a variety of contemporary faves, including pizza and big salads. One of the more popular items is fish and chips, served in newspaper.

As the name implies, teas are a specialty here. This is a good place to stop in for dessert on a weekend night and enjoy live music.

2170 Bryant Street (at Twentieth Street)
641–8458
Lunch Monday through Friday; dinner Tuesday through Saturday
Credit cards

UNIVERSAL CAFÉ

A predecessor to its neighbor, Tisane, the Universal opened in industrial surroundings, where no one expected to find a restaurant, and became an immediate hit. Maybe it was the giant coffee roaster that sits near the counter and is used to prepare some of the best coffee in town. Certainly the food is a draw. There's a limited menu featuring wonderful combinations, such as a baked chicken breast stuffed with risotto or a pan-seared filet mignon with gorgonzola mashed potatoes and string beans. At lunch pizza and focaccia sandwiches are the main draw.

Who goes there? One day I found myself eavesdropping on the conversation at the table next to me and finally joined in. I was welcomed by Dennis McNally, publicist for the Grateful Dead, the writer Burr Snider, and R. Crumb's publisher, Baba Ron Turner, all neighbors who consider themselves regulars of the café.

2814 Nineteenth Street between Bryant and Florida
821–4608
Breakfast, lunch, and dinner Tuesday through Sunday
Moderate
Credit cards

WOODWARD GARDENS

You could drive past this restaurant a million times without even realizing it's there. Under the freeway overpass at Mission and Duboce Streets is about as unlikely place to put a restaurant as I can imagine, but folks certainly find it and keep coming back. There is something about the location and the tiny dining room and the view of the minuscule kitchen that makes this an appealing adventure. What makes it pay off, though, is the wonderful food that is based on whatever is fresh and seasonal. The cooking style is California/Mediterranean with special attention to vegetables and fruits.

1700 Mission Street
621–7122
Dinner Wednesday through Sunday
Moderate
No credit cards

SOMA

SOMA stands for "south of Market Street." It's the West Coast version of Manhattan's SOHO (south of Houston Street) and has become a haven for writers, artists, and now computer programmers. They live and work in converted warehouses and other industrial buildings, so the neighborhood quality is a bit elusive, but it is there.

Actually, there are two or three distinct personalities to SOMA. In addition to all the working and creative types, this seems to be headquarters for a series of discount and outlet stores. At night SOMA is where most of the action is centered for the club scene. In fact, at midnight on Fridays and Saturdays, the intersection of Eleventh Avenue and Folsom is often overflowing with young people from all over the Bay Area who come to the "scene" to hop from one club to the next. Finally, in the area near the Waterfront, now called South Beach, apartments have sprung up like wildflowers in recent years, and a large community of youngish residents has developed.

During the day the digital culture is evident in many of the hangouts, where you will find coffee drinkers working away on their laptops. The area has been nicknamed Multimedia Gulch, and at last count more than a hundred high tech companies were clustered between the Embarcadero and Seventh Street, and Harrison and China Basin. Certainly the number of CD-ROM makers and Internet and Web-page mavens is rising. The hip bible of cyberspace, *Wired* magazine, is headquartered here, as are several other computer "zines." You won't be invited into most of these companies, but there are a few places where you can get a definite feel for the community.

SOUTH PARK

Once the home of the local aristocracy, then almost a slum in the 1950s and 1960s, this oval strip of a neighborhood built around a green park with a small playground has become gentrified and is the unofficial home base for Multimedia Gulch. Here, the lunchtime crowd gathers at cafés like the South Park Café, Ristorante Ecco, and Caffe Centro to spread the latest word about who is going broke and why someone else's program doesn't work. On a sunny day the park itself is jammed with picnickers from the nearby design and digital offices. In addition to cafés, a few clothing stores, upscale beauty salons, and other shops add a touch of style to the park.

Parking

Street parking in South Park is usually available except during lunchtime, when spaces are at a premium. If you circle the park and can't find room, look for one of the metered spaces on one of the bordering streets: Second or Third Street, or Bryan or Brannan.

LUMBINI

The most eye-catching store in South Park may appear by its name to be an Italian restaurant, but it's actually a garden and design shop with a very eclectic selection of goods. Landscape architect Topher Delaney named the place after Buddha's birthplace, and the shop is dedicated to bringing out the inner gardener in all of us. There are unusual international items hanging from every corner of the converted warehouse: beautiful pots, globes, statuary, candles, seeds, wallpapers, toys, healing herbs and lotions, books, and even an African Voodoo Container.

156 South Park. Open Monday through Saturday 10 A.M. to 6 P.M. 896–2666.

BRAINWASH

Unusual and almost unbearably hip, Brainwash satisfies a combination of interests. Recognizing that people have lots of time on their hands when they have to babysit their laundry, Brainwash opened in the early 1990s as the city's first combination laundromat–café. The sparkling machines are in the back, while the café is in the front room and extends to sidewalk tables in front.

Everything is done with a sense of humor, including the signs around the place and the decor of the rest rooms. Adding a cyberelement to the place are computer terminals connected by modem to other coffeehouses, so one can sit, do the laundry, and chat with a stranger in a connected coffeehouse across town or in another city.

The food is OK, but it's not the attraction: it's the scene, and if you are really into laundry, the lint filters are top-notch.

1122 Folsom Street. Daily 7:30 A.M. to 11 P.M. No credit cards. 861–3663.

YERBA BUENA CENTER/ARTS COMPLEX

It took more than twenty-five years and the displacement of thousands of low-income families and business, but the redevelopment of the area once called "South of the Slot" is finally near completion. The "slot" refers to the cable car tracks on Market; to the north lived the wealthy and to the south the less affluent. After years of nothing but construction sites and empty lots, a convention and arts complex finally was born. First came the Moscone Convention Center and then the Yerba Buena Center and Museum of Modern Art. Today the area is alive and bustling.

Parking

If possible, park at the Fifth and Mission Municipal Garage for the best rates. Otherwise, there are many expensive garages and lots in the area. Many parking meters are reserved for truck loading, and those that are available are good for only fifteen minutes to an hour. If you don't mind walking a bit, cruise the streets toward the bay. Sometimes you can find nonmetered spaces on side streets.

Yerba Buena gardens is about two blocks from the Powell or Montgomery Street Bart stations. Several bus lines also serve the area.

MUSEUM OF MODERN ART

With the opening of the new Museum of Modern Art in 1995, the Yerba Buena complex became the new center for art in the city. Architect Mario Botha's stunning building is reason enough to visit the museum. You can get a sense of the place from just walking into the lobby, but spend the time to explore both the changing exhibits and the permanent ones.

My personal tastes always take me to the photography section and to the unusual collections such as the art of the chair. As one who has spent a lifetime trying to find a comfortable chair, these creations, from such designers as Eames, Le Corbusier, Frank Gehry, and Mark Mack, made for entertaining viewing.

Plan to spend some time when you visit. There are many nooks and crannies on the four floors of the museum, and there is a pleasant café on the premises if you need to rest and recharge your batteries.

When to go can be a major economic decision if you are part of a large party. General admission is $7 for adults and $3.50 for students and seniors. Kids under thirteen are free. On Thursday evenings between 6 P.M. and 9 P.M., admission is half price. On the first Tuesday of each month, admission is free, but you can obviously expect the joint to be crowded. Free tours of the galleries are offered several times a day. Call the museum's voice-mail for current times and details.

151 Third Street, south of Mission. Open Tuesday, Wednesday, Friday, Saturday, and Sunday 11 A.M. to 6 P.M.; Thursday 11 A.M. to 9 P.M.; closed Monday and holidays. Advance admission tickets available at the museum or through BASS. 357–4000.

YERBA BUENA ARTS CENTER

If you're in the neighborhood and you haven't had your fill of art, cross the street and visit the Center for the Arts Galleries, which features changing exhibits and is part of the new Yerba Buena complex. Included are several gallery rooms and a performing arts center. There's also an inviting café called Opts, which creates special menus to match the featured artists.

The entire area is built around the urban renewal project Yerba Buena Gardens. Here, as a quiet counterpoint to the new modern arts buildings and the adjoining Moscone Convention Center, is a vast urban park, complete with a waterfall to mask the noise of the city. This is at the impressive Martin Luther King Memorial, which features glass panels with quotes from the slain civil rights leader. This is no ordinary waterfall. It's actually a complex fountain that spans almost the entire width of the plaza, from Third to Fourth Street.

At the top level you can sit in the sun and gaze down on the grassy esplanade while you listen to the gentle trickle of water heading for the waterfall. Your view also takes in some of the nearby skyscrapers, including the controversial Marriott Hotel, which has been described as the world's largest pinball machine. Grab a sandwich and a coffee from the Pasqua Café and relax. You'll probably be visited by a hungry bird looking for a snack. You'll be glad to know that there are public rest rooms on this level.

A ramp leads you along more water to the level below, where the waterfall comes crashing down. Beneath the water is a walkway to the panels quoting Dr. King. Be prepared to get wet if you go in for a closer look. The ceiling tends to drip. Both areas are beautifully landscaped with much greenery and colorful flowers.

You will probably be sharing the gardens with an unusual combination of conventioneers (they are the ones with the badges) from nearby Moscone Center, downtown office workers, and random sun worshippers.

For information on art exhibits and theatrical events at the center, phone 978-ARTS (2787).

ANSEL ADAMS CENTER

On the Fourth Street side of the Gardens is a museum that is a tribute to California's great nature photographer. The Ansel Adams Center is a very manageable museum with five galleries, including one showing some of Adams's most recognizable masterpieces. The other galleries show various photographers in changing shows. Save time to visit the gift shop, which has a wonderful collection of photography books in hardcover and paperback.

250 Fourth Street. Tuesday through Sunday 11 A.M. to 5 P.M. $4 adults; $3 students; $2 seniors and ages 12 to 17; under 12 free. 495–7000.

CARTOON ART MUSEUM

This place reminds me of an old story about the comedian Bert Lahr, who was known to be extremely intense and serious about his work. Getting ready to open in a play, he developed a piece of stage business and wanted his colleagues to see if it worked. As he performed, they howled with laughter, but he stopped them angrily and said, "Can't you be serious? I'm trying to see if this is funny."

In a large and attractive second-floor exhibition hall, the Cartoon Art Museum treats the comics with great respect. Its mission is "to encourage the appreciation of this original art form for its artistic, cultural, and historic merits." This is not to imply that a visit here is a sobering experience, just that the work is taken seriously by the staff. Recent shows have included a retrospective of the works of *Mad* magazine founder Harvey Kurtzman and a salute to Charles Schultz, the creator of "Peanuts."

For you, the experience might be nostalgia in finding the newspaper cartoons your dad read to you on Sunday morning or the comic books you once collected or learning about cartoon art that dates back as far as the 1700s. The collection at the museum includes more than ten thousand pieces of art. Theme shows are presented every four months.

In addition to the main gallery space, there's a separate children's gallery and a CD-ROM gallery.

814 Mission Street. Open Wednesday through Friday 11 A.M. to 5 P.M.; Saturday 10 A.M. to 5 P.M.; Sunday 1 P.M. to 5 P.M. Adults $3.50; children $1.50; students and seniors $2.50; free admission the first Wednesday of each month. 227–8666.

More museums are due to move into the Yerba Buena area, including the Mexican Museum and the Jewish Museum.

CALIFORNIA HISTORICAL SOCIETY

Around the corner from the Yerba Buena Center is the new headquarters of the California Historical Society. There are at least two good reasons to check it out. One is to see the society's collection of photos, books, paintings, and memorabilia, which cover the history of California from the Ohlone Indians on. The organization has been collecting treasures since its founding in 1871. Changing exhibits are presented in their three galleries. For serious researchers a library is available by appointment.

The other reason to visit is to see the building itself, a stark contrast to the modern architecture of Yerba Buena Center. Instead, you'll enter a renovated elegant building from the 1920s. It's a bit like walking into a stately old home with polished wood floors, a grand staircase, and art adorning the walls, even though the previous incarnations of the headquarters included life as a hardware company and an office furniture store.

678 Mission Street. 357–1848. Open Tuesday through Saturday 11 A.M. to 6 P.M. Adults $3; students and seniors $1

South Beach

This is the city's newest neighborhood and the one most in question because of plans to build a new ballpark on the waterfront. The identifying symbol of South Beach is the towering, seventy-foot-high, red-and-silver sculpture, Mark diSuvero's *Sea Change*, which moves with the wind at the corner of Embarcadero and Townsend. Below it is a grassy park that overlooks a yacht harbor and has plenty of room and even chairs for sitting and relaxing. There's no more pleasant place in town to sit and look out onto the bay on a sunny day.

Nearby, the Pier 40 Coffee Roastery provides the hangout and bulletin board for community notices. This is where you check in to find out what's going on in the neighborhood.

PLACES TO EAT

APPAM

A very attractive Indian restaurant specializing in clay pot cooking. This is the only Indian place in town that serves "Yiddish" Naan, a flat bread stuffed with beets. Go figure.

1261 Folsom
626–2798
Lunch and dinner daily
Moderate
Credit cards

FRINGALE

Although Gerald Hirogoyen's French bistro is extremely popular and he is always ranked among the city's top chefs, he has managed to retain the bustling charm of his small restaurant and keep the prices down as well. This is one of those places that is just plain fun. Chances are you will have to wait for your table even though you have a reservation, but that gives you the opportunity to see what everyone else is eating and to chat with others. Tables are so close together, you feel like trading tastes with your neighbor. But the food is great, and you'll feel like you've had a quick trip to France.

570 Fourth Street
543–0573
Lunch Monday through Friday; dinner Monday through Saturday
Moderate
Credit cards

ICON CAFÉ

Icon is a funky café that was formerly the Billboard, a haven for artists. Now it's decorated in computer art, with cyberspace metallic creations on the wall and TV monitors and video installations and world music on the box. The menu features a variety of inexpensive, hip choices. The food is decent, but the major draw is the computer in the center of the room, which allows you to browse the Internet. This is a good place to get an easy initiation into the World Wide Web. A $5 minimum on food or drink is required, but you can sit at the terminal as long as crowds and demand allow.

Corner Ninth at Folsom
415–861-BYTE (2983)
e-mail: CON@BYTEBAR.COM hours
Inexpensive
Credit cards

LE CHARM

So you thought all fine French restaurants had to be expensive. The young couple who run Le Charm are out to prove you wrong. In their light and airy space with a large outdoor seating area, they serve imaginative and surprisingly inexpensive French food. At lunch I had a delicious chicken brochette with a pasta pancake (pasta held in a seasoned pancake batter) and salad for six bucks. For dinner everything on the menu is under $10.00, and a three-course dinner is $18.50. The quality is on a par with places that charge twice as much.

315 Fifth Street, between Howard and Folsom
546–6128
Lunch Monday through Friday; dinner Tuesday through Saturday
Inexpensive
Credit cards

PAZZIA CAFÉ AND PIZZERIA

I just happened into Pazzia one day, after I couldn't get into a neighboring restaurant. What a nice find! First, they greeted me with a wonderful house-baked bread and some olive oil to dip it in, and then the waiter led me through the choice of daily grilled specials such as chicken breast and rabbit (tastes like chicken). There are four or five pastas and many thin crust pizzas available, too. Pazzia is a small spot with the feeling of a neighborhood café in Italy.

337 Third Street
512–1693
Lunch and dinner daily
Moderate
Credit cards

RISTORANTE ECCO

South Park's touch of high style is represented by this sleek Northern Italian restaurant. Ristorante Ecco is where the classy dress crowd dines in this center of activity for the multimedia world. The dining room looks out onto the park, while the larger barroom has the feeling of a clubby meeting place. In back of the restaurant, there's a takeout counter where lunchers can pick up their food to take to the park or back to the office.

101 South Park
495–3291
Lunch Monday through Friday; dinner nightly
Moderate
Credit cards

SOUTH PARK CAFÉ

Even if you've never been to Paris, you will immediately recognize the feeling of the South Park Café. The narrow dining room, the decor, the small park outside, and the specialties that are delivered to the tables are all what you would expect to find in a classic French café.

108 South Park (between Second and Third Streets)
495–7275
Breakfast and lunch weekdays; dinner Monday through Saturday; open late
Moderate
Credit cards

TOWN'S END RESTAURANT AND BAKERY

The owners of this South Beach restaurant used to have a great breakfast place called Home Plate on Lombard Street that was filled with baseball memorabilia. It must have come as a surprise to them to see that the Giants' new stadium is scheduled to become their neighbor. Breakfast is served at Town's End, and the menu has been expanded for excellent lunches and dinners. The food is California/Italian, with pastas, salads, and daily specials. Save room for dessert. The baked goods are special.

2 Townsend Street
512–0749
Breakfast daily; lunch and dinner Tuesday through Saturday
Credit cards

Nob Hill

Long before I ever dreamed of living in San Francisco, I saw a movie called *Nob Hill*, with Mark Stevens and Vivian Blaine. You probably don't remember it. It was one of those 1940s Technicolor treatments of "Old San Francisco," forgettable except for the views and drama from the top of California Street. To my memory, the film didn't bother to explain that this was where the big four railroad barons, Crocker, Stanford, Huntington, and Hopkins, and other nabobs set up their mansions, hence the nickname, Nob Hill.

Today, the only mansion that remains is the former home of another railroad millionaire, James Flood, although it is now the exclusive Pacific Union Club at California at Mason. Most of the area is devoted to luxury hotels, such as the Fairmont, Mark Hopkins, Huntington, and Stanford Court, plus the city's largest church, Grace Cathedral. This is one of the better hills for driving visiting friends and relatives around, roller coaster–style. You are guaranteed a reaction if you head east on California from Leavenworth or Jones, pointing out the hotels and attractions along the way. When you suddenly descend at Mason while your passengers are gazing at the Fairmont or Mark Hopkins, prepare for a scream or two.

For walkers the trick is to park on the level ground between California and Clay Streets. You will be able to stroll much of the neighborhood without encountering the steep hills.

The hill is dominated by luxury hotels, such as the Huntington, the Mark Hopkins, and the Stanford Court. The easiest to visit without feeling like you are supposed to have some business there is the Fairmont.

FAIRMONT HOTEL

While no longer the prize of San Francisco's extensive collection of hotels, the Fairmont is still among the most fun to visit, if for no other reason than to ride the breathtaking outdoor elevators. This moving experience of rising up above the city and the bay is still unmatched even though some other hotels have added outside elevators.

The Fairmont is the kind of hotel they simply don't make anymore. It is enormous, and everything about it is larger than life. The lobby, with its marble columns and carpet of leaves, is always abuzz with action, so much so that you can take advantage of the many comfortable chairs and sofas without feeling like you don't belong there. The same goes for the ample rest rooms and other public spaces. You can make yourself at home without feeling like an intruder. This is as opposed to the Mark Hopkins across the street, which has a smaller lobby and a sign advising that the rest rooms are for hotel visitors only.

Wander through the place. You'll pass stores and banquet rooms. If you are feeling particularly bold and are dressed properly, you can probably wander into a party and have a quick bite to eat. Many a struggling actor has survived on such a bold move, but we are not recommending it for anyone who would be embarrassed to be asked questions. In the lobby near the elevators are very graphic historic photos of the 1906 earthquake and fire, which were particularly relevant to the hotel's history. The original Fairmont was destroyed in the disaster before it could officially open. It was rebuilt and opened for business exactly one year later.

On the level below the lobby is a beautiful outdoor terrace garden that is a quiet place to stroll on a sunny day or starry evening.

There are several restaurants at the hotel, but only one that you should at least look at, perhaps even have a cocktail there. The Tonga Room is a re-created island paradise, complete with a thunderstorm that goes off every half hour. Water actually pours down into the pool in the center of the room as you sit at your table under grass umbrellas. If you don't mind missing the band, which starts at 8 P.M., the deal is Happy Hour between 5 P.M. and 7 P.M. You can get your fruit-laced drink and have your way with the buffet. Pay no mind to the TV at the bar, which was playing road races from ESPN on my last visit.

950 Mason at California.

GRACE CATHEDRAL

On the site of the former Crocker mansions, which were destroyed in the 1906 earthquake, stands Grace Cathedral. While it certainly doesn't have the historical impact or majesty of the great cathedrals of Europe, Grace Cathedral is definitely worth a visit, especially on a weekday, when nothing much is going on and you can wander at your leisure and admire the many features and when it is relatively easy to park on the street. This is the center for the Episcopal Church in the Bay Area, but its welcoming brochure proclaims it a cathedral for all people. You are invited to explore and lose yourself in the peaceful surroundings. Keep in mind that this is a "new" building, begun in 1928 and supposedly finished nearly forty years later.

The main entrance is up a series of steps off Taylor Street at California. You are greeted by a Bufano sculpture of St. Francis, for whom the city is named. To the left is a table with brochures explaining the various things to see, including a helpful self-guided tour explaining features such as the "Gates of Paradise" doors, modeled after the famed Ghiberti doors of The Baptistry in Florence, and the murals along the north and south aisles, which depict several moments in San Francisco history.

I was fascinated by the Labyrinth, modeled after the floor of the centuries-old Chartres Cathedral. Actually, there are two labyrinths: one outside and dedicated in late 1995 to the late Jewish philanthropist Mel Swig. Located in the plaza on the Taylor Street side of the Cathedral, this 40-foot-wide circle is made of gray terrazzo and is available to spiritual seekers twenty-four hours a day. You are invited to follow the one-third-mile circular path of the Labyrinth and hopefully enjoy a mystical experience. It's sort of a moving meditation that prompts you to reflect on your life and move on to the next plateau. Inside the cathedral is the woven labyrinth that has been at Grace since 1991. It's a shorter walk, without shoes, but without the distraction of the street.

There's a special section near the main entrance of the cathedral that focuses attention on AIDS and the need for understanding, empathy, and determination to find a cure. A panel from the AIDS quilt hangs from the ceiling, and the featured work of art is an altarpiece by the late Keith Haring done in gold with etchings of angels.

Admission to the cathedral is free, although donations are gratefully accepted.

California and Taylor Streets. Open 7 A.M. to 6 P.M.. Guided tours are available Monday through Friday from 1 P.M. to 3 P.M.; Saturday from 11:30 A.M. to 12:30 P.M.; and Sunday from 12:45 P.M. to 2 P.M. A particularly moving experience is the singing of Vespers every Thursday at 5:15 P.M. A schedule of services and special events is available at the door.

HUNTINGTON PARK

Across the street from the main steps to Grace Cathedral is a lovely neighborhood park that is laid out with as much care as the geometrically designed labyrinths. Usually bathed in sun, Huntington Park has a children's playground at its north end at Sacramento Street, while its southern end at California Street seems to be the province of tai chi chuan practitioners.

The centerpiece of the park is a fountain that is a copy of a sixteenth-century fountain in Rome. Everything in the park seems to be at a human scale, and although there are no signs or imposed rules, people seem to treat the park as though they were in a library. No boom boxes here. Perhaps the view helps set the tone. To one side there's Grace Cathedral, to another, the sedate Huntington Hotel, and next door, the imposing brownstone that was once the Flood Mansion and is now the Pacific Union Club.

PLACES TO EAT

HYDE STREET BISTRO

This is a charming and popular Russian Hill neighborhood spot. The cuisine crosses the border between Austria and Italy. You might start with a vegetable strudel salad then move on to a risotto or pasta, and then have a grilled fish served with spaetzle. The dessert specialty of the house is the warm apple strudel.

This is a friendly, spare restaurant, where the money goes into the food, not the decor. The chef will accommodate special dietary requests.

1521 Hyde Street
441–7778
Dinner nightly
Moderate
Credit cards

NOB HILL GRILLE

The name might be a bit intimidating, considering the neighborhood and the *e* at the end of *grille*, but this is a very informal coffee shop/diner where you can sit at the counter or hope to get a table. What you get is American food of the grilled-cheese and beef-stew variety, and it's all plentiful and good. Soups of the day are hearty, the sandwiches and salads are bountiful, and the desserts are far from low-cal. You might have lunch surrounded by women in business suits on one side with guys in overalls on the other.

969 Hyde Street
474–5985
Breakfast and lunch daily; early dinner Wednesday through Friday
Inexpensive
No credit cards

Union Street

Next to Union Square, Union Street is probably the best-known shopping area in the city. Frankly, I always thought it a bit too trendy and touristy, but if you stick to the area around Fillmore Street, you can begin to get a real neighborhood feel to the area. Parking meters are usually available, particularly if you try the north-south streets that intersect Union Street, such as Webster or Pierce Streets. Garages in the area tend to be expensive. The number 45 bus is your best bet for public transportation.

FREDERICKSON'S HARDWARE

The first signal that locals really hang out here is the fact that service shops have not been driven out by the string of boutiques and restaurants. None is more important than Frederickson's, an old-fashioned hardware store on Fillmore, off Union, that seemingly sells everything. The welcome to the store is warm, including a sign that welcomes pets as long as they are on a leash. It's worth a few minutes just browsing through Frederickson's and soaking up the atmosphere of the neighborhood.

3029 Fillmore. Open Monday through Saturday 9 A.M. to 6 P.M.; Sunday 10 A.M. to 5 P.M. Validated parking. Credit cards. 292–2950.

THE ONE BOOK EMPORIUM

For contrast walk across the street to the One Book Emporium. This is a tiny shop that is truly one of a kind. The "one book" is *The Earth-Star Service Manual*, a book its sellers promise will help you live an ever more autonomous, hilariously daring, protocreative life. The manual, also known as "The Pearl," is available only at this store and from its producers in North Hollywood.

There is more offered for sale than "The Pearl." There are T-shirts with philosophical quotes and books and videos that relate to this process of transformation. Among them during my visit were Oliver Stone's *Natural Born Killers* and Quentin Tarantino's *Pulp Fiction*. Nina, the manager and buyer, assured me that both videos fit the concept.

3024 Fillmore Street. Open weekdays and Saturday 10 A.M. to 6 P.M.; Sunday 11 A.M. to 5 P.M.; closed Tuesday. 673–5510.

BREW CITY

Down the hill on Fillmore Street is a great place for beer lovers. The name might lead you to believe that this is another in the growing trend of brew-pubs, but this is a place where you can actually make your own beer.

Ideally, it works as a social event where three or four friends share the work and the product. Brew City provides the recipes, ingredients, equipment, and the trained staff to get you going. It takes about two hours to make beer, then another two weeks for fermentation. When you return, you bottle and put on your custom label on your six cases of beer. The average cost is $115.

More than thirty varieties of beer are available: ales, stouts, lagers, pilsners, bocks, and so on. Since there are no preservatives, the beer will stay fresh for about three months. There's a small parking lot for customers, which is a definite plus in this neighborhood.

This is a popular concept in Canada where there are more than three hundred personal breweries. Brew City is the first one in Northern California and one of only fifteen in the United States, although more are planned.

2198 Filbert Street at Fillmore. Open Tuesday through Saturday 11 A.M. to 10 P.M.; Sunday 11 A.M. to 6 P.M.. The last brew is two hours before closing time. 929–2255.

PLACES TO EAT

BETELNUT

You won't find Bloody Mary chewing betel nuts here, but you will find the foods from Asia blending together for an adventure in Pacific Rim cuisine. You'll also find Bloody Marys (the beverage) and lots of tropical drinks that seem to pick up where Trader Vic left off. This is a stylish popular spot where you're likely to taste dishes you've never had before. You can enjoy a wide range of tastes by having a series of "small plates."

2030 Union Street
929–8855
Moderate
Credit cards

PANE E VINO

The name means "bread and wine," which is a subtle way of describing what you get at this popular neighborhood trattoria in Cow Hollow. This is basic food, celebrating the simplicity of fine Italian cuisine. The menu items may look like those in countless other restaurants, but here they taste special thanks to the chef's care in choosing the finest ingredients and not letting sauces and seasonings overwhelm them. Whether you have one of the many pasta dishes, meat, fish, or chicken, you will be in for a treat.

3011 Steiner Street
346–2111
Lunch Monday through Saturday; dinner nightly
Moderate
Credit cards

Pacific Heights

This is a neighborhood where the attraction is mansions of the wealthy. It's not a place where you're going to hang out or interact with residents. The usual practice is to drive up and down Broadway or Jackson or Pacific and gaze at the beautiful homes with their equally spectacular views. It's one of those neighborhoods where you wonder, "Where did so many people get so much money to afford these homes?"

The novelist Danielle Steele lives here, as does Gordon Getty. We know where they got their bucks. The fictional Mrs. Doubtfire lived at the corner of Steiner and Broadway. You're not likely to see many celebs walking around. You will see workmen, joggers, and dog walkers.

If you want to get out of your car and sit a while, there are two nice parks in the area, Alta Plaza and Lafayette Park, plus a very pleasant area with a great view of the bay from the steps at Broadway and Lyon Streets. For more on Pacific Heights, see chapter 12.

The area known as Japantown comes alive during one of its many street festivals such as the Cherry Blossom Festival in April, but most of the time it is a fairly conventional shopping area. The tradition and culture that one finds in Chinatown are missing here because the neighborhood was broken up during World War II, when Japanese-American families were sent off to internment camps. When families returned from detention, they scattered throughout the Bay Area, leaving the three-block stretch of Post Street, between Laguna and Fillmore, to become a shopping area or a place to visit for worship at one of the many temples and churches. The architecture is mostly 1960s Japanese-American, and the emphasis is definitely on commerce. The mix is eclectic: there are malls selling Japanese goods and serving Japanese food, there is a major multiscreen movie theater showing American films, and there is a well-appointed Japanese bathhouse, the Kabuki Hot Springs, where for ten bucks you can soak in hot and cold tubs to your heart's content. Massages are also available. 1750 Geary Blvd. 922–6000. Open Monday through Friday 10 A.M. to 10 P.M.; Saturday and Sunday 9 A.M. to 10 P.M. Appointments suggested for Shiatsu massage.

Your best bet for a cultural experience is to visit during one of the annual festivals, when flowers and banners decorate the Peace Plaza, a gift from the Japanese people to the community. Most festivals feature tea ceremonies, sumo wrestlers, Taiko drummers, music and dancing, and brightly dressed children.

PLACES TO EAT

IROHA

Noodle dishes are a staple of many Asian cultures. For Japanese diners this usually means a choice of either ramen, soba, or udon noodles, often served with tempura, roast pork, or even dumplings that are similar to the Chinese dumplings called pot stickers. You can enjoy all of the above at this low-key restaurant in Japantown.

1728 Buchanan Street
922–1321
Inexpensive
Credit cards

ISUZU

This popular restaurant for local Japanese families specializes in seafood of all kinds, from sushi and sashimi to fish cooked in a variety of styles. Check with your waiter to see what is fresh, and order accordingly. Your entree will be accompanied by several dishes of vegetables and salads.

1581 Webster Street
922–2290
Lunch and dinner daily
Moderate
Credit cards

CHAPTER 3

Not Quite Neighborhoods

Because the following areas are not mainly residential centers, they may not qualify as actual neighborhoods, but they are still important areas to know and good places to visit.

Embarcadero

Remember the unbearably ugly Embarcadero freeway, looming like a giant concrete creature casting ominous shadows on the road and sidewalk below? Once it came down, in the rebuilding that followed the 1989 earthquake, this entire stretch of real estate was reborn. For visitors, workers, strolling lovers, and locals just sightseeing near home, the Embarcadero is now one of the great places in the city. Eventually, much of the area will be lined with palm trees and trolley tracks, adding even more life to this revived area. By the time you read this, there may even be a brand new baseball stadium on the waterfront, along with shops and other attractions. The plan as of this writing is to build the Giants' ballpark around the Embarcadero and King Street, in the area called South Beach.

The Embarcadero follows the bay from China Basin, south of Market Street, north to Fisherman's Wharf, and has become one of the prime walking spots in the city. You can begin just about anywhere, walk in any direction, and enjoy fresh sea air, beautiful views, and, frequently, a warming sun. A three-and-a-half mile stretch is called Herb Caen Way, in honor of the city's Pulitzer Prize–winning newspaper columnist. You will probably encounter as many runners as walkers, many of them starting out from the renovated YMCA with its entrance on Spear Street between Mission and Howard Streets.

Now that the shipping industry has moved to the Port of Oakland, the concentration is on creating a scenic and educational resource. The scenery surrounds you as you walk along the Embarcadero with the bay to one side and the city's skyline to the other. The education comes in the form of a series of black and white poles, which are displays featuring different aspects of the waterfront's history. What was the "Gold Mountain"? The "White Angel Jungle"? Who were the "Frisco Crimps"? Each pole tells a fascinating story, and if you are up for a long walk, you can get a quick refresher course on San Francisco history in one of the nicest settings imaginable.

There's also something called the Promenade Project, which adds to the beauty of the Embarcadero. It is a continuous concrete sculpture with a band of glass blocks in the center. At night the glass is illuminated to create a ribbon of light along the waterfront.

During the day you can join sunbathers snacking by the water. At night couples take romantic walks along the piers that jut out into the bay. The nicest is just south of Broadway. This walkway features period lamps, benches, great vistas, and even a public toilet. On Saturday mornings the area around the Ferry Building comes alive with a Farmer's Market. The Ferry Building, by the way, is the center point for the numbering of the piers along the waterfront. Even numbers go south, odd numbers go north.

If you're a walker, there is no place more invigorating than the Embarcadero for slow stroll or, for that matter, a brisk run. Not only is the scenery spectacular, but the entire area is flat, and there is almost always a refreshing breeze.

RINCON ANNEX

The most interesting building in the area from a historical perspective is the Rincon Annex at Mission and Spear Streets. Though there are many glitzy new skyscrapers in the area, this is the most architecturally significant building, which was retired as a post office in 1979. A huge new office complex was built on the site, but the original lobby was saved and turned into museum of sorts. Grey Brechin, an architecture historian and writer who has written extensively about the site, showed me around. Rincon Annex was a spectacular WPA project that was constructed as art. Not only are the murals works of art, but so is every aspect of the building: the counters, heaters, light fixtures, windows, and so on.

The murals, by the Russian artist Anton Refrigier, were the subject of great controversy. They show a very checkered history that challenges the assumption that San Francisco has always been a liberal, accepting town. Here is a picture of the city's history with all its warts, exposing anti-Chinese, anti-labor, and anti-Indian treatment. The city fathers were aghast at this portrait of San Francisco.

The twenty-six murals tell the chronological story of the city from mission days to the building of the Transcontinental Railroad to the founding of the United Nations. Surprisingly, the artist was forced to change only one mural. In the mission scene the mural Indians are standing tall and dignified. Originally the monk in background was fat, but he had to be slimmed down because of a protest from the Catholic Church, which thought it made him look parasitic. You can still see the change in the mural.

While you're there, wander into the adjoining new building with its spacious atrium. The fountain/waterfall, which drops from a circle at the top of the ceiling without making a splash, is worth a visit in itself. The atrium features an upscale international food court of sorts and the highly rated Chinese restaurant, Wu Kong.

Corner of Mission and Spear. Historic area open 7 A.M. to 6 P.M.; atrium and restaurants open at night.

The Financial District, Formerly the Barbary Coast

San Francisco has always been both ashamed and proud of its reputation of having been one of the wildest, most dangerous cities in the world. After the Gold Rush and into the early 1900s, this was the scene of just about every imaginable vice. Someone back then likened it to the "land of the Berbers" on the shore of Tunisia, hence the nickname "Barbary Coast." Should we draw any conclusions from the fact that the area is now the center of the finance industry, with all its social prominence and respectability? Although it is no longer a place where one could get "shanghaied" on a hell ship to China or slipped a "Mickey Finn" (two terms that were invented during the heyday of the Barbary Coast), any investor will tell you that it is still possible to get fleeced in this neighborhood.

A visit here includes what you can see and what you can only imagine. Picture Montgomery Street as the shoreline of Yerba Buena Cove. It is 1851, and you are walking on sand dunes in a spot now occupied by skyscrapers. Instead of a paved street full of BMWs, bike messengers, and people closing deals on their cellular phones while waiting for the light to change, there are wooden planks underneath your feet. Out in the bay are hundreds of deserted ships, the crews abandoning all to head for the hills to find gold. You can't see any of this, but chances are you are walking on a landfill, and there is still a part of a wooden ship under the ground. There are plaques on many of the buildings, giving the various bits of history.

Parking

There are numerous parking garages in the area, most of them very expensive. The closest municipal garage is under Portsmouth Square at Kearny and Sacramento. Some parking meters are available on the street, but most of them are truck loading zones until 1 P.M.

Interspersed with the main streets like Montgomery are several back roads that provide interesting walks:

HOTALING STREET

This is a colorful pedestrian street between Washington and Jackson, with antique stores and small offices. Notice the VIPs who enter the Villa Taverna, a private restaurant. Hotaling was named after a man who owned a whiskey distillery. His buildings survived the 1906 earthquake while others around it were demolished, causing cynics to scoff at the notion that the quake and fire were divine punishment for the reckless ways of the Barbary Coast.

BALANCE STREET

Just off Jackson between Montgomery and Sansome is a narrow alley so named because a ship, the *Balance*, is said to be buried underground, one of the many ships abandoned during the gold rush. Buried treasures still turn up during excavations for new buildings.

GOLD STREET

This is a one-block road that runs off Balance Street. It's a rather picturesque narrow alley filled with offices and the popular restaurant Bix.

LEIDESDORF STREET

Leidesdorf runs between Sansome and Montgomery Streets and heads north and south between California and Clay Streets. It's named for one of San Francisco's black pioneers, William Leidesdorf, who made his fortune before the gold rush and built the first City Hall. Today, the street is filled with lunch-hour strollers, many making their way up to the park next to the Transamerica Building.

COMMERCIAL STREET

This road, three blocks long, connects the Financial District to Chinatown. It runs from Sansome Street to Grant, east to west, and is one of the few remaining brick streets (in some stretches) in the city. The main surprise on Commercial Street is a museum that is one of the city's best-kept secrets.

PACIFIC HERITAGE MUSEUM

Built on the original site of the West's first mint, the museum, once the U.S. subtreasury building, is the gift of the Bank of Canton, whose headquarters adjoin the building.

This is a beautifully appointed four-story museum that presents unusual and artful exhibits for long periods. A wonderful show on air travel in the Pacific ran for more than a year. The general theme for all shows is the link between the western United States and the people of the Pacific. On my last visit there was a presentation of wooden furniture from the Ming Dynasty. Extensive space is devoted to each subject, and a visit here is never rushed or crowded. On the lowest floor there is a permanent exhibit showing what the building was like the first time around. There are vaults with bags filled with who knows what in an area that looks like a prison for money.

608 Commercial Street. Monday through Friday 9 A.M. to 5 P.M. Free. 399–1124.

GRABHORN PARK

Just up the street from the museum, toward Chinatown, is a vest-pocket park that offers a quiet refuge to the weary. Grabhorn Park is named after the printing company that used to be in this location, and it is a tiny escape with benches, trees, and a waterfall to mask off the sounds of the city. For some reason this park seems to have escaped the homeless population, so the odds of being able to sit and not be panhandled are pretty good.

CHINESE HISTORICAL SOCIETY

It doesn't look like it exists from the street, but in the basement at 650 Commercial Street is the Chinese Historical Society of America Museum. This is a tiny space with a lot crammed into it. You will see various displays and mementos of the Chinese pioneers in California, including work tools, a shrimp-cleaning machine, a wooden wheelbarrow, artifacts, photos, Taoist altar banners, papier-mâché dragons, and weapons from Tong wars. The overall story is of the migration of the Chinese to this country and the evolution of Chinese-American culture.

650 Commercial Street. Open Tuesdays and Fridays noon to 4 P.M. or by appointment. Free. 391–1188.

Transamerica Pyramid

The pyramid has become so much a part of the landscape that most Bay Area residents take it for granted. Sure, there were screams of complaint when the building went up in the early 1970s, but now the forty-eight-story pyramid is considered a San Francisco institution.

If you've never been inside, it's worth a few minutes of your time. Park in one of the metered spaces along one of the streets to the north, such as Pacific or Jackson, or in the municipal garage under Portsmouth Plaza at Kearny if you are going to be in the neighborhood for a while.

Unfortunately, the major attraction of the pyramid, the observation deck on the twenty-seventh floor, is closed as of this writing, and there are no immediate plans to reopen it. You can stroll through the lobby, however, which features changing exhibits that vary from chocolate sculptures by the master chocolatier Joseph Schmidt to rare movie posters on loan from the Pacific Film Archive. There is also a small room with a scale model of the pyramid and a multimedia presentation on the building and the company. Here you will learn fun facts that will come in handy when you wish to dazzle—or bore—your friends. What is the smallest floor in the building? The forty-eighth and top floor, which is only 2,025 square feet. On top of the top floor is a 212-foot spire with an airplane warning light.

Redwoods Park

To the east of the pyramid is a half-acre park, appropriately called Redwoods Park. Redwood trees were brought in from the Santa Cruz Mountains to turn this portion of the concrete canyon into a natural preserve of sorts. There's also a fountain and waterfall and a small stage for lunchtime performances. This is a peaceful, quiet area, and because of the trees and high buildings, it tends to be shady and cool.

Wells Fargo Museum

A good place to spend a few minutes is the Wells Fargo museum at 420 Montgomery Street. Here you will find displays that tell the story of the gold rush and, of course, Wells Fargo's considerable role in the growth of California. Exhibits show their historic wagons, early letters and wire transmissions, gold samples, weapons, maps, and so on. If you bring the kids, make sure to take them up to the mezzanine for a simulated ride on a stagecoach. You will gain new respect for those pioneers who bumped across the West in claustrophobic discomfort. Because the company controlled overland mail and transportation in the entire West in the 1860s, stagecoaches and Wells Fargo are synonymous. If you have no shame, you can hop aboard and sing "Oh, the Wells Fargo wagon is a-coming" from *The Music Man*.

There is much to learn here on a short visit. By the way, am I the only one who assumed that the "Fargo" in the company's name referred to the city in North Dakota? Actually, the founders were named Henry Wells and William Fargo, but you knew that already, right?

420 Montgomery Street. Monday through Friday, except for bank holidays, 9 A.M. to 5 P.M. Free. 396–2619.

Jackson Square

The most elegant section of the former Barbary Coast is now the home of antique and design shops and beautifully restored old buildings. This is a four-block area, between Sansome and Columbus and Washington and Pacific, free of skyscrapers and with a historic atmosphere that reminds me of Boston's Back Bay. You can usually find a metered parking space on Jackson or Pacific; just take the time to wander. In addition to the expensive antique shops, there are several unusual stores that cater to folks with specific tastes.

THOMAS CARA

For any lover of the wonderful coffee available in San Francisco, a special pilgrimage is in order to the place at least partially responsible for it all, Thomas Cara on Pacific Avenue. This is a showroom and repair facility for fine espresso makers.

It was Thomas Cara who brought the first espresso machines to the western United States for resale. While in Milan during World War II, he bought his first machine, a huge, elaborate silver masterpiece made by La Pavoni that now sits on display at the front of the store but is not for sale. He also brought home the rights to sell La Pavoni and Gaggia machines in the United States, some forty-five years before the gourmet coffee craze hit on a national scale.

For years Cara operated on Columbus Avenue near Broadway, a logical North Beach location for his product. But when topless clubs became the rage of Broadway in the 1960s, Mama Cara decided it was time to move. They've been in the present location since 1968, and now his sons, John and Chris, run the operation.

In addition to the machines for sale and those being serviced (mine occasionally included), the Caras have on display an unusual collection of coffeemakers, which seem to fit right into the classy neighborhood of antique stores and art galleries.

517 Pacific Avenue. Monday through Saturday 9 A.M. to 5:30 P.M. 781–0383.

THOMAS BROS. MAPS

Anyone who has tried to navigate around a city like San Francisco, with streets that suddenly change names or seem to vanish into thin air, should be familiar with Thomas Bros. Maps. Here, in a renovated Victorian house they have occupied for more than thirty years, is their only store in the city, offering detailed maps of just about anywhere you would like to go, plus globes and other travel-oriented goods.

550 Montgomery, at Columbus. Open weekdays 9:30 A.M. to 5:30 P.M. 981–7520.

WILLIAM STOUT ARCHITECTURAL BOOKS

This is the equivalent of a mini-library for anyone interested in architecture or design. Stacked floor to ceiling with new and out-of-print books on architecture, this two-level store is a great resource on a single subject.

This is a place where scholars go to study the history of architecture and design. Long a fixture in Jackson Square, the shop moved from smaller quarters in a nearby alley in the mid-1990s. You might find the place a bit intimidating if you don't feel like you know the subject, but the folks are friendly and helpful.

804 Montgomery Street. Open Monday through Saturday from 10 A.M. to 5:30 P.M.; Thursdays until 9 P.M. 391–6757.

Civic Center

The Civic Center is the area surrounding City Hall, with entrances on Polk Street and Van Ness Avenue between McAllister and Grove Streets. The new Public Library, Davies Symphony Hall, the Opera House, the State Office Building, the Federal Building, the Bill Graham Civic Auditorium, and the Veteran's Building, which had been the headquarters of the Museum of Modern Art, fill out the Civic Center, giving the area a bit of a split personality. By day government reigns, while at night the activity centers on the performing arts. The truly special nights are when the two worlds join forces, as when the Symphony's biannual fund-raiser, the Black and White Ball, was held in the Civic Center. Then every building and street in the area became a stage.

Parking

This is not an area in which to look for street parking, although metered spaces occasionally do become available on Van Ness and some of the east-west streets such as Hayes and Turk. The simplest solution is to park in the municipal garage under Civic Center Plaza, although you should know there's a good chance of being confronted by a panhandler.

Because of the central location, the Civic Center is easily reached by public transportation, including BART, buses, and trolleys.

San Francisco Public Library

The brand-new, seven-story Main Library became the town's newest hit as soon as it opened in April 1996. Thousands of people turned out for the week-long series of events celebrating the 376,000-square-foot, $137-million building. There is probably not another library like it in the nation.

Pick your subject, and you will find it has a special place at the New Main. Children's books? There are more than thirty thousand in forty languages, plus audio- and videotapes, CD-ROMs, and magazines. Art? There's a collection of reproductions and photos that are stored digitally and can be viewed on special monitors. History? The history center has more than three hundred thousand photographs, plus memorabilia such as maps, menus, theater playbills, and oral and written histories. Gay and lesbian lore? The Hormel Center, donated by an heir to the meat fortune, has the world's largest collection of material about gay people. Technology? There are more than three hundred computer terminals scattered throughout the library for visitor use.

Entrances to the library are on Larkin, Fulton, and Grove streets. Open Monday 10 A.M. to 6 P.M.; Tuesday through Thursday 9 A.M. to 8 P.M.; Friday 11 A.M. to 5 P.M.; Saturday 9 A.M. to 5 P.M.; Sunday noon to 5 P.M. 557–4400.

City Hall

San Francisco's impressive City Hall is closed at this writing and is in the process of yet another earthquake-induced renovation. It was built in 1915 after the 1906 quake destroyed the previous hall. Once reopened it will certainly be worth a visit. The great rotunda in the center of the hall and the majestic stairway leading up to the mayor's office are spectacular and have been the setting for many a movie scene. The Hall's dome is modeled after St. Peter's in Rome and was purposely designed to be three feet higher than the Capitol in Washington, D.C. The primary entrance to the Hall is on Polk Street, facing Civic Center Plaza, which is often the scene for political demonstrations and a hangout for the homeless.

Rock 'N' Roll Landmarks

It's hard to imagine now that it ever happened, but in 1967 the "Summer of Love" brought kids from all over the world to San Francisco in search of sex, drugs, and world peace. Clearly, this was the center of the rock culture with bands like The Grateful Dead, Jefferson Airplane, Janis Joplin and Big Brother and the Holding Company, and many others all performing and recording in and around the city. The new magazine *Rolling Stone* was headquartered here and sent out weekly reports about the city by the bay.

Free LSD, free grass, free love, and who knows what else were plentiful on the streets of the Haight-Ashbury district and neighboring Golden Gate Park. The flower children danced and hugged and loved the world and each other in a permanently stoned state until it all came crashing down.

In less than a year LSD was outlawed. Peace and love were overcome by violence and greed. The Diggers staged a funeral that symbolized the death of the Hippie movement. Most of the kids who had come to San Francisco with flowers in their hair either left or got some "straight" clothes and went to work.

The music scene, however, flourished, and the city has remained fertile ground for veteran and new musicians. For the rock 'n' roll fan, there are many landmarks to know about, although the most you can do is look at the sites and imagine what life used to be like in the San Francisco of the 1960s.

AVALON BALLROOM

Now the Regency II movie theater, this was the venue created by the laid-back Chet Helms, who introduced his Texas friend Janis Joplin to the area. Helms was an early competitor of Bill Graham's but was soon overwhelmed by the more aggressive and better-organized Graham.

1268 Sutter Street, off Van Ness Avenue.

The Carousel Ballroom/Fillmore West

The Grateful Dead and the Jefferson Airplane decided to take on Bill Graham, too. They and most of the hippies thought that Graham was too much of a businessman and that music should be as close as possible to free. The two bands, as well as other local groups, would play there but the experiment barely lasted a year before the operation went bust.

Bill Graham took it over and ran it as Fillmore West, bringing in top acts from around the country. The building is now a car dealership.

Southwest corner, Market and Van Ness.

The Fillmore Auditorium

This is one of the few venues from the old days that is still in operation. Bill Graham opened and closed it a few times. Now concerts are presented there regularly.

1805 Geary Street. 346–6000.

Winterland

Gone now but arguably the most famous of all the San Francisco rock palaces, Winterland was the perfect size for a major show. This was the last place in town where you could see a group like The Who or Bruce Springsteen and the E Street Band and actually be close enough to see them without TV monitors. Once arena settings became the norm for high-priced acts, however, Winterland was doomed.

Every rock performer who was anybody during the decade of the 1970s performed in this former ice-skating rink. Its most famous concert was the farewell performance of The Band, which was made into a film, *The Last Waltz*, by Martin Scorcese. For the event, which featured appearances by such guests as Eric Clapton, Bob Dylan, and Van Morrison, Graham brought in chandeliers and other elegant furnishings and served Thanksgiving dinner to the entire audience. Winterland was torn down to make room for an apartment building.

Corner Post and Steiner.

JEFFERSON AIRPLANE HOUSE

This imposing pillared mansion, across from Golden Gate Park, was the private residence of members of the band for a while. Then, most of them moved to Marin County, but the house remained band headquarters until the Airplane broke up.

2400 Fulton Street.

GRATEFUL DEAD HOUSE

Along with the Airplane, the Dead was the house band of the neighborhood. In fact, under their previous name, the Warlocks, the band played for Ken Kesey's acid tests, which were chronicled by the author Tom Wolfe. Like members of the Airplane, the Dead left the Haight for quieter pastures in the late 1960s.

710 Ashbury Street.

Lesser-Known Neighborhoods (But Worth Getting to Know)

CHAPTER 4

Most of us who like to feel like insiders are always looking for new discoveries, perhaps a neighborhood that is not well known except to the people who live there. So you wander into a neighborhood and want to get a sense of what life is like there. Where do you start? A friendly, relaxed setting can open the way to conversation, which brings us to search for one or two places that appear to set the tone of the neighborhood.

Since these kinds of neighborhoods don't have visitors centers or tourist bureaus, a good place for solid information is usually the local bookstore, the one that was there before the chain operations came in. Another place is the local coffeehouse, the one that was in operation before Starbucks moved in. In the bookstore browsing is encouraged without the pressure of having to buy something. There are usually chairs for you to take a load off your feet. Bulletin boards display not only interesting personal items, but also flyers on local performances and events. And the staff is usually local and familiar with the neighborhood. On a more subtle level the decor and the book selections and displays often reflect the feeling of the territory. As for the coffeehouse, it often plays the same role as the pub in England, a place where locals meet to pass the time of day.

Noe Valley

Noe Valley is hardly unknown to most San Franciscans. In the 1970s this sunny area of affordable Victorian and Edwardian homes became the neighborhood of choice for young families. There are few housing bargains around anymore, but this is still a popular and welcoming spot for an interesting mixture of older residents, former hippies, yuppies, and just plain folks. While Noe Valley doesn't have the ethnic appeal of North Beach or Chinatown, it's a nice place to spend the day and have a genuine San Francisco experience.

Here you will find an interesting mixture of old and new. There are still old-fashioned cafés (the kind without espresso machines) like Herb's Fine Food with its horseshoe-shaped counter and its menu that hasn't changed for years. There's a neighborhood bar called the Rat and Raven. There are two used record shops, a gourmet-style supermarket, a natural foods store, a tiny news and magazine store, a locksmith, clothing shops, lots of restaurants, a New Age crystal shop, and a flower shop called Accent on Flowers, Too, that sets the tone of the neighborhood with a sign that reads, PLEASE TOUCH THE FLOWERS (CAREFULLY).

Although there are no children's attractions except for some kid's clothing and toy stores, this is a nice place for a family visit. On one sunny midday visit, I counted twelve children in strollers within ten minutes of arriving. Also noticeable were the number of dogs on leashes.

If you follow our suggestions for getting to know a neighborhood by visiting the local bookstore or coffeehouse, you will have plenty of choices. There are at least four bookstores of note and more choices for a cappuccino than you'll find on the average street in Rome.

Parking

There is metered parking on the main drag of Noe Valley, Twenty-fourth Street, and it's usually easy to get a space during the week. Saturdays can be a problem, though. Fortunately, the surrounding blocks are pretty flat, and you can usually find something within a few blocks of Twenty-fourth Street. There are no major parking garages in the area, but there is a small metered lot on Twenty-fourth Street, between Castro and Noe, where you can park for fifty cents an hour if you can get a space.

Bus and trolley service is also available to the area.

BOOKSTORES

COVER TO COVER

This is a good place to start your exploration of the neighborhood, especially if you have a child with you. Located in the heart of the commercial section of the valley, Cover to Cover is a small, well-stocked store featuring a special children's section in back with a playhouse where kids can hide away and look at books to their heart's content while Mom and Dad browse the new selections in front and talk to the salespeople about the neighborhood.

This is one of the many independent bookstores that are highly vocal in fighting off the big chains that have become such a factor in the marketing of books. It's also a shop that has some longevity in the neighborhood and can tell you about where and how to enjoy yourself. Author readings are frequently held here, including many by children's book writers.

3910 Twenty-fourth Street. Open Monday through Saturday 10 A.M. to 9 P.M.; Sunday 10 A.M. to 6 P.M. 282–8080.

PHOENIX BOOKS

In their corner location at Twenty-fourth and Vicksburg, this small shop sells mostly used books and music. Because they must be so selective in what they buy and therefore think they can resell, the books on the shelves can give you some insight into the kind of people who live in the area. Subjects covered follow the general interests of thirty-something parents: childcare, self-help, poetry, and literature. Phoenix is a low-key spot where you can pick up some bargains and talk to the friendly clerks about the neighborhood.

3850 Twenty-fourth Street. Open daily from 10 A.M. to 10 P.M. 821–3477.

CARROLL'S BOOKS

Now this is another kind of used bookstore entirely. First of all, it's off Twenty-fourth Street on Church, and you probably wouldn't know it's there unless you sought it out. One look inside the tiny entryway, however, tells you are in an unusual store. Amid the clutter in the doorway is a rack for community publications with the sign that reads NO REAL ESTATE JUNK. Walk into the back and you enter a world of used books in a space that seems to keep growing.

In the center of a large open room, you'll find a couch that looks like a Goodwill Industries reject, some chairs, and a birdcage with some chirping canaries. There's also a community bulletin board for personal notices. And the books? You won't know where to start, with belles lettres, old fiction, mysteries, science fiction, biographies, or the endless collection of *National Geographic* magazines. The racks of used and rare books appear to be endless. Hang around for a while and you are guaranteed to meet at least one local character who will give you a special flavor of Noe Valley.

1193 Church Street. Open Sunday through Thursday 10 A.M. to 9 P.M.; Friday and Saturday 10 A.M. to 10 P.M. 647–3020.

SAN FRANCISCO MYSTERY BOOKSTORE

Although this destination store for mystery lovers could probably be in any part of the city, Bruce Taylor has been operating in Noe Valley for twenty years. If you've been looking for the earlier novels by a writer who's hot now or if you want to read a detective story that takes place in Savannah, Georgia, he has it. He also has reading copies and first editions.

Bruce has seen his share of changes in the neighborhood. He watched the old Meat Market Coffeehouse become Miss Millie's. The knish store now sells Tom's Peasant Pies. Bud's Ice Cream, where there used to be lines of eager fans at the corner of Castro, is now Rory's Ice Cream. Mostly, though, he says the main changes have been more in the center of the commercial area, around Noe. According to Bruce, you can now go from coffeehouse to coffeehouse during a rainstorm without getting wet.

4175 Twenty-fourth Street, between Castro and Diamond Streets. Open Wednesday through Sunday 11:30 A.M.to 5:30 P.M. 282–7444.

COFFEÉHOUSES

SPINELLI'S AND MARTHA AND BROS.

Indeed there are too many places for coffee to mention. One indication of the neighborhood is that many folks point to the Starbucks on the corner of Twenty-fourth at Noe as "that interloper from Seattle."

Local loyalties seem to be with two venerable establishments: Spinelli's, Twenty-fourth Street commercial district between Noe and Sanchez; and Martha and Bros., farther east between Vicksburg and Church Streets. Both feature good coffee, some pastries, and outdoor benches where you can sit in the sun and strike up a conversation with another coffee fiend or a passerby.

LOVEJOY'S ANTIQUES AND TEA ROOM

If coffee is not your style, check out the charming and tiny Lovejoy's. This place started out as an antique store that served tea, but because of customer demand reversed the emphasis of the operation. Now it's a tea room that sells antiques. Basically, anything and everything in the place is for sale, which translates into the pictures on the wall, the lovely china tea cups and saucers, even the chairs and tables. The other antiques are now offered at the M and M Exchange at Twenty-third and Sanchez.

Tea, crumpets, traditional English sandwiches, quiches, and pâtés are served along with a selection of teas in this pink storefront with Victorian furnishings. It's all terribly civilized.

1195 Church, just north of Twenty-fourth Street. Breakfast, lunch, and afternoon tea daily. 648–5895.

PLACES TO EAT

BACCO

Noe Valley's stylish Northern Italian restaurant specializes in a variety of interesting pasta dishes that are a long way from the old spaghetti-and-meatball, tomato-sauce fare of the Italian places I grew up with. The emphasis is on fresh, tasty ingredients.

737 Diamond Street, at Twenty-fourth
282–4969
Dinner nightly
Moderate
Credit cards

BARNEY'S

This is part of a group of hamburger joints that started in Oakland. Every variety of burger imaginable, and some you never thought of, is offered, plus bountiful salads and side dishes. These are juicy, three- or four-napkin burgers. Also, try their curly spicy french fries, but be prepared for a huge portion. For those who don't want to eat beef, they have chicken and turkey burgers, too.

4138 Twenty-fourth Street, west of Castro
282–7770
Lunch and dinner daily
Inexpensive
No credit cards

FIREFLY

I hope they named this eclectic and sometimes humorous Noe Valley restaurant after the Groucho Marx character, Rufus T. Firefly. There is nothing too outrageous for the chef to try, from seafood pot sticker dumplings to "swamp stompin' bayou gumbo." The menu changes weekly and offers food from around the world, all served with California sensibilities.

4288 Twenty-fourth Street
821–7652
Dinner Tuesday through Sunday
Moderate
Credit cards

MISS MILLIE'S

This is a whimsically decorated café in the former Meat Market coffeehouse, which was a former meat market. The big draw here is breakfast, with such regulars as omelettes and french toast, plus specials like souffléed lemon pancakes and roasted root veggies as an alternative to home-fried potatoes. Good coffee drinks, too.

4123 Twenty-fourth Street, west of Castro
285–5598
Breakfast Tuesday through Friday; brunch Saturday and Sunday
Credit cards

RORY'S

Ensconced in the former location of Bud's Ice Cream, Rory's is an excellent ice cream parlor. For a decadent treat, have a few scoops in a hot chocolate waffle cone.

Corner of Twenty-fourth and Castro
Open daily 11 A.M. to 11 P.M.

Potrero Hill

Overview

If the fog is covering most of the city and you are frantically searching for some sunshine, one of your best bets is to head for Potrero Hill. It's the last hill before you get to the bay, and skies are often blue even when the rest of San Francisco is gray.

Potrero Hill is actually a continuing series of hills offering some of the best views of the city skyline. The bottom of the hill on the north side is basically industrial with a mix of warehouses and chic designer marts. The bottom of the hill on the south side is a rough mix of housing projects and industry, perhaps best known as the childhood home of O. J. Simpson. The top of the hill is a self-contained village of artists, craftspeople, and young urban dwellers.

The area that best captures the neighborhood is on Eighteenth Street between Texas and Connecticut. In these two blocks you can get a sense of the laid-back, iconoclastic lifestyle of the place. Between Texas and Missouri you will find mostly locals standing in line for one of the sandwiches or salads from Hazel's Kitchen. This is a tiny takeout spot offering fresh food at very inexpensive prices. Customers sit on the benches outside and enjoy their lunch while they gossip with neighbors. Then many folks head two doors down to Farley's Coffeehouse for their cappuccino and a dessert. No Peet's or Starbucks around here.

Across the street is a Potrero institution, Bloom's Saloon, which still displays its BIKERS WELCOME sign, as if to announce that there is nothing overly chic about this neighborhood.

Things do change a bit at the corner of Eighteenth and Connecticut. You'll notice that the customers in the restaurants are dressed differently, as though they have come from business and office buildings rather than just from the neighborhood. There are at least three destination restaurants at this corner: Asimakopoulous, which has been serving Greek food at this location for years; the newer and more stylish Aperto for Italian cuisine; and the rather snazzy Hunan and Mandarin restaurant called Eliza's. Rounding out the corner is the popular Goat Hill Pizza, where once a month family night features all the salad and pizza you can eat. Locals say that at least once in your life you should experience breakfast at the Just for You Bakery/Café, which is a no frills hole in the wall with a counter and a few tables known for its huge portions.

Parking in the area is usually no problem, if you don't mind parking at a 45-degree angle and bench-pressing your car door as you try to get in and out of the car.

CHRISTOPHER'S BOOKS

The best place for an introduction to the area is the corner shop at Eighteenth and Missouri. Tee Minot runs Christopher's and is usually there with her dog, Mavis. Dogs are a main theme here, as you will immediately notice by the collection of Polaroid photos of customer's pets. Tee greets the animals, hauls out her camera, and even has some treats on hand as she welcomes dogs and even nonreaders into the store.

Tee is a big booster of the neighborhood and can give advice on where to eat, where to shop, and how move into the area. She describes it as a real family neighborhood filled with artists and writers and others who choose to live in a friendly, nonchic area. The bookstore joins forces with the neighborhood coffeehouse, Farley's, to hold readings for kids once a month on Tuesday evenings.

If you do happen to bring a dog into Christopher's for a photo op, you should also know that Jackson Park at Seventeenth and Arkansas is the scene of a nightly dog party at 5 P.M. The neighbors convinced the park department to make it a leash-free area as long as they keep it clean and sanitary.

1400 18th Street at Missouri. Open daily 10 A.M. to 10 P.M. 255–8802.

FARLEY'S

This is a local coffeehouse that looks like a local coffeehouse. Low-key is the generous way of describing the furnishings. Wooden tables and chairs of varying styles are scattered around the room, as are newspapers, magazines, and community notices. Kids may be coloring while their parents stoke up on caffeine. On sunny days the crowd moves outside on benches and wherever else they can perch.

Everyone seems to know everyone else, and chances are you will find yourself in a conversation, if you want one.

1315 18th Street. Open Monday through Friday 7 A.M. to 10 P.M.; Saturday and Sunday 8 A.M. to 10 P.M. 648–1545.

BASIC BROWN BEAR FACTORY

Back on the bottom of the hill on the north or city side is a "can't-miss" stop if you are trying to entertain the kids. The factory claims to be one of the last manufacturers of stuffed animals in the United States and offers free tours of the facility daily except Sunday. In fact, the entire factory appears to have been set up for tours with friendly workers and signs pointing to "stuffing," "cleaning," and "cutting."

Before you get too caught up with the word "free," you should know that you will spend some money here. The tour allows kids to pick an unstuffed bear from the many styles offered and then stuff the bear at the stuffing machine. Then they can watch as the workers sew and groom their bear. Kids also can bathe the bear and pick all the accessories and clothes. Of course, you end up buying the products. Bears range from the $9.00 Baby Bear to the giant $129 California Bear. The Basic Brown Bear sells for $26.00.

444 De Haro Street. Open daily 10 A.M. to 5 P.M.; Sunday 12 noon to 5 P.M.; drop-in tours daily at 1 P.M. and Saturday at 11 A.M.; for tours of eight or more, call to reserve a time; street parking is available around the neighborhood. 800–554–1910.

ANCHOR STEAM BEER

Just across the street from the Basic Brown Bear Factory is another San Francisco institution that is well worth a visit, without the kids. In fact, as families exit the factory and the kids hug their new bears, you will see parents sniffing the air and fighting the olfactory pull to the Anchor Brewing Company.

In this former Chase and Sanborn coffee plant, Anchor Steam beer is made, and free tours are offered to the public. Here the word "free" is without strings—in fact, you even get some free tastes at the conclusion of the tour. There is a hitch, though. The tours are popular, and there is usually a waiting list of a few months.

Still, if you plan ahead, you will find it worthwhile. I'm not even a beer drinker, and I was fascinated by equipment like the huge copper brewing kettles from Germany, the brewing process, and the historical posters in the attractive barroom. I also must admit that I am a sucker for any assembly line like the one that brings in washed bottles, fills them, then caps and labels them. Too many "Industry on Parade" films from early TV, I guess.

Anchor Steam is the brainchild of Fritz Maytag, the washing machine heir, who is considered the dean of the American microbrewery movement. Compared to most of the newer microbreweries, this is a major operation, but it would still fit into a corner of the Budweiser plant in Fairfield.

1708 Mariposa Street. Tours from one to ten people available by reservation Monday through Friday; the tours last one-and-a-half hours; free. 863–8350.

THE REAL CROOKEDEST STREET

Sure, everybody knows about Lombard Street. It's a major tourist attraction as tourists get in line to take very slow rides down what is billed as the crookedest street in America. If you won't mind the crowds, it's OK. But for a backroads experience, you might as well take a brief ride on the real crookedest street in San Francisco. It's on Potrero Hill at 20th and Vermont Streets, and while the scenery isn't as upscale or as pretty, you won't have to get in line, and you won't have to dodge a lot of tourists who are not watching the road.

According to the city, there are eight turns on Lombard that average 131 degrees of arc. There are only five turns on Vermont, but they average 160 degrees of arc. You feel it as you go down what is fortunately a one-way street.

PLACES TO EAT

APERTO

The choices are easy at this small neighborhood trattoria with an open kitchen. They don't try to overwhelm you with menu selections. At lunch you could have pasta or panini (sandwiches such as roast chicken with red peppers and aioli on focaccia) or one of the daily specials. At dinner they bring on the arrosti (roast chicken, veal, and the like) as well as specials. The emphasis is on fresh ingredients, prepared without fuss.

1434 Eighteenth Street
252–1625
Lunch and dinner daily
Moderate
Credit cards

ASIMAKOPOULOUS

This café and deli has been a fixture on Potrero Hill for years. It's one of the few Greek restaurants in a city that seems to have scores of places in every ethnic dining category. Asimakopoulous is very informal, serving such specialties as chicken-lemon soup, Moussaka, skewered lamb, and chicken dishes.

288 Connecticut Street, at Eighteenth
552–8789
Lunch Monday through Friday
Dinner nightly
Credit cards

ELIZA'S

The big splashy neon sign on top of Eliza's advertises Hunan and Mandarin food. The menu seems to appeal to a mostly Caucasian crowd interested in familiar items such as pot stickers, sesame chicken, mu-shu pork, and Mongolian beef. Whatever you call it, the food is very good and plentiful, and no MSG is used. The kitchen is glad to make your dishes as spicy or mild as you like. Special lunch plates are mostly under $5.

1457 Eighteenth Street
648–9999
Lunch and dinner daily
Inexpensive
Credit cards

HAZEL'S KITCHEN

Let's say you want to grab a bite on the run but wouldn't be caught dead in a fast-food franchise joint. If you happen to be on Potrero Hill, you're in luck. Get in line at Hazel's, which is sort of a closet that opens out onto Eighteenth Street. Every day there's a freshly made soup, a daily special such as lasagna, several salads, and a choice of sandwiches using top ingredients. Take your meal with you, or sit with the locals on the benches and planters on the street.

1331 Eighteenth Street
647–7941
Open daily for lunch
Inexpensive
No credit cards

SAN FRANCISCO BBQ

The look of this Potrero Hill café might lead you to expect a scene out of Memphis or Austin, but this is Thai barbecue. There's a grill with marinated chicken, ribs, sausages, fish, and whatever else is available, served best over noodles with chopped peanuts, lime, and cilantro. You can also get sticky rice and carrot salad, as well as occasional dessert specials.

1328 Eighteenth Street
431–8956
Lunch Tuesday through Friday; dinner Tuesday through Sunday
Inexpensive
Credit cards

Bernal Heights

In 1984 I found myself living for a few months in a friend's house in Bernal Heights, which was then a very marginal neighborhood that many young people were betting on becoming the next hot neighborhood. Twelve years later it's finally starting to happen, particularly on Cortland Street, which is the neighborhood's main drag. Once the province of gangs at night, Cortland Street, which runs from Mission Street to Bayshore Boulevard, is now more of a family spot. This area is never going to be another Noe Valley, mostly because the homes are generally too small for the kind of investment that leads to gentrification. Here is a neighborhood with a real mix of socioeconomic groups, with enough unusual attractions to make it a destination for those who like the feel of a small town in the middle of a big city. There are destination restaurants, like the Liberty Café, and old established haunts, such as the Wild West Saloon, whose slogan is "beyond trendy."

If you want proof of the small-town atmosphere, just wander around the twisting roads in the hills. You will stumble across some of the only dirt roads remaining in the city and will probably see some chickens clucking in a neighborhood backyard. We will not give you exact directions because we would hate to create traffic nightmares for the dirt road residents.

Parking

No problem. There is ample metered parking on Cortland and plenty of free spaces on the side streets.

BERNAL BOOKS

As with most burgeoning neighborhoods, there is a local bookstore that could just as well serve as the community center. Rachel Pepper opened Bernal Books in the spring of 1995, and it immediately became a fixture. Chances are she will be behind the counter when you walk in, trying to sort out all the special orders that have come in for her customers. She competes with the giant chain stores by offering personal services, in store classes, readings, and twice monthly story hours for preschoolers.

Bernal Books has all the community notices and newspapers, as well as pictures of the neighborhood. On most shelves are little notes from Rachel, telling you that she selected each children's book herself, that selected authors are Bernal residents, or that magazines can by ordered by request. There's also a sign advising that dogs are welcome, and there's a good supply of Clifford, Carl, and Spot books to make them feel at home.

401 Cortland Avenue. Open Tuesday through Friday 10 A.M. to 7 P.M.; Saturday 10 A.M. to 6 P.M.; Sunday 10 A.M. to 4 P.M. 550–0293.

THE BARKING BASSET CAFÉ

Dogs seem to be a continuing theme in the businesses of the neighborhood, including the area's local coffeehouse. This is a very informal spot that serves California/Mediterranean food and also serves as a hangout for folks who want to linger over a coffee and pass the time of day. This is another good place to find out what life is like in Bernal Heights.

803 Cortland Avenue. Breakfast and lunch. Wednesday through Monday; dinner Thursday through Saturday. Inexpensive. No credit cards. 648–2146.

The first big draw from outside the neighborhood was the aforementioned Liberty Café, which drew rave reviews in the San Francisco papers for its fresh, imaginative food. But other shops and cafés add to the feeling of life on the street. Some of the more notable are as follows:

DOGTOWN

This is a colorful arts and crafts store devoted to dogs. They've got dog post-cards, dog art, dog bowls, dog pins, dog jewelry to bedeck Fido's collar, leashes, hand puppets that feature dog faces, and even miniature dog altars made by the artist/owner.

328 Cortland Avenue. Hours are irregular. 648–3506.

HEARTFELT

Although it looks more like an art gallery from the outside, this is a colorful card and gift shop with every inch of space filled with fun items. Heartfelt is run by the same woman who owns Dogtown, Kathleen Dunphy.

436 Cortland. Open daily from 11 A.M. to 8 P.M.; Sundays 11 A.M. to 5 P.M. 648–1380.

TEODOSIA

This is an arts and crafts shop featuring works by local artists, kids, street people, and whoever else wants to show their stuff. When Teodosia began in 1995, 14 artists contributed their works. Within a year the number had risen to nearly 150. There are some very attractive folk art pieces in here, plus small items like postcards. The attractive young lady behind the counter told me that she is a third-generation resident of Bernal Heights and that she is both happy and sad with the recent changes in the neighborhood. Whereas she now feels safe on the street and loves the new cafés and stores, she can no longer afford to buy a house in her neighborhood now that it's been "discovered."

430A Cortland. Open Tuesday through Friday 1 P.M. to 8 P.M.; Saturday and Sunday 11 A.M. to 7 P.M. 642–0223.

The Prince Charming Barber Shop

Just to show that the neighborhood hasn't become too upscale, there is an old-fashioned barber shop next to Teodosia with fading photos of Elvis Presley, Marilyn Monroe, and Clark Gable in the window. I can't vouch for the haircuts.

PLACES TO EAT

LIBERTY CAFÉ

Some restaurants can be intimidating when you walk in alone without a reservation. At this bright and open neighborhood spot, you are made to feel at home right away, and if you get there before or after the lunch or dinner rush, you should have no trouble finding a table.

The food is straightforward American with the emphasis on fresh and organic ingredients. The menu changes monthly but usually features such items as pizza and chicken pot pie. A wonderful eggplant, mozzarella, and sun-dried tomato sauce sandwich on focaccia with salad cost me $6.50.

Save room for dessert. They make great pies and cakes here, plus the only chocolate creme brulée I have ever tasted.

410 Cortland Avenue
695–8777
Breakfast, lunch, and dinner; closed Monday
Moderate
Credit cards

HUNGARIAN SAUSAGE FACTORY

This cozy little Bernal Heights café and deli doesn't look much like a factory. They do make sausages in back, but out front there's a charming dining room where you can have a sandwich or a salad or sample their Hungarian specialties, such as stuffed cabbage and, of course, sausages. Outside there are a few tables for sunning while you enjoy some of their pastries and a coffee or tea.

419 Cortland Avenue
648–2847
Lunch and dinner daily; takeout all day
Inexpensive
No credit cards

The Richmond

A short walk down Clement in either direction will give you a quick idea of this neighborhood, called the Richmond district. Many call it the new Chinatown, a place where the twenty- and thirty-something generation of Asian-Americans and often their parents move into less crowded surroundings. Chinese markets and Asian restaurants dominate on Clement Street, along with a wide range of shops that reflect an even broader ethnic mix. The area called the Richmond takes in quite a bit of territory, from Golden Gate north to the bay, and from Arguello Boulevard west to the ocean. It's a multicultural area with its most recent wave of immigrants coming from Russia to the area around Geary Boulevard and Nineteenth Avenue.

The weather is likely to be cool and foggy in the summertime. Oddly enough, winter often brings sunny days even when the rest of the city is in clouds.

Parking

No fun. Finding a space is always a challenge around Geary and Clement, where the stores and restaurants are clustered. It takes patience and circling the block a few times. There are few parking lots in the area. The best deal, although it is probably temporary, is the fifty-cents-an-hour garage run by Kaiser Medical Center between Fourth and Fifth Streets, south of Geary Boulevard.

Public transportation is best served by the Geary bus, but if you're just roaming, there are considerable distances to cover on foot.

Sixth Avenue

Instead of exploring the endless shops and cars on busy east-west streets like Geary and Clement, you might want to consider a north-south tour, where you can find street parking and sample the feeling of smaller neighborhoods within the larger Richmond district.

Green Apple Books

If you wanted to find the opposite of the new bookstores of the Borders or Barnes and Noble variety, venture into Green Apple. It's like entering the attic of an old house that has been stuffed to the rafters with books. There is a funky feeling to the place as you walk the wood floors, climb the various stairways, and settle down to read on the rickety chairs that are randomly scattered throughout the store.

Green Apple is a three-story store for new and used books. Near the cash register someone is usually turning in a collection for cash or credit. It's fascinating to listen in and see which books bring in the big bucks and which ones have little or no resale value. Somehow it reminded me of an idea a friend of mine once had while packing for a move. He felt that it made sense for everyone to simply leave all their books behind and automatically get a new collection at their new home.

What you get at a new and used store like Green Apple is a varied selection and the chance for finding surprise gems that won't be stocked in a new-only store. You also find people who live in the neighborhood who can lead you to other places to visit. Some of the best finds we've had in years of exploring the back roads came from simply asking residents about their favorite places and experiences.

506 Clement Street at 6th Avenue. Open weekdays 9:30 A.M. to 11 P.M.; weekends 9:30 A.M. to midnight. 387–2272.

HAIG'S DELICACIES

San Franciscans still come from all over the city to get their sauces and spices from Haig's, which was one of the pioneer international food shops. We suspect one reason is to be helped by the friendly bald gentleman behind the deli counter, who proudly offers a taste of what he proclaims to be the world's best hummus. He may be right.

This is another browsing store, where you can find exotic cans and jars from around the world, plus some interesting items from around the United States. Chances are pretty good that you will be tempted to buy something.

642 Clement Street. Open Monday through Friday 9:30 A.M. to 6:30 P.M.; Saturday 9 A.M. to 6 P.M. 752–6283.

SAM AND HENRY'S COOL BEANS

Take Sixth Avenue one block north to California and there is a coffeehouse that feels like a throwback to another era. Before the big operators like Starbucks and Peet's took their cookie-cutter design shops into neighborhoods all over the Bay Area, there were little hangouts like Sam and Henry's. Here the decor is clearly the work of the owners and the customers, with hand-painted walls, funky art, snapshots of customers and friends on the wall, and a few chess tables with lots of newspapers.

If you're a stranger when you walk in, you won't be for long. Sam or Henry will engage you in a conversation, and soon you will feel like a regular. This is the kind of place where you can sit at leisure and become a part of the neighborhood.

4342 California Street. Open daily 7 A.M. to 7 P.M. 750–1955.

ANTIQUE STORES

While you're in the neighborhood, with nonmetered street parking by the way, there are two antique shops that might be of interest to you just north of California on Sixth Avenue.

Sixth Avenue Antiques carries an interesting selection of furnishings and collectibles, while across the street, Brighton Beach Antiques carries large wooden pieces of furniture as well as collectibles such as old bottles. Down the street on California near Fifth is another large shop called Antique Traders.

BALBOA STREET

You could head south and hang out for a while on Balboa, which is a quiet street compared to Geary and Clement, despite its United Nations atmosphere between Fifth and Seventh Avenues. In these two blocks you will find two Russian restaurants; the Cinderella Bakery/Café; Katia's; O'Keefe's Irish Bar; Hawaiian Pizza; Jakarta Indonesian Restaurant; three Chinese restaurants (including the upscale China House Bistro); the more low-key Melissa's; the Emperor Palace; and the local caffeine parlor, Javaholics. You will hear a variety of languages spoken in this neighborhood.

IN THE SPOTLIGHT

On my last visit there was also a one of a kind shop called In the Spotlight, which features Barbie collectibles. The tiny store was crammed to the ceiling with product and boxes, and the owners, Rudi and Rowena, were looking for larger space nearby, so the location may have changed by the time you read this.

According to Rudi, what makes the store different is the assortment of Barbies and accessories that are imported from all around the world, with emphasis on Asia. Many of the items are one of a kind. Their main business is mail order, but for the Barbie-conscious, the store is something of a museum of doll fashion.

515 Balboa Street. Check for new location. 387–9432.

PLACES TO EAT

ALAIN RONDELLI

This is one of the city's premier restaurants, serving imaginative French cuisine served out on the Richmond district. A favorite of food critics.

126 Clement Street
387–0408
Dinner Tuesday through Sunday
Expensive
Credit cards

CHINA HOUSE BISTRO

The word *bistro* gives you the first clue. This is not your typical neighborhood Chinese restaurant. China House is a stylish, continental dining room serving specialties from Shanghai. You will be served dishes that may be new to you in a more sedate setting. This is a restaurant for a romantic and adventurous evening rather than a place to take the whole family and let the kids be kids.

The best way to order is to let your waiter or the hostess/owner, Cecelia Chung, help you choose.

501 Balboa Street
752–2802
Dinner nightly
Moderate
Credit cards

CINDERELLA BAKERY AND CAFÉ

Long before the latest wave of Russian immigrants to the city, there was the Cinderella Bakery and Café. Since the 1940s regulars have been coming in for hearty soups with dark Russian rye bread, piroshki, beef stroganoff, and especially pelmeni, which are meat-filled dumplings served in soup or with sour cream. Waitresses speak Russian and some English and hug the folks who come in every day and don't even have to announce their order. I confess I couldn't take my eyes off an eightyish woman who looked like the lost Princess Anastasia.

The bakery is in front and the café in back.

436 Balboa Street
751–9690
Breakfast, lunch, and dinner daily
Inexpensive
No credit cards

KATIA'S

One block down the street from the venerable Cinderella Bakery and Café is a prettier, more Americanized version of the Russian café. Katia serves all the Russian favorites: borscht, pelmeni, and shaslik, but the treatment is more delicate, and the atmosphere is more contemporary.

600 Fifth Avenue
688–9292
Lunch and dinner Wednesday through Sunday
Credit cards
Inexpensive to moderate

LAGHI

In a neighborhood of Chinese restaurants, Laghi has carved out a loyal clientele who come to this friendly trattoria for food from the Emilia Romagna area of Italy. The decor is nondescript; all the effort here goes into the food, and you come away the winner. Many consider the chef's region of Italy to be the dining capital, and Laghi is out to prove it. Save room for the tiramasu that beats all tiramasus. If you're not familiar with this popular Italian dessert, it's usually made with ladyfingers, mascarpone cream, whipped cream, espresso, and chocolate.

1801 Clement Street (figure on spending time looking for a parking place)
386–6266
Dinner Tuesday through Sunday
Moderate
Credit cards

LA SOLEIL

Across the street from Alain Rondelli is a popular and very good Vietnamese restaurant that shows touches of the French colonial legacy in Indochina. The menu is extensive, and the flavors of lemongrass, coconut, and curry dominate.

133 Clement Street
668–4848
Lunch and dinner daily
Moderate
Credit cards

PAT O'SHEA'S

Famous as a sports bar with TVs blaring three or four events at a time and for its sign that proclaims WE CHEAT TOURISTS AND DRUNKS, Pat O'Shea's Mad Hatter is a surprise food mecca. This is where Nancy Oakes started putting out sumptuous dishes before she opened the wildly popular Boulevard restaurant. You can still get wonderful dishes there. It's also one of the better places in town for a big juicy burger, which seems to fit the general atmosphere more.

3848 Geary Boulevard
752–3148
Lunch and dinner daily; weekends during football season tend to be very
   crowded
Inexpensive
Credit cards

When I moved to the Bay Area in 1975, Polk Street was always linked to Castro as the gay areas of town, partly because of shops with names like Hard On Leather and Sukker's Likkers and partly because of the amount of cruising and hustling that went on. Now the area between Geary and Broadway is without a singular personality.

This all changes, though, once you cross Broadway and head up to Union. For three blocks this is a Russian Hill neighborhood with an incredible mix of stores and cafés and a feeling that people actually live in the area. There are at least three groceries, four cleaners, three beauty shops, two antique shops, a drugstore, a bookstore, movie theater, a magazine and smoke shop, a range of restaurants and cafés from snack bars to the highly ranked La Folie, and five coffeehouses, including Starbucks, Peet's, Spinelli, Bohemian Cigar Store, and Royal Ground.

As opposed to many of the city's busy neighborhoods, Upper Polk offers reasonably available metered parking during the daytime.

PURE T COMPANY

Certainly the most unusual place in the neighborhood is a shop called Pure T, which offers free tastes of tea ice cream. In this inviting and peaceful Asian-decorated storefront at 2238 Polk, they sell such exotic tea ice creams as Moroccan mint, chamomile, German fruit, Thai, lemongrass coconut, black currant, jasmine, Earl Grey, Indian chai, and bourbon vanilla, plus a sorbet of the day. The ice creams are creamy and flavorful, and regular customers swear they are also guilt-free.

Apparently, the owners have been asked so often how they got the idea to make varieties of tea ice cream that they have printed their story as part of their brochure of offerings. Basically, the proprietors—Sherry, Deborah, and Hanif—were at a Japanese restaurant, where they were served green tea ice cream. Hanif asked what other flavors were available, and when the waiter said none, they instantly decided to go into business. After much research and experimentation, Pure T was born.

A wide selection of brewed teas is available for drinking, along with tea cookies and even T-pops.

2238 Polk Street. Open daily except Tuesday noon to 10 P.M. 441–7878.

RUSSIAN HILL BOOKSTORE

The neighborhood bookstore sells only used books but carries a well-chosen variety. It's connected to another storefront offering one of the most interesting and extensive selections of cards and journals in the city. This is a pleasant, friendly operation where you can inquire about the goings-on in the neighborhood but not the kind of place where you sit and read for a while. All the sidewalk cafés on the street appear to take care of that need.

2234 Polk Street, between Vallejo and Green. Open daily 10 A.M. until 10 P.M. 929–0997.

PLACES TO EAT

BELL TOWER

If size is a consideration, you might want to try the half-pound burger at this neighborhood bar and café in the Russian Hill section of town. The burger is cooked as you order it and served with lettuce, tomato, onion, pickle, and a heaping mound of french fries. Sometimes, the little things make you feel good about a place. For example, I asked the waitress to hold the onions, and she wanted me to know that there were some onions mixed into the burger in case I wanted to change my order.

This is a cozy corner bar with daily specials such as meat loaf, fried chicken, and lamb stew.

1900 Polk Street at Jackson
567–9586
Lunch and dinner daily
Moderate (the burger was $6.50)
Credit cards

LA FOLIE

The French chef Roland Passot and his family own a charming restaurant that combines the cooking techniques of France with the style and ingredients of California. Every plate of food is artfully decorated. This is a special-occasion restaurant, rated among the best in town.

2316 Polk Street
776–5577
Dinner Monday through Saturday
Expensive
Credit card

REAL FOOD DELI

A spinoff from the Real Foods Market up the street, this corner café has become a busy Russian Hill hangout. Take your choice of specials displayed in the huge deli case: tortas, pasta salads, quiche, sandwiches, soups, and desserts. The emphasis is on natural and vegan foods. Place your order, and it will be delivered to your table, inside or streetside. There is pleasant classical music playing on the stereo, and the atmosphere is comfortable for anyone eating alone.

2164 Polk Street
775–2805
Open daily 8 A.M. to 8 P.M.
Inexpensive
Credit cards

Marina District

The last major tourist wave to the Marina district came in the aftermath of the Loma Prieta earthquake of 1989, when everyone from network news anchors in limousines to the merely curious came to witness the devastation. On television this was the neighborhood shown to make most of the world think the entire city had been destroyed. Built on soft landfill, homes and apartments simply collapsed as the ground under them gave way. But within a few years the area looked as though nothing had ever happened.

This is still prime real estate with many homes having spectacular bay views and all the neighborhood sharing the expansive Marina Green as their local park. The Green is a wonderful place to take kids for Frisbee throwing, playing ball, or watching kite-fliers show their stuff. It also fronts a marina filled with boats of all sizes, including some impressive rigs from the nearby San Francisco Yacht Club. Also in the neighborhood is the Palace of Fine Arts and its ingenious museum, the Exploratorium.

Chestnut Street is the main business street for the Marina. Like much of the city, it is a neighborhood in transition. Perhaps most symbolic of the change was the closing in 1996 of Ed's newsstand, which had been a long-time fixture but fell victim to rising rents. Before that, the local Woolworth's made way for a more expensive chain operation, the area's longtime book-store/café shut down, and store names that you see everywhere else started popping up.

Still, it's a pleasant and busy street with many nice shops and loads of places to grab a drink or a bite. A casual walk down Chestnut during the middle of a weekday afternoon raises the question, "Where did all these twenty-something's come from, and how can they afford to be here without working?" This is where you will find a preponderance of attractive, hetero-sexual singles who look like they just came from an audition.

THE GROVE

Even though Peet's and Starbucks face off against each other from practi-cally next door, the hangout of the moment seems to be a place called The Grove. In a rustic setting with dark wood floors and wood tables and chairs, The Grove serves Illycafe, imported from Italy, and makes all espresso drinks exceedingly well. They also appear to touch all the bases, serving a few hot entrees, soups, salads, sandwiches, pastries, special teas, and Noah's Bagels, even though there is a Noah's outlet a few blocks down the street.

Mainly, though, this is a place to hang out and either meet people or casually eavesdrop on a conversation. I enjoyed my double cappuccino while shamelessly listening to a couple of actors assure each other of their mutual talents and how work was certainly around the corner. There are lots of newspapers and local notices around, which you can appear to read while you are secretly listening to your neighbors.

The sure sign that this is a place where people hang out rather than grabbing something on the run is a sign that imposes a ninety-minute time limit per table.

2250 Chestnut Street. Open daily from early in the morning until late at night. 474–4843.

PLACES TO EAT

CAFÉ MARIMBA

This brightly colored, splashy restaurant might first look like a folk art gallery, but in fact Marimba offers Mexican food that goes far beyond the taco and burrito. Food from many regions of Mexico is featured, as are colorful drinks. Experiment. Go for a series of the small dishes for a variety of delicious and often spicy tastes.

2317 Chestnut Street
776–1506
Lunch Tuesday through Sunday; dinner nightly
Moderate
Credit cards

E'ANGELO'S

According to a Herb Caen column in the *San Francisco Chronicle*, a fan recognized Robin Williams on the street one evening and expressed his admiration. Williams responded by suggesting that the fan have dinner where he and his family were heading, to E'Angelo's. This is a neighborhood institution in the Marina, where families pile in for pasta, pizza, and other traditional Italian-American dishes. Robin won't always be there, but do expect crowds and a joint that is always jumping.

2234 Chestnut Street
567–6164
Dinner Tuesday through Sunday
Moderate
No credit cards

JUDY'S CAFE

There is nothing trendy about Judy's. This Chestnut institution has been serving huge portions of omelettes and other breakfast treats, plus soups and sandwiches. This is not low-fat diet food. Their promise is that you'll feel like you're dining at Grandma's house. They've even bucked the trend and don't have an espresso machine. The food is good and wholesome and the decor would please Grandma, too.

2268 Chestnut Street
922–4588
Open every day for breakfast and lunch
Moderate
Cash only

PLUTO'S

Certainly Pluto's is destined to become a chain operation. The initial café on Scott Street was designed to be duplicated, and it's an idea that should catch on. You order cafeteria-style from a selection of roasted poultry and grilled meats, salads, vegetables, and beverages, and you get to pick from a variety of fixings and condiments. The food is fresh and tasty, and there's nothing on the menu above $5.75.

3255 Scott Street off Chestnut
775–8867
Lunch and dinner daily; breakfast Saturday and Sunday
Inexpensive
Credit cards

PART 2

Gotta Shop!

Would it surprise you to learn that I would rather have my fingernails removed than join Catherine in her favorite pastime, shopping? So what is a couple to do when trying to enjoy each other's company in the city? Our solution: find shopping areas that offer something for both of us. That usually rules out Union Square and large department stores where one of us can't get enough while the other can't leave soon enough. Instead, we head jointly for interesting small neighborhood shops that are usually near coffeehouses and cafés where the shopping-impaired partner can sit and read the paper. What follows are our suggestions for the most interesting, neighborhoodlike shopping streets.

CHAPTER 5

Not Your Average Strip Mall

Fillmore Street

The flags that adorn this shopping area between Bush and Washington say, WELCOME TO FILLMORE, THE 5-STAR STREET. It's not made clear who or what those five stars are, but there are several reasons to make this a destination for shopping. There are lots of hip clothing and home-design stores (most of them between Bush and California Streets), several coffeehouses and restaurants, ice cream parlors, doughnut shops, and banks. High fashion and style definitely prevail. One indication of the upscale nature of the area is a place called Jet Mail, at 2130 Fillmore. This is as snazzy a post office alternative business as you'll find anywhere, complete with a stylish window display.

The real find, however, is the number of thrift shops where you can go treasure hunting. Not your typical Salvation Army or St. Vincent De Paul's outlets, but shops run by organizations whose donors live nearby in Pacific Heights. You won't find a concentration of thrift, or used, stores like this anywhere else in the city. Three of them are on the same block, between Sacramento and Clay Streets.

Parking

First check the small metered lot on California Street between Fillmore and Pierce Streets. It costs fifty cents an hour, and the turnover is good. Otherwise, look for metered parking on Fillmore on any of the side streets to the west. To the east the pickings will be slimmer on the street because of the nearby California Pacific Medical Center.

There is good public transportation via the Number 1 California Trolley.

THRIFT SHOPS

NEXT TO NEW

Run by the Junior League, this shop has the widest selection of clothing, including kids clothes, which are usually outgrown before they are worn out. The best items are in the window display. Ask when they will go on sale, and then try to get there early on that day. Some shrewd buyers who have scouted in advance will show up in the predawn hours to grab an incredible bargain. Everything goes on a first come, first served basis. Keep in mind that there is a lot of shmutz mixed in with the good finds, but if you look hard, you can find name labels such as Talbot and Ralph Lauren at incredibly low prices.

2226 Fillmore Street. Open Monday through Saturday 10 A.M. to 4:45 P.M. 567–1628.

SECONDS TO GO

This is the thrift shop of the schools of the Sacred Heart scholarship fund. Here you will also be able to sift through the racks for that surprise evening gown or those silk pumps that someone wore only once or twice.

2252 Fillmore Street. Open Monday through Saturday 10 A.M. to 4:45 P.M. 563–7806.

REPEAT PERFORMANCE

Across the street from the previous two stores, this thrift shop is operated by the San Francisco Symphony and like the others offers the bargain detective a good time. Here you will find clothes, housewares, fixtures, books, and collectibles.

2223 Fillmore Street. Open Monday through Saturday 10 A.M. to 3:45 P.M. 563–3123.

VICTORIAN THRIFT SHOP

A few blocks to the south the California Pacific Medical Center has its thrift shop, and again the buys are waiting to be mined. Catherine found a complete ski outfit for just $15. Does she ski? No, but she might some day, and look how ready she'll be. Besides, a deal is a deal, and who knows when we'll have the next blizzard around here.

2033 Fillmore Street. Open Monday 11 A.M. to 4 P.M.; Tuesday through Saturday 10 A.M. to 5 P.M. 567–3149.

BOUTIQUES

Now that you've saved all that money, you can go to the other extreme on Fillmore Street at a few of the more expensive boutiques.

AVANT PREMIERE PARIS

This is the old-fashioned kind of salon, where the husband sits in a cushy chair and watches as his wife tries on clothes. The customers are some of the same "ladies who lunch" who might end up donating their elegant woolen or silk suits to the thrift shops. The emphasis on design is on sophisticated, well-tailored goods—nothing flashy.

1942 Fillmore Street. Open weekdays 11 A.M. to 6 P.M.; Saturday 10 A.M. to 6 P.M.; Sunday noon to 6 P.M. To give you an idea of how they fancy the store to be a French salon, the hours are posted in French. 673–8875.

CIELO

One might imagine that the hip daughters and sons of the customers of Avant Premiere come here for the most current Italian designer fashions. The room is open and airy, that spare look that has become known as industrial chic. Clothes are sexy, high style, and expensive, the kinds of items that you see in the TV stories on fashion shows but never seem to see in the department stores.

2225 Fillmore Street. Open Monday through Saturday 11 A.M. to 7 P.M.; Sundays noon to 6 P.M. 776–0641.

COMPANY STORE

Big is beautiful is the concept of this high-fashion store featuring women's clothes in sizes 14 to 24.

1913 Fillmore Street. Open Tuesday through Friday 11 A.M. to 7 P.M.; Saturday 10 A.M. to 6 P.M.; Sunday noon to 6 P.M. 921–0365.

CHEAP CHIC

BETSEY JOHNSON

The ultrahip New York designer has a shop on Fillmore offering tight-fitting cotton dresses and outfits worn by either the very young or the very fit.

2031 Fillmore Street. Open Monday through Saturday 11 A.M. to 7 P.M.; Sunday noon to 6 P.M. 567–2726.

WE BE BOP

Flash and dash in kicky styles, also with sizes for larger women.

1903 Fillmore Street. Monday through Saturday 11 A.M. to 7 P.M.; Sunday noon to 7 P.M. 771–7294.

CROSSROADS FASHION

This is one of two good vintage clothing stores in the area featuring clothes from the 1950s and 1960s with some new items mixed in. These are MTV fashions with the kind of nondescript shirts and loose-fitting jackets that rock stars wear, plus some women's items last seen worn on *Josie and the Pussycats*. The store operators call their stock "found fashion."

1901 Fillmore Street. Open Monday through Saturday 11 A.M. to 6:30 P.M.; Sunday noon to 6 P.M. 775–8885.

DEPARTURES FROM THE PAST

The vintage (in other words, used) clothes here, dating from the 1940s through the 1970s, reflect more elegant tastes. If you need that special outfit for a costume party where you need to look like Rosalind Russell or Ralph Bellamy, look here.

2028 Fillmore. Open Monday through Saturday 11 A.M. to 7 P.M.; Sunday noon to 6 P.M. 885–3377.

HATS

In a time when so few people wear hats, it's interesting to note that there are two hat shops on Fillmore Street. Both stores make women's hats and also sell men's hats.

MRS. DEWSON'S HATS

2052 Fillmore Street. Open Monday through Saturday 10 A.M. to 6 P.M.; Sundays until 4 P.M. 346–1600.

COUP DE CHAPEAU

1906 Fillmore Street. Open Tuesday through Saturday 11 A.M. to 6 P.M.; Sunday noon to 5 P.M. 931–7793.

HOME FURNISHINGS

Fillmore Street is a destination for people whose homes might appear on the pages of *Metropolitan Home*. There are about twenty shops that offer home furnishings and gifts, most of them expensive. Stylish stores like Nest, Mike Furniture, Pascual's, and Dover-Foxcroft Ltd. are all on the block between California and Sacramento Street and are worth checking out. The original drawing card on the block is still going strong.

FILLAMENTO

One of the longer-standing shops in the area, Fillamento began as a house-wares store and now also carries large furniture items such as couches, tables, and chairs. On its three levels Fillamento carries a wide range of interesting merchandise from affordable dishes and silverware to designer tablecloths. They appear to have items before they show up in other stores, many of them from local artisans.

2185 Fillmore Street. Open Monday through Friday, 10 A.M. to 7 P.M.; Saturday and Sunday 10 A.M. to 6 P.M. 931–2224.

We also took a fancy to a few stores between Bush and Pine Streets:

CEDANNA

Billing itself as a gallery and a store, Cedanna is dedicated to artful living. On display are furnishings and furniture such as tables, chairs, dressers, and mirrors created by contemporary craftspeople. There's also a special section of one-of-a-kind children's clothes and books. This is a striking, attractively designed browser's store filled with interesting and often expensive items.

1925 Fillmore Street. Open Monday through Friday 11 A.M. to 9 P.M.; Saturday 11 A.M. to 7 P.M.; Sunday 11 A.M. to 6 P.M. 474–7152.

MAIN LINE

One of the many splashy stores on Fillmore, Main Line looks from the outside like a fifties diner. Inside you will see colorful displays of gifts and things for the home, particularly table settings and items for entertaining.

This is a good place to find that unusual refrigerator magnet you've been searching for.

1928 Fillmore. Open daily 10 A.M. to 7 P.M. 563–4438.

ZINC DETAILS

The works of local artists and craftspeople are featured in this home furnishings store. Glass appears to be the hot item, in the form of decorative vases and bottles. Some larger pieces of furniture are on display, too.

1905 Fillmore. Open daily 10 A.M. to 7 P.M. 776–2100.

SURPRISE PARTY

Part of the surprise is finding this tiny shop. The rest of the surprise is their stock, which consists of a colorful selection of beads and seashells. Why seashells? The owner says Father Neptune came to her in a dream and told her to do it. Why beads? "Why not beads? They are colorful and fun to work with," she says. Customers include fashion designers, who buy items to decorate their creations, and folks who just like beads and shells and the necklaces and other items made from them.

1900A Fillmore Street. Open daily from 11 A.M. to 6 P.M.; Sunday noon to 5 P.M. 928–1885.

BROWSER BOOKS

The neighborhood bookstore is Browser Books, which is a narrow but deep shop with lovely classical music on the stereo. The staff is very friendly and helpful, rattling off three or four books if you mention that you are looking for a new book about vivisection but can't remember the name or author. They also won't bug you by asking that you check your bag at the register.

In the rear of the shop are several chairs and a table for sitting and reading. I passed a pleasant half hour waiting for a downpour to stop and found a paperback mystery by Carl Hiaasen that I had not seen elsewhere. (The minister did it.)

2195 Fillmore Street. Open Monday through Saturday 10 A.M. to 10 P.M.; Sunday 9 A.M. to 10 P.M. 567–8027.

FOR THE PAMPERED PET

GEORGE

Just off Fillmore Street in California is a one of a kind store devoted to dogs. George has everything Fido could dream about: dishes, collars, sweaters, toys, treats, beds, cosmetics, brushes, and some items your pooch didn't know existed, such as attractive place mats for dog dishes. Much of the merchandise is made specially for the store and for their mail-order operation. In the spirit of equal time, they do carry a few cat items, too. The store is named after the owner's dog.

2411 California Street. Open Monday through Saturday 10 A.M. to 7 P.M.; Sunday noon to 5 P.M. 441–0564.

FOOD FOR THE EYES

LE CHANTILLY

This is a bakery—or more properly a pastry gallery that is a pleasure to look at, although I must admit I've never tasted anything from their glittering cases. I'm more of a chocolate fudge guy than a genoise and marzipan devotee. Still, every cake is a work of art. As my mother would say, "They look too pretty to eat." I'm sure the shop's owners have a different point of view, but judge for yourself. You won't see anything like this in your average neighborhood bakery, but this ain't your average neighborhood.

2119 Fillmore Street. Open Monday through Saturday 9 A.M. to 6 P.M.; Sunday 11 A.M. to 6 P.M. Expensive. 441–1500.

COFFEEHOUSES

There has not been a recorded case of caffeine deprivation on Fillmore Street for years. You name it, it's here. Peet's, Starbucks, Spinelli's, Royal Ground, and several other coffee places.

Hayes Valley

There's a hand-painted sign on the wall of a building on the south side of Hayes Street near Franklin that reads, WELCOME TO HAYES VALLEY. It's hard to tell if it's the work of a neighborhood association or a graffiti artist, but the sign's colors and lettering portend what is to follow on the three blocks that make up one of the hottest new shopping areas in San Francisco. Except for the well-respected Hayes Street Grill, there wasn't much of a reason to go there for years. Then came a gym, Muscle System, that drew a crowd of very fit gay men, and then came some art galleries. But it took the Loma Prieta earthquake of 1989 to create what is now the Hayes Valley. The quake damaged the freeway exit that used to hover over the street and keep it in perpetual darkness. Once the ramp was torn down, the sun came in and so did the merchants and stylish, well-heeled customers.

Located between Franklin and Laguna Streets, west of the Civic Center, this three-block compact shopping area once housed plumbing-supply places and hardware stores, plus Mom and Pop groceries. As is often the case with gentrification, the services are mostly gone now, and style is in, but it's a different style than you'll find, say, on Fillmore Street. This is a quirkier, more cutting-edge area, where you usually find things you didn't know existed. On the street during the day, you'll see a mix of cultures from upscale patrons of the arts (the Symphony, Opera, and Ballet are nearby), to the folks from the housing projects to the west who still hang out in front of the remaining grocery stores.

Despite the still-funky nature of the street, this is not a place for bargain hunters, although you may find an occasional treasure on a sale rack. You will find unique new vintage and antique items for the home and body.

Parking

There are meters on Hayes Street that are usually available. Street parking is also most likely around Laguna Street.

CLOTHING

560 HAYES

Billed as a vintage boutique, this store buys, sells, and consigns vintage clothing for men and women. Their stock is the creme de la creme from thrift stores. Here's where you'll find those pointy-toed pumps you've been looking for, that Doris Day–like peignoir, or leather chaps for men and women. In other words, a man looking for a pair of high heels would feel right at home here. So do the ladies who have wandered over from Pacific Heights, as well as young women with black lipstick from Haight Street. Every space in the store is filled with merchandise that includes collectibles like salt and pepper shakers, figurines, and vases. To add to the atmosphere, there's the store dog, Sacca, who looks like the pooch from the Our Gang comedies, and the disco and Judy Garland music blaring from the stereo.

560 Hayes Street. Open daily from noon to 7 P.M. 861–7993.

DARBURY STENDERU

This place may defy description. Darbury is a Seattle-based artist who has obviously had her share of caffe lattes. The store is a gallery of her clothes and home furnishings, all done in fabric art. Her medium is silk velvet, which she dyes herself into sexy, sensual prints. The multicolored fabrics are used to create flowing, often diaphanous clothing designs and to cover pillows, settees, mirror frames, and whatever else strikes her fancy.

Why did an artist from Seattle open a shop on Hayes Street? A San Francisco customer urged her to come and took her to see the store called Zonal (see below), and that did the trick. "We don't belong on Fillmore or

Union Street," says the manager. "It's too conservative. We could only be on Hayes Street."

541 Hayes Street. Open Monday through Saturday noon to 7 P.M.; Sunday noon to 5 P.M. 861–3020.

ONE BY TWO

This is an ultramodern clothing store, offering women's and unisex designs. During our last visit they were taking 1960s-type fashions and re-creating them with 1990s fabrics and cuts. Who knows, by the time you read this, maybe the 1970s revival will be hot. They also specialize in windbreakers with hats to match. Asked to describe their clothes, the saleswoman said, "Contemporary street wear." Clothes are designed and made on the premises, in the basement. The street level boutique is open, airy, and cheerful. Ask for one of their very hip business cards—it's a transparent slide.

418 Hayes Street. Open daily 11 A.M. to 7 P.M. 252–1460.

BULO

In his wildest dreams, Al Bundy (of TV's *Married with Children*) never imagined a shoe store like this. Here, the shoe is elevated to an art object, a piece of sculpture. The owner, Enrico Parella, showcases his products on pedestals in the window and throughout the store. He sells Italian imports but not the brand names that you see in every department store. Some are outlandish, like the ones with nine-inch heels and three-inch platforms that Enrico assured us were comfy. He said he sold two pairs to a woman from Los Angeles who said they would be perfect for her job. Sorry, he forgot to ask what she did for a living. You'll also find shoes for more conservative tastes, as might be worn by a businessman from Milan. Like most works of art, these shoes are expensive.

437A Hayes Street. Open Monday through Saturday 11:30 A.M. to 6:30 P.M.; Sunday noon to 5:30 P.M. 864–3244.

GIMME SHOES

Across the street from Bulo is yet another stylish shoe store. In fact, Enrico Parella decided to open Bulo partly because there was a fine shoe store across the street and he figured that Hayes Street could become a destination for people looking for unusual shoes. The owner of Gimme Shoes apparently was not impressed by that logic. When I relayed the story to him on the phone, he hung up. Anyway, Gimme Shoes carries fine men's and women's shoes plus accessories such as belts, earrings, and sunglasses. Italian designs are featured here, too, and the emphasis is on hip.

416 Hayes Street. Open daily 11:30 A.M. to 6:30 P.M. 864–0691.

COULARS

Many of the customers who come into this small boutique know the owner, Marylie, by name. They like her taste and figure she'll have something that's right for them. This was the first semi-upscale store on Hayes, opening when the freeway was still overhead and crime was a daily concern. Now, the addition of all the new neighbors has made the pioneering venture pay off.

All the clothing and accessories in the shop are things Marylie would choose for herself, which seems to fit in with the desires of society ladies looking for something to wear while out shopping for something else to wear. Everything is soft and feminine and a bit understated. Younger women who like to be stylish without a hard edge will find items here, too. There's a large selection of accessories such as hairclips, earrings, combs, and barrettes. What distinguishes Coulars from its counterparts on Union or Fillmore Streets is its small size and personal touch.

327 Hayes Street. Open daily from 11 A.M. to 6:30 P.M. , but as Marylie says, "If you come and I'm still here, I'm still open." 255–2925.

FOR THE HOME

"FORMERLY" COUNTRY STARK JAVA

Remember that ornate sultan's bed you had a strange dream about? They have it here. This is a home store that might be described as Arabian Nights meets Mendocino glass blowers. It actually started as an art showcase, then turned into a furniture and furnishings store. There are huge ornate pieces of furniture along with handblown glass vases and lamps. The original store name was meant to indicate that they presented stark country furniture made from materials from Java. Unfortunately, many people came in looking for a coffeehouse. So a name change was in order, although the right one hasn't been chosen as of this writing. The leading candidate: Urban Habitat.

572 Hayes Street. Open daily noon to 6 P.M. 552–2767.

ZONAL

The slogan of the store is "Always repair, never restore." It will probably be a new concept to you, but the idea is to make distressed merchandise chic, sort of like charging a high price for torn jeans. On display are rusted bed frames, window frames, screen doors, and whatever else is distressed, all presented and ready to go. Some of the work is quite clever, such as the various kinds of old mailboxes that are sold as CD holders, or the ceiling sculpture of twisted old bedsprings.

568 Hayes Street. Open Tuesday through Saturday 11 A.M. to 7 P.M.; Sunday 11 A.M. to 5 P.M. 255–9307.

VICTORIAN INTERIORS

The name says it all. If you are remodeling a Victorian home, you should stop in here and see the collection of wallpaper, fixtures, tassels for curtains, toys, books, carpets, tiles from England, and moldings. Two designers own the store, and their basic work is in restoring the interiors of Victorian houses. They also sell retail.

575 Hayes Street. Open Tuesday through Saturday 11 A.M. to 6 P.M.; Sundays noon to 5 P.M. 431–7191.

SAN FRANCISCO WOMEN ARTISTS SALES AND RENTAL GALLERY

This is not only a lovely space to view art, complete with a garden in back, but the work is interesting and affordable. You'll find ceramic figurines, video art, painting, sculpture, and the like, all at prices less than you would expect to pay at a gallery downtown. The art is all the work of members of the cooperative that runs the gallery with works presented in rotating shows chosen by an independent jury.

370 Hayes Street. Open Tuesday through Saturday 11 A.M. to 6 P.M.; Thursday to 8 P.M. 552–7392.

ZEITGEIST

This is a combination sales and repair shop specializing in rare and unusual watches and clocks. The displays of art deco timepieces, pocket watches, old electric clocks, and hip new wristwatches are worth seeing, and if you are in need of watch repair, they'll work on almost anything.

437B Hayes Street. Open Tuesday through Saturday noon to 6 P.M. 864–0185.

Upper Grant

Upper Grant in North Beach has always had a funky-artsy quality to it. Until the mid-1990s, it was home to places like the venerable Schlock Shop, where you could find old hats, lamps, trinkets, and anything else the owner felt like keeping in stock. When this institution folded, it signaled the end of an era and the beginning of a new one. Now Upper Grant is as hip as they come, with small shops featuring stylish clothing, household items, and cultural artifacts. The entire strip runs only two short blocks so you can browse at leisure and take advantage of North Beach's many restaurants and cafés.

As of this writing, three more storefronts were being renovated on Grant, and you can expect the avenue to be brimming with stylish, informal shops.

Parking

There are metered spaces on Grant that offer one-hour parking, but they may be hard to get. The Vallejo Street Garage, on Vallejo between Stockton and Powell, is just a few blocks away, and rates are good.

QUANTITY POST CARDS

The store has been on Grant for quite some time, but they used to be across the street in a much smaller and less snazzy space. Now, the outside window promises a fun-house atmosphere, and, indeed, inside there are token-operated amusement park–like collectors' items on display but not for sale. They do sell postcards of every kind, from the classic gags like the famed Jack-a-lope card to vintage valentines, greetings from just about everywhere, used cards sent to and received by people who are complete strangers to most of us, and modern artsy postcards. Prices range from a dime to $5.00 for postcards. This is a browser-friendly, very loose store.

1441 Grant Avenue. Open daily "about 11 A.M. to 11 P.M.," unless they take the day off. 986–8866.

CLOTHING

Men and women can find unique fashions on Grant that are beyond what you'll find in department stores. Many of the boutiques are owner-operated; they open around 11 A.M. or noon, whenever he or she can get there.

DONNA

If Catherine is looking for a one-of-a-kind special occasion dress or is in the mood to shoot a wad on some casual wear, this is the first place she'd check out. The store, named after its owner/operator, also carries interesting costume jewelry and accessories. If you happen to be searching for a gift for a friend named Donna, check out the store's inexpensive canvas bags with the store name.

1424 Grant Avenue. Open Monday through Saturday 11 A.M. to 7 P.M.; Sunday noon to 7 P.M. 397–4447.

GRAND

Across the street from Donna, this boutique for both men and women features clothes by local artisans. Especially nice are the one-of-a-kind shirts for men. Expect bold splashes of colors. One of the featured items during a recent visit was a neon green umbrella that would brighten any gloomy day. The women's fashions at Grand have much more of an edge than the men's, but what would you expect?

1435 Grant Avenue. Open daily noon to 7 P.M. 951–0131.

KNITZ AND LEATHER

As the name implies, here's where to find fine knitwear for both men and women, plus leather jackets and bags. The knits in this tiny shop include an attractive and stylish selection of handcrafted sweaters, vests, and scarves. They don't come cheap. Knitz and Leather is an old-timer in the neighborhood, having opened in 1984.

1429 Grant Avenue. Open daily noon to 7 P.M. 391–3480.

RAGE ACCESSORIES

Just around the corner on Union Street is a little jewel of a store. In a closet-sized display space, the owner, Tracey Murray, opens shutters onto the street and shows her handmade jewelry and hats. There's barely enough room for Tracey to stand while she shows her wares, but you'll have plenty of room on the sidewalk. Tracey makes much of the merchandise and also carries the work of local artists.

524 Union Street. Open daily noon to 7 P.M. 781–6355.

FOR THE HOME

SLIPS

Want to beautify that funky old couch that looks like it was dipped in juice drink and Nestlé's Quik? This is a very modern, very hip, and also very expensive place for custom-made slipcovers and curtains. You choose the fabric and can watch the workers sewing away in the back of the store. There's also a select showing of modern furniture and a few antiques for sale.

1534 Grant Avenue. Open Tuesday through Saturday 11 A.M. to 7 P.M.; Sunday noon to 6 P.M. 362–5652.

COLUMBINE DESIGN

This is a one-of-a-kind flower shop, offering flora as sculpture. They feature unique floral arrangements, many decorated with scenes created with natural phenomena such as colorful seashells or dried butterflies. One can picture a customer coming in for a centerpiece for a dinner party or even for a special single flower. Everything is top quality and worth the lofty price.

1541 Grant Avenue. Open Monday through Saturday 11 A.M. to 7 P.M. 434–3016.

CHAPTER 6

Outlet Stores

This is a special category for bargain hunters who know how to sift through piles of merchandise until they strike gold. Some of these outlets, such as the Espirit Factory store, at Sixteenth and Illinois Streets, are tourist destinations. Although there are various outlet stores around the city, the center for outlet shopping is the South of Market area, anchored by the big Burlington Coat Factory building (also called Yerba Buena Square). Most of the stores are geared to women.

On her research tour Catherine chose a variety of places that she would return to, from absolutely low-end bargain rack shops to classy, tiny workshops where you buy directly from the maker of the product.

FRITZI

On the plain-pipe-rack end of the clothing-store scale, Fritzi takes the prize. In an ugly cement building near the Transbay Bus Terminal, this outlet store sells sportswear and dresses for women and girls. The most expensive item Catherine could find was $20, and there were racks of skirts for kids for just $4 each. The items were of the quality you might find in middle-range department stores.

This is the kind of place where men are lined up in chairs in front of the store while their wives run amok. Overheard was one guy saying to his neighbor, "She'll clean out a whole rack."

218 Fremont Street. Open Monday through Thursday 9 A.M. to 5 P.M.; Friday and Saturday 8 A.M. to 5 P.M. (Every Friday there's an early bird sale with additional discounts and lines of customers waiting for the store to open.) 979–1399.

By the way, if you happen to hear a strange sound nearby, it's probably coming from the parking lot under the bus ramp. A bagpipe player practices there on occasion, apparently choosing a spot where he's unlikely to get complaints about noise.

MARGUERITE RUBEL

Ms. Rubel makes and sells classy quilted jackets and raincoats in her second-floor factory. Her colorful creations are made of either velvet, poplin and silk-like polyester, or combinations thereof. Not everything is discounted here, but you can find various overruns and irregular items for up to 50 percent off. If you want to have a custom raincoat or jacket made, she'll do that, too. There are good deals here on accessories, such as headbands and scarves.

543 Howard Street, between First and Second Streets. Open Monday through Saturday 10 A.M. to 5 P.M.

JESSICA MCCLINTOCK/GUNNE SAX OUTLET

You'll know you're in the right place when you approach this huge warehouse. Just follow the legions of women walking with determination and purpose. Mothers and daughters will be searching for discounted wedding gowns from $30. Teens will be looking for that perfect prom dress. Moms and little girls will sift through the racks of kids dresses in velvet, satin, and lace. The discounted items are either last season's overruns or irregulars, but they are all from either the traditional Jessica McClintock, hipper Scott McClintock, or informal Gunne Sax lines.

The second floor is filled with stuff they want to move out quickly. You'll find bolts of fabric, trims, buttons, and other items that are great for the person who sews.

This place is a scene. The dressing room is open and far from private, with little dramas of decision played out at every mirror.

35 Stanford Street, off Brannan near Third Street. Open Monday through Saturday 9:30 A.M. to 6 P.M.; Sunday 11 A.M. to 6 P.M. 495–3326.

Georgiou

The whole range of women's clothes, from business suits to vacation wear, is on sale at the Georgiou outlet. All the clothes are made from natural fibers. The outlet store is the repository for overruns, last season's clothes, and irregulars, and there are some real bargains to be had, particularly on accessories such as belts, earrings, and bracelets.

Unlike most of the other outlet stores, this one has pleasant physical surroundings and a helpful sales staff. Like all the other stores, you have to pick through a lot of stuff you don't want in order to find the gems.

925 Bryant Street, between Seventh and Eighth Streets. Open Monday through Saturday 10 A.M. to 5 P.M.; there is a parking lot at the rear of the store, off Langston.

Martha Egan

You have to search for the understated sign out front of this tiny clothing factory, where Martha and her helpers make fine women's clothes. As you walk in, you'll see someone cutting fabric and someone else further back sewing.

Here you can buy hip, 1940s-inspired dresses and separates, including casual evening wear in comfortable fabrics. The bargains are at the end of season 50 percent off rack and in the piles of leftover fabric that are for sale. Shopping here is a much lower-key experience than the larger discount operations, but you might find a lovely one-of-a-kind item.

1127 Folsom Street, between Seventh and Eighth Streets. Open Monday through Friday 10 A.M. to 6 P.M. 252–1072.

Siri

Siri's fashion studio is tucked away on a street I didn't know existed. You might know of her sophisticated women's clothes from high-fashion boutiques. The shop is where she designs and makes elegant and chic outfits, from business suits to sports and evening wear. Prices can be high for retail items, but if you search for discontinued styles or seconds, you could save as much as 50 percent.

7 Heron Street, off Eighth Street between Harrison and Folsom Streets. Open Monday through Friday 10 A.M. to 6 P.M.; Saturday 10 A.M. to 5 P.M. 431–8873.

CHRISTINE FOLEY

This is another tiny, owner-operated outlet where you can buy retail as well as hunt for bargains. Christine Foley makes top-of-the-line hand-loomed cotton sweaters for women, children, and men. Using bright colors and unusual patterns and designs, she creates unique sweaters that sell for big bucks in high-fashion department stores and boutiques.

For bargains, check out the discontinued styles. Some irregulars, with the imperfections marked for you to see, sell for as much as 70 percent off the retail price.

430 Ninth Street. Open Monday through Saturday 10 A.M. to 4 P.M. 621–8126.

TIGHT END

The clever title award for an outlet store goes to this shop for workout clothes. This is the factory outlet for "Urban Athlete" cotton, Lycra, and ribbed sports and street clothes for men, women, and kids. Discounts are available on overruns, samples, and discontinued items.

434 Ninth Street. Open Monday through Saturday 10 A.M. to 4 P.M. 255–8881.

ALLEN ALLEN, USA

Billed as a women's clothing catalog factory outlet, Allen Allen offers deals on first-quality and irregular clothes. These are sophisticated, casual skirts and blouses in jersey rib, Lycra, fleece, linen/rayon, denim, and cotton cashmere at from 30 percent to 70 percent off. They have some items for little girls, too.

1301 Harrison Street at Ninth Street. Open Wednesday through Saturday 10 A.M. to 4 P.M. 431–3295.

City Lights

This is not an outlet for the famous North Beach bookstore, nor is it a place for lighting fixtures. The product here is fashionable and comfortable work-out and dance wear made mostly of stretchy cotton. Discounted items are in the various bargain bins.

333 Ninth Street. Open Monday through Saturday 10 A.M. to 6 P.M. 861–6063.

CHAPTER 7

Farmer's Market and the Flower Market

Farmer's Market

Every Saturday morning on the Embarcadero, across from the Ferry Building, there's a party of sorts for food lovers, as farmers from around the Bay Area bring their fresh produce to sell. Bakers, candlestick makers, and everyone else with an item that would grace a dinner table also show up to peddle their wares. There are several farmer's markets throughout the Bay Area, and this is one of the biggest and best attended. The prices are good because the farmers can eliminate the middlemen and sell directly to the consumer, and the freshness of the seasonal produce can't be beat.

FLOWER MARKET

If you're an early riser or too wired to turn in after a night on the town, the action spot in the city in the predawn hours is at the Flower Market. Around 4 A.M., the place is jammed as florists hunt for the best bargains. They get the wholesale prices, but the public is also invited after 9 A.M. to pick through the rest. Most of the wholesalers in the warehouses close by 10:30 A.M. Frankly, I don't know my hydrangea from my hibiscus, but I do know that you will find flora of all kinds from local growers and from around the world.

The week starts with a bang with Monday madness day, when the trade gets an extra 10 percent discount from participating suppliers. If you have a friend who can get you some trade credentials, this is when to score big.

The largest section of the market closes at 12:30 P.M., but many stores stay open to the public until midafternoon, as does the busy Flower Market Café at 698 Brannan.

Main entrance off Sixth Street, above Brannan. 781–8410.

PART 3

Enjoying the Great Outdoors

CHAPTER *8*

Urban Picnicking Sites

There are few cities in the world that can compare with San Francisco in offering outdoor recreation. The combination of the physical setting, the year-round moderate weather, the usually clean air, and the abundance of parks and waterfront attractions draws people outside at all hours of the day.

San Francisco is a wonderful place for a picnic. If there is going to be a sunny time of day, chances are it will be between 11 A.M. and 3 P.M., at which time the wind is also likely to calm down to a pleasant breeze. Office workers who are stuck inside all day flock to the city's many choice outside eating spots, which range from small public parks to large courtyards and plazas provided by the builders of San Francisco's newer skyscrapers.

343 SANSOME STREET

The most hidden of these oases is the rooftop garden at 343 Sansome Street at Sacramento. After an elevator ride to the top floor, you can dine in your own corporate penthouse setting overlooking the financial district, courtesy of the building's owners, the Hines Company. There are tables and benches arranged in a nicely landscaped setting. Those who are daring can sit right out on the ledge, looking east to the Bay Bridge and Oakland.

There are many delis and cafés nearby where you can get takeout lunches.

Rock fans will be interested to know that the rooftop garden is some. fourteen floors above what used to be the art-deco, one-story building that housed KSAN-FM from 1976 until it switched to a country format in the early 1980s. The building was demolished to make way for the skyscraper.

YERBA BUENA CENTER

One of the newest urban picnic areas is in the Yerba Buena Arts complex, complete with a waterfall to mask the noise of the city. This is at the impressive Martin Luther King Memorial, which features glass panels with quotes from the slain civil rights leader. This is no ordinary waterfall. It's actually a complex fountain that runs almost the entire width of the plaza.

At the top level you can sit in the sun and gaze down on the grassy esplanade while you listen to the gentle trickle of water heading for the waterfall. Your view also takes in some of the nearby skyscrapers, including the controversial Marriott Hotel, which has been described as the world's largest pinball machine. Grab a sandwich and a coffee from the Pasqua Café and relax. You'll probably be visited by a hungry bird looking for a snack. There are public rest rooms on this level.

A ramp leads you along more water to the level below, where the waterfall comes crashing down. Beneath the water is a walkway leading to the panels quoting Dr. King. Be prepared to get wet if you go in for a closer look. The ceiling tends to drip. Both areas are beautifully landscaped, with much greenery and colorful flowers.

You will probably be sharing the gardens with a combination of conventioneers (they are the ones with the badges) from nearby Moscone Center, downtown office workers, and random sun worshippers.

There are often metered spaces on Third Street, between Harrison and Howard Streets. Your best bet, though, is to head for the municipal garage at Fifth and Mission Streets.

MARATHON PLAZA

Another convenient urban picnic area is at the Marathon Plaza office building at Second Street and Folsom. Again, a fountain is used to mask off the noise of the city traffic and construction, and seating is on several levels, on less-than-comfortable concrete booths. You can get something to eat from Max's Eatz or a frozen yogurt or coffee at Oh-La-La and enjoy eating out in the sun. It's a pretty good bet you can find a one-hour parking meter not too far away.

EMBARCADERO CENTER

The Embarcadero Center, an office and shopping complex that begins on Battery Street between Sacramento and Clay Streets and continues to the Embarcadero, is studded with nooks and crannies that offer good places for a bite to eat or just to sit in the sun. On many of the plazas connecting the buildings, there are a few chairs and stone benches. On warm days the steps will also be filled with lunchtime picnickers. On the street level, beyond Four Embarcadero, is the expansive Justin Herman Plaza and the controversial Vaillancourt Fountain. Not only is this an appealing place to sit and eat, but there is usually some form of entertainment available, from volleyball in the summer to ice skating in the winter.

There is often metered street parking available on the Embarcadero behind Vaillancourt fountain. Otherwise, the Embarcadero Center lots offer reduced rates for validated parking if you buy something that costs at least $5.00. If you know you are going to make a purchase at one of the stores, your parking will be at about half the regular price.

SIDNEY WALTON PARK

If you would prefer smaller crowds and more greenery, take the escalator to the top floor of One Embarcadero, go past the Cineplex, and you'll come to a walkway that takes you across Washington Street and onto the lawn of the Alcoa Building. This is a lightly populated area. Or you could continue across the plaza to Sidney Walton Park, which is bordered by Davis, Jackson, Pacific, and Front Streets. This is an inviting place to have lunch in the sun for several reasons. First of all, there are rolling hills of green grass, fountains, shade trees, and good wind protection from the surrounding office and apartment buildings. There is also some interesting art in the form of two sculptures. One is a whimsical portrait of the artist Georgia O'Keeffe by Marisol, and the other is Jim Dine's bronze *Big Heart on Rock*.

The park is surrounded by restaurants, including Square One, MacArthur Park, and several takeout shops, making it easy to get whatever you feel like eating.

You might also find yourself on the local TV evening news. The park is convenient to both Channel 5 and Channel 7, and when they need to get a quick "man on the street" reaction to a story, they often head in this direction. Have your sound bite ready, just in case.

REDWOODS PARK

To the east of the Transamerica Pyramid is a half-acre forested oasis appropriately called Redwoods Park. Redwood trees were brought in from the Santa Cruz Mountains to turn this portion of the concrete canyon into a natural preserve of sorts. There's also a waterfall and a small stage for lunchtime performances. This is a peaceful, quiet area but not a place for sun worshippers. Because of the trees and high buildings, it tends to be shady and cool. There are plenty of delis nearby, and Chinatown is just a few blocks away for takeout food.

WASHINGTON SQUARE PARK

If there is a community center of North Beach, it is Washington Square Park, which is bordered by Columbus and Stockton, and Union and Filbert Streets. It's a gently sloping expanse of green lawn and trees, with some park benches and walkways. At Columbus there is also a small children's playground. The neighborhood is loaded with Italian delis and bakeries that will supply the perfect picnic for you. It's not at all unusual to see groups of office workers in a circle on the lawn, lunching together. There are also benches ringing the park.

For striking up conversations, generally the benches have their own patterns of occupancy. On the Filbert Street side, the street people and wandering musicians usually take their place in the shade of the trees. On the Stockton Street side, there's a pretty good mix of people who stop for a few minutes while passing through and those who like to read their papers and magazines while facing the afternoon sun. On the Union Street side, the local Italian-Americans usually hold court and are a great source of stories about North Beach, past and present.

Your best chances for a street space, with a parking meter, is on Upper Grant or Union Street between Columbus and Stockton. I usually head directly for the Vallejo Street municipal garage, between Stockton and Powell.

LEVI PLAZA

When Levi Strauss built its brick-and-glass corporate headquarters in the early 1980s, it commissioned the famed landscape architect Lawrence Halprin to design a public park in front of the building. The result is one of the nicest open spaces in the city, with fountains, benches, and a large scale reminiscent of the piazzas and plazas of Europe. The main plaza is a mosaic of brick and concrete, broken up by trees and planters. Across Battery Street, the open space becomes more parklike, with rolling green lawns and a fountain with a waterfall that blocks the sound of traffic from Battery Street and the Embarcadero.

Try to find a metered space on Battery, the Embarcadero, or any of the side streets. The Plaza runs from Battery to Sansome Streets, and from north of Union to south of Greenwich.

WAVE ORGAN

Would you like to get out on the water, listen to the sounds of the bay, sit in the sun (or fog), and have a great view of San Francisco without having to board a boat? If the answer is yes, then you might want to lunch at the Wave Organ. It's another brainchild of the folks who bring you the innovative exhibits at the Exploratorium, and it's not only easy to get to, but it's also free.

The Wave Organ is basically a series of pipes that have been sunk out in the bay, terminating in several benches and other listening areas. Find yourself a comfortable perch and just listen while you look at San Francisco skyline or at Alcatraz and the bay. The sounds vary, depending on the size of each pipe, its location, and the action of the tides. Benches that double as listening booths are well-placed to catch the midday sun.

Don't expect Bach or anything resembling music. Just relax and go with whatever subtle sounds the bay is producing at the moment.

To get to the Wave Organ, enter the driveway to the San Francisco Yacht Club, which is just before the Golden Gate Bridge entrance off Bay Street. Continue past the Yacht Club until you can drive no farther. Park your car and walk to the end of the narrow strip of land to the Wave Organ.

HUNTINGTON PARK

Across the street from the main steps of Grace Cathedral on Nob Hill is a lovely neighborhood park that is laid out with as much care as the cathedral's geometrically designed labyrinths. Usually bathed in sun, Huntington Park has a children's playground at its north end at Sacramento Street, while its southern end at California Street seems to be the province of tai chi chuan practitioners.

The centerpiece of the park is a fountain that is a copy of the sixteenth-century tortoise fountain in Rome. Everything in the park is at a human scale, and although there are no signs or imposed rules, people seem to treat the park as though they were in a library. No boom boxes here. Perhaps the view helps set the tone. To one side there's Grace Cathedral; to another, the sedate Huntington Hotel, and next door, the imposing brownstone that was once the Flood Mansion and is now the Pacific Union Club.

ALTA PLAZA PARK

This is one of the neighborhood parks for tony Pacific Heights, running east and west from Steiner to Scott and north and south from Jackson to Clay. Its location practically insures that it is well-maintained and safe. There is nothing particularly remarkable about the park, but it does have all the amenities: a pleasant children's playground, tennis courts, lots of trees, views, and some impressive homes on its borders.

The southern tip of the park, off Clay, is at the bottom of a steep hill, and there are some challenging steps up to the top. They ascend a series of lovely terraces that look down on the city to the south. On a sunny day you'll find folks sitting on the steps, having a picnic or just soaking up some rays. In any weather, you'll see dogs walking their masters and mistresses. The easiest entrance is from the north around Jackson and Scott Streets. It's reasonably flat here and a short walk to the playground.

LAFAYETTE PARK

Similar in layout to Alta Plaza Park, this four-block park has all the usual elements: a small children's playground, lots of green grass, many dogs and their walkers, and a tree-filled hilly area. On one visit I was surprised to also find a small meadow between the trees on the eastern side of the park, where male sunbathers stripped down to their shorts and beyond.

Despite the mansions that surround it, Lafayette Park does not have as much charm as Alta Plaza. Lafayette Park is between Sacramento and Washington Streets, and Gough and Laguna Streets.

CHAPTER 9 — Golden Gate Park

One of San Francisco's treasures for locals and visitors alike is Golden Gate Park, the three-mile stretch of green grass, trees, ponds, and gardens that runs from Stanyan Street to the ocean. Most remarkable is that the 1,000 lush acres were originally sand dunes on which the designer of New York's Central Park, Frederick Law Olmstead, told city fathers no respectable trees would ever grow. But thanks to the landscaper John McLaren and the engineer William Hammond Hall, the dunes were transformed into one of the world's great parks. McLaren is said to have planted more than a million trees in the park during his fifty years as park superintendent.

There is public transportation available to the park but none inside it, although you can rent bikes and skates on Stanyan Street. There is one main road in the park: John F. Kennedy Drive runs all the way from the main entrance at Stanyan and Fell Streets to the ocean, cutting through the center and northern portions of the park. There are several additional entrances off Fulton to the north and Lincoln to the south.

Weekends and the summer tourist season are the most crowded times to visit the park. During the week traffic and parking are relatively easy. One of the best features of the park is that it is so user friendly. You will encounter no KEEP OFF THE GRASS signs.

McLaren Lodge

The first building you see on entering the park is the headquarters, named after its longtime gardener, John McLaren. On weekends, if you enter the driveway on Stanyan Street north of Fell, you can often find a parking place behind the lodge. In any event, you could begin a visit by stopping inside on a weekday and picking up a free, detailed map of the park. When the office is closed on weekends, refer to the big map out in front of the building.

CONSERVATORY OF FLOWERS

One could devote a lifetime to exploring the various treasures to be found in Golden Gate Park. Most people know about the great glass Conservatory of Flowers that greets you shortly after the entrance on Kennedy Drive. This is the oldest building in the park and was designed to resemble the Palm House at London's Kew Gardens. There is a small admission fee. Be advised that it is hot and steamy inside. At this writing the future of the conservatory is in grave doubt. Storms in late 1995 caused millions of dollars of damage, and the city is still trying to figure out whether to demolish the building or somehow raise the funds for restoration. My bet is that the building will be saved.

Just to the east of the conservatory is a grassy area where you might be treated to an impromptu vaudeville show. This is where amateur and professional jugglers meet on most Sundays to show their stuff and share their talents. It fronts on Kennedy Drive, at the main area for roller skaters and bladers on weekends when the road is closed to motorists.

CHILDREN'S PLAYGROUND

If you bring the kids to the park, you might want to let them watch the jugglers, even take a few lessons, and then work your way to the south on Bowling Green Drive to the children's playground area and the beautifully restored carousel. This is a wonderful, large playground with swings, slides, sandboxes, and climbing structures to challenge a variety of age groups, plus plenty of room to run up and roll down small hills. Bring a picnic and stay awhile. There are also important necessities, like water fountains, rest rooms, and snack bars. There is a parking lot off Bowling Green Drive. With luck and patience, you should be able to get a spot.

MUSEUM CONCOURSE

The major destination in the park is the music concourse, which is surrounded by the De Young Museum, the Japanese garden, and the California Academy of Sciences. Each of these worthy attractions is likely to be jammed during the summer and on weekends but easy to visit at other times. One delightful free offering is the Sunday afternoon concert at the band shell by the venerable Municipal Orchestra. There is a certain "good old days" charm to these performances, straight out of Meredith Willson and *The Music Man*.

ACADEMY OF SCIENCES

Again, if you are spending your time in the park with kids, the Academy of Sciences is a good bet. A single admission buys access to the Museum of Natural History, the Morrison Planetarium, and the Aquarium. There are three connected buildings making up this complex, with a large open courtyard in the center. The Wattis Hall of Man is filled with exhibits on various stages of life in cultures throughout the world. The displays are lively and interesting to most age groups, and there is space for kids to run off some steam. The Steinhardt Aquarium is the most surefire attraction for kids. There are nearly two hundred tanks of colorful and exotic fish, plus a fish roundabout that gives you the feeling of being surrounded by marine life. Dolphin and seal feeding becomes a performance of sorts, viewed from bleacher seats. Feeding begins at 10:30 A.M. and continues every two hours until closing.

If you are at the Academy of Sciences, take a look at the totem pole in the courtyard. It might come as a surprise to learn that the roots of this structure are in rock 'n' roll.

Here's the story: in the 1970s, when I was general manager of KSAN-FM, the legendary rock station, we were approached by a promotion person from an airline who had recently learned of a tribe of Indians in Canada called the Gitksan. The called themselves Ksan for short. Somehow this led to an on-the-air contest to fly some lucky winners to visit the Indian village and watch the master carvers make their totem poles. In return some Gitksan craftsmen were brought to San Francisco to erect a totem pole at the academy.

One sunny day in the late 1970s, a major dedication was held with both rock and Indian chants, and the pole was dedicated as a permanent fixture. Now people pass by it everyday, having no idea that it all started with a contest on the "Jive 95."

Open daily 10 A.M. to 5 P.M.; Memorial Day to Labor Day 9 A.M. to 6 P.M. Admission: adults $7.00; ages 12 to 17 $4.00; ages 6 to 11 $1.50; children 5 and under, free. Free-for-all the first Wednesday of each month. Separate admission for Planetarium and Laserium shows. 750–7145.

JAPANESE TEA GARDEN

The most popular garden in the park is the Japanese Tea Garden, which dates back to the late 1800s and the Midwinter Fair, which was San Francisco's first big international festival. The tea garden is one of the fair's few remaining sites, the others being the De Young Museum and the Music Concourse. Unfortunately, because of the popularity, the crowds often overwhelm the tranquillity of the landscape, bridges, and waterfalls. This is a lovely spot to visit, *if* you peek inside first and determine that it is not too jammed. Summertime is probably best avoided, unless it's a cold, foggy day and the tourists stay away from the park. The best time to visit is in April, when the cherry blossoms add yet another touch of beauty.

Located at the southwest end of the concourse. Open daily from 9 A.M. to 6:30 P.M. There is an admission fee to the garden, and for another charge, you can have tea and rice cakes in the tea house pagoda. Admission is free on the first Wednesday of each month. 752–1171.

OTHER GARDENS

There are many small gardens within the park, each spectacular during its prime blooming season. One of the most imposing is the twenty-acre rhododendron garden where you can simply get lost among the giant flowering bushes. The fuschia garden near the Conservatory of Flowers is usually in bloom from July to October. The rose garden, off Kennedy Drive, is a restful, flat area for those who want only a short walk.

SHAKESPEARE GARDEN

Hidden behind the Academy of Sciences is the lovely and peaceful Shakespeare garden. An archway marks the entrance to this small oasis of Elizabethan design, which features flowers and plants mentioned in the bard's writings. You walk down a brick pathway to a wall of quotes. From *Othello:* "Our bodies are our gardens, to the which our wills are gardeners. . . ." Or from *The Tempest:* "You would I give a thousand furlongs of sea for an acre of barren ground. . . ." Many benches, inscribed with dedications from their donors, are placed throughout the garden. Of particular interest to local theatergoers is one that reads TO BILL BALL [founder of the American Conservatory Theater] FOR HIS ENCOURAGEMENT, ARTISTRY AND GENIUS—STEVE SILVER [creator-producer of *Beach Blanket Babylon.*] Silver passed away a few years after providing this memorial for his fellow local theater legend.

AIDS MEMORIAL GROVE

A more recent sign of the times is the AIDS Memorial Grove in the eastern end of the park, across from the tennis courts. Here once again the presence of Steve Silver is felt because the stone entrance to the grove was his gift a few months before he died of AIDS. At this writing the grove is a work in progress, with volunteers gathering once a month to weed and plant and spend quiet time together in memory of lost loved ones.

Even during renovation there is much here to create a setting for reflection, remembrance, and mourning. Giant redwood trees share the grove with dogwoods, ferns, and wildflowers as the oval path takes you from the darkness of shade to the brilliance of sunlight or the damp mist of fog. There is a large semicircular bench of wood and limestone for those who simply want to sit. If your life has been touched in any way by AIDS, prepare for a moving experience.

Strybing Arboretum

The horticultural gem of the park is the Strybing Arboretum, which is a seventy-acre showplace of some five thousand labeled species of plants. As one gardener explained to me, it's all possible because of the unique four-season climate—spring, fall, spring, and fall—which allows the arboretum to grow plants from around the globe, particularly those areas with Mediterranean climates. Among the highlights are the Japanese Moon viewing garden; the succulents garden, highlighting plants from Mexico and Africa; the California native garden, which is awash with wildflowers in the spring; and the New World Cloud Forest, where sprayers create a constant fog, which seem like overkill on certain summer days.

Everyone should try the garden for the visually handicapped. Here you can follow a wall and enjoy the fragrance and touch of the many species of plants along the path.

Open daily. Free tours are given of the Strybing Arboretum daily at 1:30 P.M. They begin at the bookstore, whose entrance is on the south side of the park at Lincoln Way and Ninth Avenue.

Other Park Highlights

Stow Lake, in the center of the park, where you can rent a paddle boat for two or simply walk around the perimeter and watch the ducks. This is the largest lake in the park and even has its own island.

The Buffalo Paddock, where bison, not buffalo, roam, is the gift of Richard Blum, the husband of Senator (and former Mayor) Dianne Feinstein. When I last visited, the bison were being cared for by a volunteer who also happened to be an usher at the San Francisco Opera. He would sing arias to the apparently appreciative beasts while setting out their daily feasts.

Spreckels Lake, which is really more of a small pond than a lake. The fun here is to watch the operators of remote-controlled model boats maneuver their craft around the water. Some of the boats are typical speed jobs, while others are remarkable handmade works of art. Spreckels Lake is near 35th Avenue and Fulton, on the northern side of the park.

The Anglers Lodge and Casting Pond, located behind a rustic log cabin lodge, is the site of a series of ponds connected by walkways where members of the lodge and visitors can practice fly fishing and get some tips from the pros.

Presidio

I've always believed that the best real estate in California, or most places for that matter, is owned by the military. Certainly that was the case for the Presidio, which was first established as a military base by the Spanish settlers in 1776. There is no better location in all of San Francisco. After serving as a base for the Mexicans and then the United States, this historic area was turned over to the National Park Service in October 1995, creating the largest urban national park in the country. How large? Try some of these statistics:

- nearly 1,500 acres, more than half of it open space
- 510 historic buildings; many others scheduled to be removed
- 11 miles of hiking trails
- 14 miles of biking trails
- 44 miles of roads
- an 18-hole public golf course
- several tennis courts
- a bowling alley
- more than 400,000 trees, all in a lush environment fronting on the Pacific Ocean and San Francisco Bay

The park's future development will be decided over the next several years. Money is going to be a major factor. Unfortunately the new park was created as part of an economy move as the Defense Department closed obsolete bases. The Park Service inherited the land during a time of severe budget cutting, and no one is quite sure where the necessary funds are coming from to fix up the Presidio. One of the first private tenants was Mikhail Gorbachev's international peace think tank, which is housed in a lovely Coast Guard home overlooking the bay. There are also major environmental research groups coming in. At this writing a trust has been established to take over much of the business operation under the watchful eye of the Park Service. The trust would be charged with making the Presidio pay for itself. There is considerable controversy over whether or not this means overcommercialization or simply survival. So far the entire area is remarkably free of commercialization, except for a bowling alley and a Burger King with a whopper of a view. It's in a former mess hall on Lincoln Boulevard with a million-dollar view of the water and the Golden Gate Bridge.

VISITOR CENTER

The logical place to begin a visit to the Presidio is at the visitor center, which is in a row of red-brick barracks on the Main Post, across from the parade ground. As of this writing there is ample parking on the grounds, but there are plans to return the entire area to nature and have all parking elsewhere, presumably at Crissy Field. There will be signs pointing you to the current choices. There are also three MUNI bus lines serving the Presidio. At the visitor center you can pick up maps and brochures and find out what services are available. A ranger will also be on duty to answer questions. There are large display boards throughout the park, giving the history of a particular site.

Building 102, Montgomery Street. Open daily 10 A.M. to 5 P.M. 561–4323.

MAIN POST WALK

The Main Post Walk would be a good way to get steeped in the history of the Presidio and to see most of the historic buildings and the new Herbst International Exhibition Hall, housed in a remodeled commissary. It's a mostly flat stroll of about a mile, and there is a self-guided brochure available at the visitor center. You'll see how the Presidio evolved. The tour usually takes about an hour, but you can make it as long as you'd like if you linger in some of the buildings, such as the Presidio Museum, which is housed in the former Post Hospital. Assuming that the cannon and Nike missiles are still on display, keep in mind that a shot was never fired from the Presidio, except for drills. This is a military museum, with several interesting historical displays and artifacts. The most detailed exhibit chronicles the army's considerable role in helping San Francisco recover from the 1906 earthquake.

Just above Lincoln, to the south of the visitor center. Open Wednesday through Sunday 10 A.M. to 4 P.M.

As you walk back up the Post walk, you'll pass the 6th Army Headquarters, which will remain at the Presidio. The barracks buildings housed enlisted men, while the officers were around the corner. If you're a film buff, check out the four Queen Anne/Stick–style homes that face one another at the corner of Funston Avenue and Presidio Boulevard. Can you recognize the one that was Sean Connery's house in the movie *Presidio*? By the way, they're called stick houses because of the posts on the front porches.

Funston Avenue could be used for a movie setting for Main Street, U.S.A., with its white shingle homes and picket fences, set off by shade trees and green lawns. This was not a bad place to be stationed, particularly for officers.

All of these locations are well indicated on the current map of the Presidio that is free at the visitor center.

HIKES AND RIDES

For nature lovers there are several ways to enjoy the Presidio. With a map in hand from the visitor center, you can take off on any number of hiking or biking trails. Within minutes from the Main Post, you will enter a wilderness area of surprising quiet and beauty. Many of the best trails take you to places you could never see by car.

And you can choose between land and sea.

The Ecology Trail is an energetic hiking or mountain bike trail that leads from Pershing Square near the Main Post in a loop through a forest with lovely meadows. In the thick of the cypress, eucalyptus, and redwood trees, you are completely removed from the city and the ocean, which is only a mile or so away. About midway through the trail, there's a very pleasant picnic area at El Polin Spring. Continue along the trail, and you hook up with Lover's Lane, which begins at the Presidio Boulevard Gate and runs all the way to Funston. This is a downsloping, well-lighted stroll, but, of course, you eventually have to get back up the hill.

There's a completely different hike, no bikes allowed, on the coastal trail that winds along the bluffs overlooking the Pacific. The trail runs from Baker Beach to the Golden Gate Bridge, and the views are spectacular. You will also come across some of the coastal defense batteries, most of them dating back to the turn of the century. These are huge concrete bunkers where cannon and other weapons were poised to fire on intruders at sea.

For a flatter surface for walking and running, the Golden Gate Promenade hugs the bay and is a favorite spot for folks who usually begin at the Marina Green and can run or walk all the way to Fort Point.

Bicycles will be available also. For information, check the desk at the visitor center.

FORT POINT

Perhaps the architectural treasure of the Presidio is in its most remote northwestern corner, under the Golden Gate Bridge. The brick, steel, and granite Fort Point was built during the Civil War to guard the the young but gold-rich city from attack from the sea. Although the fort was an aesthetic success, it was obsolete by the time it was dedicated because the bricks didn't offer protection against the newer weapons of the day. In fact, you might be surprised by the displays of cannonballs in the museum that is inside the fort. Some of them look more harmless than many children's toys of today.

On a visit here wander through the museum to see the early weapons, uniforms, and other artifacts. The high point of the day comes when there's a demonstration of loading and firing the Civil War cannon in the courtyard.

The schedule varies with demand from school groups.

If you can handle the winds, climb up to the top of the Fort for a wonderful view of the bay and the Golden Gate Bridge. You'll probably also see some intrepid surfers riding the waves and the rocks next to the fort.

To get to Fort Point, look for the exit off Lincoln Boulevard. Open Wednesday through Sunday 10 A.M. to 4 P.M. Tours by appointment; the schedule will change when the retrofitting of the Golden Gate Bridge begins, probably around late 1997. 556–1693.

THE FUTURE

The exciting thing about the Presidio is that changes are happening on a regular basis, and there are big plans. You can expect several things to happen in the next several years. Look for some of the classic officers' homes to be turned into bed and breakfast inns. Look for more restaurants and cafés along the Crissy Field shoreline. Expect theaters and other attractions to bring people to the park. Expect pedestrian malls with several roads closed to motor traffic. Look for the refurbishing of existing museums and the creation of new ones. There will definitely be a transportation hub near a large parking lot. The hub will have shuttle buses to and from various locations within the Presidio. And while all the development is going on, look for an increase in open space as nearly three hundred structures are demolished. There are plans to re-create a marshland with foot bridges and hiking paths. The hope is that the former military site will continue to be a site for protection of natural resources and ideas for the future. Of course, there is no reason to wait for the future to enjoy the Presidio. There is much to do and see now; so much that it will probably take several visits.

Treasure Island

Even more uncertain is the fate of Treasure Island, another former military installation that becomes San Francisco property in 1997. This man-made island under the Bay Bridge was built for the 1939 World's Fair. After a series of plans failed, including locating the city's airport there, the navy took over and ran the island until the recent rash of base closings. Although the navy will basically vacate in 1997, it will take a few more years to clean the island of any contamination. Also turned over to the city will be the woodsy neighboring island of Yerba Buena.

Treasure Island is built on more than 400 acres of flat landfill that has housed hangars, homes, office buildings, and the kinds of services that are needed to operate a military base. Only one building is open to the public so far, the Treasure Island Museum, which offers interesting exhibits on navy history and the 1939 World's Fair. It also provides a great view of the city from its parking lot.

The future? Take your pick. The plans that are being kicked around at this date cover a wide range of interests, from social service to hucksterism: a center for the homeless, providing housing, schools, and training programs, a major film studio (some of the island's buildings are already being used as sound stages), a theme park, another world's fair, a resort with waterfront hotels, and fancy shops and restaurants. Meanwhile, get to know the island with a visit to the museum.

Take the Treasure Island exit off the Bay Bridge. Open daily from 10 A.M. to 5 P.M.

CHAPTER 11

More Places to Walk, Run, Ride a Bike, and Enjoy Nature

LAKE MERCED

As lovely as Golden Gate Park is, it's sometimes hard to forget that you are still in a bustling city. At Lake Merced, to the south of the park, it's hard to believe that you are still within the city limits. Once you enter the gate at Harding Road from Skyline Boulevard and park your car, you are truly transported to a country setting.

Park in the ample lot and start walking. You will be on a strip of land surrounded by fresh blue water. There are picnic tables along the slopes of the lake's banks. You'll see and hear birds and follow pathways to great expanses of green lawn. One road leads to the public Harding Park golf course. The setting is beautiful, and the fees are about as low as you'll find in the area. The scene can't beat on a clear sunny day in winter.

Back at the parking lot is the Lake Merced Boating and Fishing Company. This is a friendly little store that has everything for the fisherman or woman, including beginners. Here you can get the necessary permits as well as rent a boat or canoe. It costs $9 per hour if you paddle, more if you rent a motor. You'll also get plenty of fishing advice. If you don't want to take a boat, all you have to do is walk a few steps and drop a line. The lakes are stocked with trout. Most of the fishing is in North Lake, which is the deepest section.

Windsurfing instruction is also available from 9 A.M. to 1 P.M. on South lake. This is a great place to just sit or walk around. Regulars walk all the way around the lake, along Skyline, John Muir, and Lake Merced Road. You might notice a historical marker off Lake Merced Road. This is the site of the city's last known legal duel, between State Supreme Court Justice David Terry and U.S. Senator David Broderick in 1859. The markers that tell the story of the fight (Broderick's pistol accidentally fired into the ground before the duel could begin, and Terry calmly shot him dead), which led to the out-lawing of duels in the state.

This entire area on the southwestern limits of the city offers many lovely outdoor getaways. Lake Merced is only a block or so from the ocean and the Great Highway.

FORT FUNSTON

Just down Skyline Boulevard is Fort Funston, which offers one of the best free shows in town, weather permitting. If it is clear and windy, which it is much of the time at this ocean-front former military installation, the hang gliders show up to dive off the cliffs and soar like birds through the air. There is a convenient parking lot a short walk from the cliffs. This is also a good place to park for a long hike along the coastal trail. You can walk from here to Fort Point at the foot of the Golden Gate Bridge and enjoy wonderful scenery and manageable terrain. This is a nine-mile hike with some hills, but you can cut it short and still have a good stroll.

LINCOLN PARK

For a shorter walk, start in the area of Lincoln Park and the Palace of the Legion of Honor. Parking may be a bit tricky at the popular museum, so continue down the road to El Camino Del Mar and park around Thirty-second Avenue. On the ocean side of the street, a marker gives you some history of the area and the mileage to various points. Nearby there is a round platform with a great view and steps leading down to a more remote platform. There I happened upon a couple kissing and also found myself trapped by my own generational prejudices. Instead of Cary Grant and Kim Novak, it was a guy wearing a baseball cap with the bill facing the back and a girl with black fingernail polish and spikes on her leather skirt. I'm sure they were nice kids, but I must admit that I laughed instead of sighed.

Heading back up the hill, you can walk to Lincoln Park, keeping an eye out for flying golf balls from the course that is on both sides of the road. The refurbished Palace of the Legion of Honor Museum is the focal point of the park, and it is certainly worth seeing. Check the local papers for current art show-ings. Almost hidden from view on the ocean side of the parking lot is a moving permanent art installation that is dedicated to victims of the Holocaust.

GOLDEN GATE BRIDGE

What is there to say about the Golden Gate Bridge? Of course, it's a San Francisco treasure, a symbol of the city. It's just that most of us who live in the area seem to take it for granted, except for people who commute every day to and from Marin County. For them it's a mixed blessing of great views and harrowing traffic jams.

The best way to see and appreciate the art deco masterpiece is not to drive on it but to view it from a variety of angles. You can pull off at the last San Francisco exit before entering the bridge and park in metered spots with all the tour buses. This leads you to some pathways that begin the pedestrian walkway along the nearly two-mile bridge, until recently the longest suspen-sion bridge in the world. From the parking area walk down some of the paths instead of up to the bridge. There are nicely landscaped gardens with benches and views looking up at the magnificent structure. Despite the crowded parking lot, you will find few people here. Most of the tourists will be heading in the opposite direction, to the gift shop or to begin the walk on the bridge.

Should you walk across the bridge? That depends on your sense of adven-ture, and your expectations. Be prepared for the smell of fumes from the passing traffic and for high winds and cold breezes, but you will be able to say that you did it. My preference is to get a taste for the experience by walk-ing to the first tower and then returning. One look straight up from the bot-tom of a 746-foot tower will give you a new perspective on the size of this engineering marvel.

MARINA GREEN TO FORT POINT

One of the more popular runs in San Francisco is from the parking lot at the Marina Green, along the bay, all the way to Fort Point. The breezes come in from the Golden Gate to keep you cool, the water laps against the shore to provide invigorating sound effects, and you can take the six-mile round trip jaunt enjoying some of the city's best scenery without encountering traffic. It makes for a very nice walk, too.

MOUNTAIN LAKE PARK

One of the nicest urban parks you'll find anywhere comes as a complete surprise to all but the lucky neighbors of Mountain Lake Park. We found it one foggy afternoon while roaming around Lake Street, near Park Presidio. If you walk north on Twelfth Avenue, the street reaches a dead end a half block beyond Lake, and you enter the park.

At first it looks as though this is simply a nice playground with two levels of swings and climbing structures for kids. Then you see a lake filled with ducks and geese, three tennis courts, a soccer field, lots of green lawn, trails, and a vast stretch of open space. The park runs up to Seventh Avenue, with trails leading into the Presidio and on to the ocean and bay. There are many benches scattered throughout and much room to play, run, or seek quiet and solitude.

If you want a real challenge, take the trail down to Baker Beach and run the "sand ladder." It's part of the course in the grueling "escape from Alcatraz" triathlon, an event my athletic wife Catherine conquers annually.

WATERFRONT WALK OR RUN

Now that the Embarcadero Freeway is just a dim memory, the city's waterfront is fast becoming the prime spot for exercisers. Eventually, the area will be lined with palm trees and trolley lines, adding even more life to this revived area. You can walk or run all the way from China Basin to Fort Point, although most of the action appears to be north or south from the YMCA between Mission and Howard Streets.

San Francisco Stair Masters

The city has several stairways that are necessary to navigate some of the steeper hills. These can be genuinely challenging but also scenic. You might want to warm up by climbing the hills around the Noe Valley, Portrero, and the Castro districts. Then head up for the bigger challenges:

- Fillmore Street, from Green to Broadway—going back down the hill gives you a spectacular view of the bay
- the Greenwich steps, from Sansome Street up to Coit Tower
- the Filbert steps, from Sansome Street to Montgomery—a walk that takes you past one of San Francisco's most scenic streets and one of the last wooden sidewalks in town, Napier Lane; the gardens and quaint homes make this a memorable walk.

CHAPTER 12

Great Views and Drives

Views

In a city of great views, it's difficult to pick favorites. Some of the better known viewing spots, such as Coit Tower and Twin Peaks, are on the itineraries of most of the tour buses, but there are still some terrific spots that could qualify as back road finds. For example, did you ever wonder where those TV guys are when they stand with the city in the background as they introduce their story? Well, one of the best sites for what are called "stand-ups" is directly below the ugly giant TV antenna tower on Mt. Sutro.

TANK HILL

It's a slight climb up some wooden and dirt steps to one of the best views of the city. From this usually windy perch, you can see all of the southern part of San Francisco, most of the downtown and financial districts, the pricey community of Seacliff, much of the Presidio, both the Bay and Golden Gate Bridges, much of the bay, parts of Marin and the East Bay, and more, depending on the weather. In summer the late afternoon usually lets you see the various microclimates in action in the city, as North Beach and the Mission and Portrero and Bernal Hills are bathed in sun while the western parts of town are shrouded by the inflowing fog.

   The best way to get there: take Stanyan Street south (uphill from Golden Gate Park) to Belgrave, then turn left until it ends, and park. In case you're wondering about the hill's name, this used to be the location for a large water tank.

PORTOLA STREET

If you'd like to stay in your car and still enjoy an overview of the city, looking west to east, take Clipper Street from Noe Valley all the way up to Portola. Park and look over the edge.

RUSSIAN HILL

A less expansive view, again looking west to east, is from the top of Russian Hill. Enter Russian Hill from Jones Street, between Vallejo and Green Streets, and drive a few blocks to a small parking area with room for about five cars. There is a lovely overlook here, plus paths leading around a small hillside park.

Macondray Lane

While you're in the area, walk back up Jones Street for a half block or so to one of the city's hidden gems, Macondray Lane. This is a tree-shaded pathway between charming cottages and apartments that ends in a wooden stairway down to Taylor Street. Macondray Lane was the setting for Armistead Maupin's celebrated serial *Tales of the City*.

ALAMO SQUARE

Perhaps the most photographed view of the city is from Alamo Park, particularly from Hayes Street, just above Steiner. From here you can look down on the famous painted ladies, six elaborate Victorian homes that have become a signature image of the city. What makes the view so special is the way the homes set up the city's skyline in the background. If you're looking for a photo opportunity, try the afternoon when the sun will be at your back.

This is a good stop when you're on your way to a destination. It's not necessarily a destination of its own.

BROADWAY AT LYON

While exploring Pacific Heights, pull over at the corner of Broadway and Lyon. Here the view is of the Palace of Fine Arts below and then the Bay and the Golden Gate Bridges. This is a very scenic and comfortable spot, with wide steps leading down the hill and several areas for sitting and taking in the sights.

TREASURE ISLAND

One of the great views of the Bay Area is from the Bay Bridge as you head into the city. If your traffic luck is with you, it's an all too brief passing view. The best place to see the city from the east is from Treasure Island, the last outpost of the San Francisco city limits. Simply take the Treasure Island exit from the Bay Bridge and head for the museum parking lot. From there, you have a wonderful view of the city.

FROM ABOVE

There are several hotels offering rooftop views of the city. The outside elevator ride at the Fairmont is certainly breathtaking in more ways than one, as the speed in which it ascends usually provokes gasps from the passengers. The Top of the Mark cocktail lounge at the Mark Hopkins Hotel gives you a 360-degree view from Nob Hill. Perhaps the best view of all is from the top of the Bank of America building, from the windows of its fancy restaurant, the Carnelian Room.

Great Drives

PACIFIC HEIGHTS: HOME TOURS

San Francisco is a city of beautiful homes, most of them with beautiful views. It's not everyone's idea of a good time, but many of us enjoy the precarious thrill of looking at someone else's showplace. As they say, it doesn't cost anything to look.

The most obvious place to explore the homes of the rich and famous is Pacific Heights, which runs generally from California to Broadway Streets north and south, and from Franklin Street to the Presidio. (Some of the western portion of the area is also called Presidio Heights. Actually, the boundaries between Pacific Heights, Presidio Heights, Russian Hill, and Cow Hollow are up for individual interpretation. For those of us who don't live there, the main thing to know is that it's all pretty swell.) The entire area was developed after the 1906 earthquake, when society folk had to leave the destruction of Nob Hill and find new sites for their mansions.

The best way to enjoy the sights is to pick an east-west street and then cruise for a while. I like to start on Broadway around Webster and head west. At Divisadero, turn left and then head back east on Pacific. When you feel like it, turn down a block and head back west on Jackson and so on. You will see buildings of every type: Victorians, Edwardians, Italianate villas, high-rise apartments, and foreign consulates.

These are some of the more notable homes you will pass:

Spreckels Mansion

The Spreckels Mansion at 2080 Washington Street at Octavia was built for the sugar baron Adolph Spreckels. The block-long stone fortress has twenty-six bathrooms, which should be enough for its present occupants, the novelist Danielle Steele and her thirteen children.

Bourne Mansion

The Bourne Mansion at 2250 Webster Street at Pacific was designed by the famed architect Willis Polk for William Bourne, who made a fortune in the gold country and also brought water from the foothills of Yosemite to San Francisco. If that wasn't enough, Bourne owned what became the Pacific Gas and Electric Company. He had a few dollars to spend on a home.

Flood Mansions

Two of the most imposing homes ever built in San Francisco now house private schools. The mansion at 2120 Broadway is the Hamlin School, which is designed to look like an Italian stone palazzo but is actually built of wood. You will recognize the building by the twin lions that flank the entrance gate, between Fillmore and Webster Streets on Broadway. Down the street is an even grander palace, built for the Floods shortly after the 1906 earthquake, which destroyed their original Nob Hill brownstone. The Floods wanted to make sure they wouldn't lose another mansion to an earthquake, so they built a secure fortress this time. They imported granite for the foundation and had the house built of solid pink Tennessee stone. This hotel-size home is now the elementary School of the Sacred Heart.

Haas-Lillienthal House

The Haas-Lillienthal House at 2007 Franklin Street is the only Pacific Heights mansion that is open to the public. This is a classic gabled Victorian that is now operated as a museum by the Foundation for San Francisco's Architectural Heritage. Inside, the decor reflects the evolution of the time the family lived there, from the late 1880s until 1972.

Open for tours on Wednesdays noon until 4 P.M.; Sundays from 11 A.M. until 5 P.M. $5 for adults; $3 for children and seniors. 441–3004.

PACIFIC HEIGHTS WALKING TOURS

The Foundation for Architectural Heritage also offers two-hour walking tours of Pacific Heights. Sundays 12:30 P.M. Admission is $5.00 for adults; $3.00 for children and seniors. 441–3004.

City Guides, operated by Friends of the San Francisco Library, operates free one-hour walking tours of the area; for information, call 558–3981.

ASHBURY HEIGHTS

Rising above the hodgepodge of posthippiedom that is Haight Street, you will find surprisingly beautiful neighborhoods and some of the more interesting Victorian homes in the city. A suggested drive takes you up Masonic Street from Haight; turn left on Frederick Street to Buena Vista West. Drive all the way around Buena Vista Park. Among the landmarks will be yet another Spreckels Mansion at 737 Buena Vista West. This home was once a bed and breakfast inn and is now the residence of the actor Danny Glover and his family. Next door is the former home of the musician Graham Nash.

After making the circuit back to the top of the park, make your way to Java Street, wind over to Delmar, and then cruise down Ashbury. You will see a spectacular array of homes.

COASTAL DRIVE

If you'd like a miniature version of the great coastal drive between San Francisco and Los Angeles, just follow Lincoln Drive past the Golden Gate Bridge to Lincoln Park. In about ten minutes you'll wind through the edge of the Presidio forest, looking down at Baker Beach and other spectacular ocean views.

PART 4

Tourist Destinations

CHAPTER *13*   A Survival Guide

You know the cliché about the New Yorker who's never been to the Statue of Liberty or the Parisian who has never seen the Eiffel Tower. San Francisco is a bit different. Because it is so small and because many of its tourist destinations are genuinely worth seeing, locals do get to the tourist areas. Some, like the cable cars or the Golden Gate Bridge, are treasures for all of us. Others, like Fisherman's Wharf, have seen better days. Still, whether on your own or showing visitors around the city, we can make several recommendations.

CABLE CAR RIDES

When I moved here in 1975, the cost of a cable car ride was 25 cents if the operators ever got around to collecting. Now it is two dollars, making one think twice before hopping on for a ride of a few blocks. Still, if you have to get somewhere along the cable car route, there is no more enjoyable method of transportation. Why let visitors to the city have all the fun?

The views and sounds and thrill of climbing and descending hills is an exhilarating experience, one of those moments when you love the fact that you live in the Bay Area.

CABLE CAR MUSEUM

The local TV newscasts made quite a hoopla in 1996 when one of those magazines that comes up with top ten lists named the Cable Car Museum one of the top free attractions in the United States. We don't know about that ranking, but it certainly is free, and it is impressive to see the inside workings of the cables and pulleys and massive pieces of equipment that keep the cars moving around the city. The museum section of the building is a small room of photos and artifacts, including scale models of cable cars. The real attraction is the powerhouse, where you see how cables and gears keep the cars moving. Be forewarned that it is incredibly loud, as one might expect with all that grinding and gnashing of metal parts, so if you're at all sensitive to noise, you will want to make it a brief visit.

It's also practically impossible to park around here, so your best bet is to arrive and leave by cable car, making it all one experience.

Corner Washington and Mason Streets. Open daily 10 A.M. to 6 P.M. during spring and summer; other times 10 A.M. to 5 P.M. Free. 474–1887.

FISHERMAN'S WHARF

We can't recommend many reasons for you to visit Fisherman's Wharf, with its high percentage of shlock stores and attractions. But if you must go, or out-of-town visitors insist on it, we suggest a ride on a bicycle-pulled carriage. First of all, it's effortless, for you at least. Your pedaling guide will also take you beyond the glitz to the actual wharf areas where you can watch the seals from the pier and maybe even see a fisherman. You may feel like a tourist, but the ride is fun and painless, although when we videotaped a *Bay Area Backroads* TV story, the driver forgot that cameraman Jeff Pierce was hand-holding a forty-pound camera and almost bumped it and him out of the seat. Moral of the story: if you are taking pictures, hold on to your equipment.

PIER 39

Pier 39 is the best way to look through the eyes of the average tourist to San Francisco. At the entrance you'll see all they are confronted with, including people hawking boat trips, bus tours, seaplane tours, T-shirts, and souvenirs. Part theme park, part shopping center, the pier consists of a series of shops, restaurants, and attractions that follow a usually sunny walkway that meanders out into SF bay.

By accident one of the the major attractions at Pier 39 has become the sea lions who chose to make their home at the pier's K dock. At first considered to be noisy nuisances, they are now promoted as a stellar feature. To see them, walk all the way to the bay on the left of the mall.

The newest and most ambitious attraction at Pier 39 is Underwater World, a separate building that houses a 400-foot see-through tunnel that surrounds viewers with some two hundred species of water creatures. Admission is expensive: $12.95 for adults, $9.95 for seniors, and $6.50 for children from three to eleven.

In addition to all the typical shops selling souvenirs and just about anything imaginable to eat, you can enjoy a carousel, a virtual reality center, bumper cars, video games, and a stage for street performers. It's a scene you should see at least once. Some of the more interesting and fun shops include Wound About, a store filled with wind-up toys; Left Hand World (OK, I'm a southpaw . . . you may not be interested); and Calido Chile Traders, a store filled with hot stuff. For the many foreign visitors, there's a currency exchange center.

Open daily from 10:30 A.M. to 8:30 P.M., with extended summer hours. Admission is free, and and so are some performances; separate admission for various attractions (there's a parking garage across from the pier). 981–7437.

GHIRADELLI SQUARE

Ghiradelli Square is still a rather amazing project, filled with good open spaces and views of the bay. This was the first in what turned out to be a series of urban transformations of old industrial buildings that include New York's South Street Seaport, Baltimore's Harborplace, and Boston's Quincy Market. By turning the old Ghiradelli Chocolate Factory into a multilevel collection of shops and restaurants, the city's run-down harbor was beautified and became a major tourist attraction. With its huge glittering sign and bright lights, Ghiradelli is something of a showplace.

The trouble is, locals seldom go there, assuming it's just for tourists. In fact, while I must admit that the only time I go there is to show it to a visitor,

I always enjoy myself there. Walk around the plentiful open spaces and watch and listen to the many street performers. Sit and relax near the center mermaid fountain, and enjoy sea breezes and great views of the bay. The shops change as frequently as the restaurants, but there are often treasures mixed in with the tourist shops. One unusual place is the art gallery run by the National Institute for Arts and Disabilities, featuring the imaginative works of disabled artists.

Between Larkin and Polk Streets and North Point and Beach Streets.

CHAPTER 14

High-Profile Local Institutions

COIT TOWER

A ride or walk up to the top of Telegraph Hill to Coit Tower is one of those things most of us do when showing visitors the city. Chances are you will try to park in the circular parking lot, gaze out at the view, and then head off to the next destination. (A better idea would be to take the number 39 bus from Washington Square up to the top.)

When you have more time, go inside the tower to view the murals, which were restored a few years ago. They tell a dramatic story of the depression years, when they were created by a collection of forty-four artists and assistants as part of a WPA project. The murals were completed in 1934, around the time of the violence that surrounded the San Francisco longshoremen's strike. At that time the city fathers considered the art so controversial that they closed the tower to the public for several months.

The murals, most of them in the style of Diego Rivera, show various phases of California life from agriculture and industry to city life. Each painting has subtle and not-so-subtle political commentary as each of the artists put his or her personal touch to the group project.

You can also take an elevator ride to the top of the tower for a view of the North and East Bays. Actually, the elevator takes you to a loggia near the top, and then you have to negotiate about forty steps to the very top.

The tower was built thanks to one of San Francisco's fabled characters, Lillie Hitchcock Coit, who was known for her fascination with the Fire Department. In her will she bequeathed $100,000 for the city to build a suitable monument to the city's firemen. The tower that bears her name was the result.

Top of Telegraph Hill. Open daily 10 A.M. to 5 P.M. No admission for viewing the murals; there is a fee for the elevator ride.

GOLDEN GATE BRIDGE

A recent survey found that three out of every four visitors to San Francisco visit the Golden Gate Bridge. In many ways it's the symbol for California. The best way to see and appreciate the art deco masterpiece is not to drive on it, when you must concentrate on the road, but to view it from a variety of angles. You can pull off at the last San Francisco exit before entering the bridge and park in metered spots with all the tour buses. This leads you to some pathways that begin the pedestrian walkway on the nearly two-mile bridge, which used to reign as the longest single suspension bridge in the world. From the parking area, walk down some of the paths instead of up to the bridge. There are nicely landscaped gardens with benches and views looking up at the magnificent structure. Despite the crowded parking lot, you will find few people here. Most of the tourists will be heading in the opposite direction, to the gift shop or to begin the walk on the bridge.

Should you walk across the bridge? That depends on your sense of adventure and your expectations. Be prepared for the smell of fumes from the passing traffic and for high winds and cold breezes, but you will be able to say that you did it. My preference is to get a taste for the experience by walking to the first tower and then returning. One look straight up from the bottom of a 746-foot tower will give you a new perspective on the size of the bridge.

LOMBARD STREET

After being closed for several months for repairs, the fabled Lombard Street is again taking tourists on very slow rides down what is billed as the crookedest street in America. If you won't mind waiting in line, it's OK. But for a backroads experience, you might as well take a brief ride on the real crookedest street in San Francisco. It's on Portrero Hill at Twentieth and Vermont Streets, and while the scenery isn't as upscale or even as pretty, you won't have to get in line, and you won't have to dodge a lot of tourists who are not watching the road.

MISSION DOLORES

Except for schoolchildren on their obligatory tour of the California missions, most area residents never quite get around to visiting San Francisco's oldest building, Mission Dolores. Pity. It's worth a stop and could well set the stage for a pleasant day in the Mission district.

Most of us think of California as the "new" America, but consider that the first mass at Mission Dolores took place five days before the Declaration of Independence, on June 29, 1776. The present site was built with Indian labor sixteen years later. Thanks to its adobe construction with giant beams fastened by leather straps, it has survived major earthquakes and fires.

The mission is small and welcoming. Don't miss the adjoining cemetery, where you will see the markers for many early settlers whose names became city streets: Noe, Arguello, Bernal, Valencia, Guerrero. This and the veteran's cemetery at the Presidio are the only remaining cemeteries in the city. Because of the shortage of available land, the town of Colma became the home for San Francisco's dearly departed. If you're a film buff, this location will feel familiar to you. This is where Kim Novak was spotted by Jimmy Stewart in Hitchcock's *Vertigo*.

Folks who work at the mission say their visitors are mostly from out of town. They are struck by the fact that locals rarely take the time to visit, even though the mission is in the heart of San Francisco and is a continuing monument to the beginning of life in the city.

MUSEUM OF MODERN ART

The architecture competes with the paintings, photographs, and sculpture at this center for the Yerba Buena arts complex. See page 45.

151 Third Street, south of Mission (parking tip: if possible, park at the Fifth and Mission municipal garage for the best rates). Open Tuesday, Wednesday, Friday, Saturday, and Sunday 11 A.M. to 6 P.M.; Thursday 11 A.M. to 9 P.M.; closed Monday and holidays. Advance admission tickets available at the Museum or through BASS. 357–4000.

PALACE OF FINE ARTS

The Palace of Fine Arts is one of San Francisco's most visible landmarks, yet most people only see it on their way to the Exploratorium, which is a wonderful place to take the kids. Next time, save a couple of hours to wander the grounds and explore the crowning work of the noted Bay Area architect Bernard Maybeck. He was one of many architects enlisted to build the magnificent Pan-Pacific Exposition in 1915, which was designed to show the world that San Francisco had recovered from the devastating earthquake of 1906.

For the site of the exposition, landfill was brought in to create nearly 650 acres on what used to be the bay. That site eventually became the Marina district, which suffered so badly in the 1989 earthquake because of the soft landfill.

In 1915 there were actually eleven palaces as part of the exposition. The remaining structure is the sole survivor. You can wander the grounds on your own, or you can stop at the information desk at the Exploratorium and take a free guided tour. I was lucky enough to be led around by John Galt, he of the white flowing beard, impeccable dress, walking stick, and twinkling eye. John is a great admirer of Bernard Maybeck and has many a story to tell.

According to John, Maybeck described his creation as a "place representing an old Roman ruin, surrounded by a garden of greenery in a peaceful pond called dreaming waters." Maybeck summed it up pretty well, but John adds touches of his own. He'll show you where the architect designed the echo in the giant rotunda. He'll point up to the statues of the backs of some sixty women who, according to Maybeck, were looking into and weeping over plants that never got planted—apparently, the architect's little inside joke for the landscapers.

This isn't the original palace. That one was built of flimsy materials to last as long as the exposition, but when it started to fall apart in 1960, it was reconstructed in concrete.

When you come, be sure to bring your camera. There is a photo angle from just about everywhere, which explains why you will see so many bridal parties and modeling sessions on the grounds. John Galt thinks it's the most romantic spot in San Francisco, but you be the judge of that.

Marina Boulevard at Lyon Streets. Free tours are offered from 11 a.m. to 5:00 Tuesday through Sunday. There is a large free parking lot on the premises. 563–7337.

CLIFF HOUSE

Don't be put off by the tour buses that are always parked in front of the Cliff House. This is still a spot to visit if you thrill to the sight of waves rolling down an endless beach and seal lions barking on nearby rocks. What's more, there is rich history in this area, plus some amusing attractions.

First of all, the house itself: this is the third incarnation of the Cliff House, and its least spectacular. Built in 1909, it has withstood storms and quakes because it is such a fortress. After being remodeled several times over the years, the building became part of the National Park Service in 1977. The service maintains a visitor center on the lower oceanfront level, which is a good place to stop in for information. The Cliff House we all wish we could have seen was built by the financier and former mayor Adolph Sutro, who also built the elaborate Sutro Baths, the ruins of which you can see across the way. It was an eight-story French-style chateau with an observation tower that survived the 1906 earthquake but burned down in a raging fire the next year.

Visitor Center

If you walk down the steps on the outside of the Cliff House, you'll come to an arcade of sorts with vista points looking out at the seal rocks and other sites. Directly under the Cliff House are two places that will be open: the visitor center and the Musée Méchanique. At the visitor center, you can get more of the history of the Cliff House from books, pamphlets, and answers from the ranger on duty. Take a look at the rare photos of the Sutro Baths in their splendor. Then step back outside and look at the ruins; or better yet, walk across to them. The area is now maintained by the Golden Gate National Recreation Area, and tours are available by rangers or from the city guide service of the public library.

Across the aisle from the visitor center is one of the city's delightfully quirky attractions, the Musée Méchanique.

Musée Mechanique

The French title is a bit grand for this very low-key collection of wonderful coin-operated games and attractions, collected and shown by the Zelinsky family of local paint-contracting fame. I had always described this place as a pre–high tech video arcade, but during my last visit, what should I find in the back but the unmistakable sound and sight of several electronic video games. Still, they are way in the background. The main attraction here is still the kind of arcade games that our grandparents might have played. There are the player piano machines, the fortune tellers, the love tester, and the test-your-strength machines.

Of historic note is Laughing Sal, the rather grotesque statue of a laughing woman that used to be a symbol of Playland-at-the-Beach, the ten-acre amusement park that was to the south of the Cliff House. Don't miss the toothpick fantasy: a glass-encased amusement park complete with roller coaster, built out of toothpicks by San Quentin inmates. Also check out The Wizard, which looks like the same machine that turned Tom Hanks into a premature grown-up in the movie *Big*.

I am ashamed to admit that I couldn't resist putting a quarter into one 3-D device that was probably at least eighty years old to see "what a belly dancer does on her day off." You gaze through the stereopticon and see a series of changing photo cards. I won't spoil it for you in case you want to try it, but I will give you a hint: she takes a bath.

Lower level of Cliff House, 1090 Point Lobos Avenue. Open weekdays from 11 A.M. to 7 P.M.; weekends 10 A.M. to 8 P.M. Admission is free, but brings lots of quarters to play the machines. 386–1170.

Camera Obscura and Holographic Gallery

Directly across the walkway from the Musée Méchanique is a small little building that is usually boarded up to keep out light. Knock on the door to see if it is open, and if so pay your dollar to glimpse the Camera Obscura, one of the city's quirkier attractions. Inside is a parabolic disc which projects a fascinating 360-degree image of the ocean. Your guide will also explain how the idea dates back to a brainstorm by Leonardo Da Vinci.

1096 Point Lobos Avenue. Open when it's open. Admission $1.00. 750–0415.

Parking

A good place to park for your visit to the Cliff House and Sutro Baths is up the hill off Point Lobos. Turn into the lot on Merrie, and you can park as long as you want. This lot overlooks the ruins of the baths. From here you can walk down the hill to the Cliff House.

FORT MASON

"Asphalt National Park" is the nickname for Fort Mason according to Mark Kasky, who has been director since the obsolete military base became an arts center in the late 1970s. It is a national park, part of the Golden Gate National Recreation Area, and it is devoid of green, save for the famous Zen vegetarian restaurant Greens.

In the former fort some fifty nonprofit organizations fill several hangars and office buildings, set at the edge of San Francisco Bay. There are eight museums and galleries, four theaters, environmental groups, restaurants, and frequent attractions in some of the hangars, such as the annual garden show and the San Francisco City Fair.

Fort Mason used to be the principal embarkation point for troops to the Pacific. During World War II, more than 1.5 million servicemen shipped out from here. When air transport made the fort obsolete, the National Park Service took over. Now there is always something of interest going on. You can pick up maps and schedules of events at headquarters in building A.

The choices are truly varied, from browsing through the Museum of Modern Art's rental gallery, where you can actually rent paintings and sculpture to see if you and the work are compatible (or to impress the boss when you invite her to dinner); or bring a pole or crab net and fish right off the pier.

According to Kasky, architects say the fort, with its giant hangars, looks like it's still standing at attention; his job is to put it, and you, at ease.

The entrance to Fort Mason is off Marina Boulevard and Buchanan.

MUSEUM OF THE CITY OF SAN FRANCISCO

The Cannery, a three-floor shopping complex that was developed after the success of its better-known neighbor, Ghiradelli Square, has a congenial courtyard where you are likely to see a juggler or hear a folk singer. The surprise here is that it's also the home of the only museum about the city of San Francisco, in space donated by the Cannery's operator, Chris Martin.

The small museum, which has already expanded twice since it opened a few years ago, has several assets, probably the most important being Gladys Hansen, who was the historian at the city's public library for many years and now is the curator of the museum. No one knows more about San Francisco than Gladys; in fact, the new computer at the San Francisco Library is named for her.

Among the highlights at the museum are the permanent earthquake exhibits, which pay special attention to the devastating quake and fire of 1906. Also notable is the window with I. Magnin dolls from a 1970s Christmas display; the room full of thirty or more rare old projectors, highlighting the early movie days of the city the three-and-a-half-foot head of the Goddess of Liberty, which sat atop City Hall before the 1906 earthquake and is one of the few surviving parts of the building; the Sutro Bath display; and the photos showing the development of the Cannery.

The Cannery at North Point and Leavenworth. Open Wednesday through Saturday 10 A.M. to 4 P.M. Free, but donations encouraged. 928–0289.

MUSEUM OF OPHTHALMOLOGY

OK, it's not an actual museum, but if you have a half hour to spare and are at all interested in the history of eyeglasses, this is a good place to know about.

In the offices of the Foundation of the American Academy of Ophthalmology, just across the street from the Cannery, there is a lobby filled with display cases that contain spectacles and other seeing devices through history. The collection is quite remarkable if you have any fascination for such items as the kind of pince-nez eyewear favored by Calvin Coolidge or the lorgnettes of prerevolutionary France.

Did you know, by the way, that bifocals were invented by Benjamin Franklin in 1784? Or that the first glasses in the Western world were believed to have been invented by a monk in Pisa, Italy? (My guess is that he felt something was wrong with his eyes when he looked at the town tower and it appeared to be leaning.) These and other useful facts are available in a free brochure chronicling the history of spectacles, which you'll find at the front desk.

655 Beach Street, Suite 300. Open Monday through Friday, 8:30 A.M. to 5 P.M. Free. 561–8500.

The American Carousel Museum

This place is going to take a little advance work for a visit. Several years ago the American Carousel Museum was open to the public on a regular basis, but more recently it has switched to an appointment-only policy. Tours can be arranged, and the space is available for private parties.

Inside, in a beautiful and spacious gallery, exquisitely restored carousel animals are displayed like the works of art they are, with pedestals and dramatic lighting. Each figure is identified by its maker and where it formerly carried riders. All of the pieces are the collection of the Freels Foundation, which operates the museum. If you just happen to be in the neighborhood of the Cannery or the Museum of Ophthalmology next door, take a peek. You may be lucky enough to find someone there to let you in.

633 Beach Street. Phone for information on tour appointments. 928–0550.

As for parking while visiting the City, Ophthalmology, or Carousel museums, look for metered street parking on Columbus Avenue or nearby streets. There is a garage in the Cannery, but it's expensive.

CARTOON ART MUSEUM

This place reminds me of an old story that's told about the comedian Bert Lahr, who was known to be extremely intense and serious about his work. Getting ready to open in a play, he developed a piece of stage business and wanted his colleagues to see if it worked. As he performed, they howled with laughter, but he stopped them angrily and said, "Can't you be serious, I'm trying to see if this is funny."

In a large and attractive second-floor exhibition hall, the Cartoon Art Museum treats the comics with great respect. Its mission is "to encourage the appreciation of this original art form for its artistic, cultural, and historic merits." This is not to imply that a visit here is a sobering experience, just that the work is taken seriously by the staff. Recent shows have included a retrospective of the works of *Mad* magazine founder Harvey Kurtzman and a salute to Charles Schultz, the creator of "Peanuts."

For you, the experience might be nostalgia in finding the newspaper cartoons your dad read to you on Sunday morning or seeing the comic books you once collected or learning about cartoon art that dates back as far as the 1700s. The collection at the museum includes more than ten thousand pieces of art. Theme shows are presented every four months.

In addition to the main gallery space, there's a separate children's gallery and a CD-ROM gallery.

814 Mission Street. (the best parking is in the municipal garage at 5th and Mission Street). Open Wednesday through Friday 11 A.M. to 5 P.M.; Saturday 10 A.M. to 5 P.M.; Sunday 1 P.M. to 5 P.M. Adults $3.50; children $1.50; students and seniors $2.50; free admission the first Wednesday of each month. 227–8666.

FEDERAL RESERVE BANK

Unless you're a fan of Alan Greenspan's, what could sound less exciting than a visit to the Fed? Well, surprise, the San Francisco fortress of the Federal Reserve Bank knows how to put on a show, and it's free. First of all, the building itself is impressive, with its massive columns and its enormous lobby. In the lobby there is a block-long presentation, "The World of

Economics," which consists of a series of exhibits and interactive games designed to help you understand money and the economy. You can invest some serious time and get a quick cram course on finance; or you can play computer games like the one that lets you run your own muffin shop, trying to keep income ahead of expenses. One game lets you play president of the United States and figure out how to balance inflation, unemployment, and the rate of economic growth. Supposedly one former Federal Reserve chairman tried the game on a visit to San Francisco and failed miserably.

There's a 50–50 chance you will have a better understanding of the economy after a visit here. There is an even better chance you will see why economists never seem to agree on anything.

There are two other attractions at the Fed. In the lower level the enormous thick vaults are filled with who knows how much money. You can take a guided tour about the process of making and storing currency. Tours were suspended during some remodeling and presumably will be open again by 1997.

The other attraction will take some pull. If you know somebody who works in the building, ask him or her to take you on an art tour. The walls of the upper floors are filled with incredible paintings and sculptures.

101 Market Street. Open Monday through Friday 9 A.M. to 4:30 P.M. Free.
974–3252.

CIRCLE GALLERY

America's greatest architect, Frank Lloyd Wright, is represented by only one building in San Francisco. Fortunately, it is a gem and is open to the public. It's the Circle Gallery on Maiden Lane, a half block east of Union Square.

In a fairly small space Wright designed what turned out to be the forerunner of his Guggenheim Museum in New York. Built in 1948 as the V. C. Morris gift shop, the building is distinguished by its sand-colored brick wall and its circular, cavelike entrance. The building was changed considerably when it was the Helga Howie boutique, but then the Circle Gallery bought it and restored it based on the original plans, which were still in the basement.

Whether or not the art on display strikes your fancy, it's worth a few minutes of your time to walk up the circular ramp and to take in the views and the sounds from various vantage points. There's no other building like it in town.

This is a place to visit when you happen to be shopping in Union Square. Park in the Union Square Garage or the garage across from Macy's on O'Farrell between Powell and Stockton.

140 Maiden Lane. Monday through Saturday 10 A.M. to 6 P.M.; Sunday noon to 5 P.M. 989–2100.

CHAPTER *16*   Kid Stuff

San Francisco is a kid-friendly city where hills can be as exciting as rides in an amusement park and things like outside hotel elevators in fancy hotels and cable car rides are treats for kids of all ages. Many of the neighborhoods that are attractive to adults, such as North Beach and Chinatown, are just as attractive for kids. In addition, there are several places that are extra special for children. Several of them are previously noted in earlier chapters.

ACADEMY OF SCIENCES

A trip to Golden Gate Park becomes a memorable experience for any kid if you visit the Academy of Sciences with its Museum of Natural History, Planetarium, and Aquarium. See page 147.

Open daily 10 A.M. to 5 P.M.; Memorial Day to Labor Day 9 A.M. to 6 P.M.; adults $7.00, ages 12 to 17 $4.00, ages 6 to 11 $1.50, children 5 and under free; free for all the first Wednesday of each month; separate admission for Planetarium and Laserium shows. 750–7145.

GOLDEN GATE PARK CHILDREN'S PLAYGROUND

This is a wonderful, large playground with swings, slides, sandboxes, and climbing structures to challenge a variety of age groups, plus plenty of room to run up and roll down small hills. There's also a beautifully restored carousel. Bring a picnic and stay awhile. There are also important necessities like water fountains, rest rooms, and snack bars. There is a parking lot off Bowling Green Drive. With luck and patience, you should be able to get a spot.

BASIC BROWN BEAR FACTORY

Free tours are offered at this unique factory where kids can help make their own teddy bear. See page 85.

444 De Haro Street. Open daily 10 A.M. to 5 P.M.; Sunday noon to 5 P.M. Drop-in tours daily at 1 P.M., plus Saturday at 11 A.M.; for tours of eight or more, call to reserve a time. Parking is easy around this section of Potrero Hill. (800) 554–1910.

EXPLORATORIUM

Good news for parents! You will have as much fun and be as challenged and excited as your kids at this museum of learning. Located in a cavernous space inside the Palace of Fine Arts, the Exploratorium is a fun house of science and discovery. There are more than six hundred exhibits on such subjects as light, sound, electricity, and animal and plant life, plus changing exhibits on subjects such as understanding AIDS.

One of the most popular attractions is the Tactile Dome, in which you feel your way through the darkness and discover new touch awareness and sensations. A separate admission charge is needed, as are reservations.

For the toddlers there's a special area with art supplies, building blocks, books, and other activities. There is also a helper or two on hand to encourage your youngster, but parents are encouraged to stay with their child.

The Exploratorium can be expensive for an average family of three or four, but plan to spend the day there. There is much to do, and there is a decent café on the premises. Also, you won't have to pay for parking. There is plenty of space in the Palace of Fine Arts lot.

3601 Lyon Street, between Bay and Marina Boulevard. Open Tuesday through Sunday 10 A.M. to 5 P.M.; Wednesday until 9:30 P.M.; closed Mondays except for holidays; holiday schedules may vary; free the first Wednesday of each month. Children under 3 free; 3 to 5 $2.50; 6 to 17 $5.00; adults $9.00. 561–0360 (for Tactile Dome reservations, call 561–0362).

The Jungle

Sometimes a kid needs to just go wild and burn off some energy. There is no better place than the Jungle, especially if the weather forces you indoors. Perched on the second floor of a block-long discount shopping complex (with neighbors like Trader Joe's and Toys R Us), the Jungle is a series of giant play structures that allow kids from toddlers to preteens to climb, jump, crawl, roll, bounce, throw, hang, and fall to their hearts' content, all under the watchful eye of staff attendants. There's a separate sections for tots up to three years old.

The grownups who take youngsters there can watch from some comfortable tables or hide away in the glass-enclosed quiet room, shielded from the nonstop cacophony of songs from kids movies and TV shows.

One admission fee pays for the kids, with adults admitted for free. There are other ways to spend money, of course, with an ample snack bar and loads of high- and semihigh-tech games that allow kids to collect tickets to exchange for prizes.

It's all very well thought out, with large clean rest rooms, easy parking, and a genial atmosphere.

555 Ninth Street. Open Monday through Thursday 10 A.M. to 8 P.M.; Fridays until 9 P.M.; Saturdays and Sundays 9 A.M. to 9 P.M. Children's admission: Monday through Friday before 5 P.M. $4.95; after 5 P.M. $2.95; weekends $5.95. 552–4386.

Mountain Lake Park

If you're just looking for a nice park where junior can play for a while, one of the nicest urban parks you'll find anywhere is off Lake Street, near Park Presidio. If you walk north on Twelfth Avenue, the street reaches a dead end a half block beyond Lake; you then enter the park.

At first it looks as though this is simply a nice playground with two levels of swings and climbing structures for kids. But then you see a lake filled with ducks and geese. To the right are three tennis courts, a soccer field, lots of green lawn, trails, and a vast stretch of open space. The park runs up to Seventh Avenue, but trails lead into the Presidio and on to the ocean and bay. There are many benches scattered throughout and much room to play, run, or seek quiet and solitude.

One father who was playing with his son told me the park is the jewel of the neighborhood, his daily salvation. The park's entrance is on 12th Avenue at Lake Street.

MUSÉE MECHANIQUE

A free museum that houses a wonderful collection of antique arcade games that will fascinate kids and adults. See page 182.

Lower level of Cliff House, 1090 Point Lobos Avenue. Open weekdays from 11 A.M. to 7 P.M.; weekends 10 A.M. to 8 P.M. Admission free, but bring lots of quarters to play the machines. 386–1170.

SAN FRANCISCO ZOO

The city's zoo has been steadily upgrading its formerly sagging facility and is now attractive, kid-friendly, and easy to visit. Having researched the zoo by going along with a group of sixty kids from my daughter's school, I can vouch for its appeal and its comfort. Spread out over several well-landscaped acres of mostly flat land, the zoo offers adequate rest room access, a pleasant picnic area with a decent snack bar/café, and lots of benches along the pathways for those who need a rest. There are also strollers, wagons, and wheelchairs available just inside the main entrance.

For the past few years the zoo has been undergoing a major transformation, gearing up to greet the millennium with a totally updated facility. Improvements include more creative and open habitats for the animals who, in most cases, are no longer caged in. Instead of living in drab confinement, they now are given environments similar to those of their homelands. Streams and deep ravines are among the devices used to separate the animals from visitors. When possible, animals are clustered together as they would live in their native habitat, such as the Australian Walkabout with its emus, koalas, and kangaroos.

The usual assortment of nature's progeny is on display. If you're lucky, the monkeys will put on a gymnastics show, the Siberian tiger will stretch and stare right through you, and the penguins will strut in their formal attire. Note that the penguins are fed daily at 3 P.M., and it's quite a show.

Don't expect the animals to perform for you. During our visit the lions slept, and one baboon actually hid under a garbage can. Then again, what would you do if sixty screaming five- and six-year-olds were staring at you? One gorilla came up to the crowd and started to jump up and down. As the delighted crowd cheered, the gorilla danced more frantically, beat his chest, and then threw something at the group. It was then that we read the placard which said that gorillas are very sensitive and should not be teased or yelled at. Moral: read all the placards which describe the animals and their characteristics.

For young kids there's a children's zoo within the zoo, where the youngsters can pet and feed more domesticated animals.

Be advised that the zoo is at the ocean's edge and will probably be foggy and cool in the summer.

Sloat Boulevard at Forty-sixth Avenue. Open daily from 10: A.M. to 5 P.M.; children's zoo open from 11 A.M. to 4 P.M. Admission: adults $7.00; ages 12 to 16 and over 65 $3.50; ages 3 to 12 $1.50; under 3 free; admission is free for all the first Wednesday of each month. 753–7061.

(There is public transportation to the area. An information directory is available on their phone line. Parking is free and plentiful along Sloat Boulevard.)

JOSEPH RANDALL JUNIOR MUSEUM

This is a very low-key museum for kids tucked away on a hillside behind Buena Vista Park. Most kids are immediately attracted to the animal room, where they can pet and interact with a variety of small critters. On the downstairs level there are many arts, crafts, and science classes held. Preregistration is necessary, except for Saturday at 12:30 P.M., when drop-ins are accommodated on a first come, first served basis.

199 Museum Way. Open Tuesday through Saturday 10 A.M. to 5 P.M.; the animal room is closed each day between 1 P.M. and 2 P.M. Free. (Museum Way is a bit tricky to find: take Fourteenth Street from Market up the hill to Roosevelt, and follow Roosevelt to Museum Way). 554–9600.

WELLS FARGO MUSEUM

The history of the gold rush is on display, plus kids can ride in a historic stagecoach. See page 69.

420 Montgomery Street. Open Monday through Friday 9 A.M. to 5 P.M. , except for bank holidays. Free. 396–2619.

PART 5

Lodging and Special Occasions

CHAPTER 17

Romantic Getaways

Let's face it. Most talk about romance eventually leads to the bedroom, which leads us to the search for a romantic place to stay in San Francisco. Picking a spot for someone else's romantic adventure is always a tricky proposition. So much depends on personal taste. Some people find action and glitter romantic, whereas others prefer quiet and seclusion. When I am asked to suggest ideas for a romantic getaway, I usually have one basic suggestion: try to go with someone else.

There is certainly no shortage of hotels, which operate at nearly a 75 percent occupancy rate during good years. Much of the space is taken by business travelers and conventioneers, which is good news for Bay Area residents who want a weekend in the city because many hotels and inns are not heavily booked then and offer special rates. But you have to ask for them. Just keep in mind that a hotel would rather fill empty space for a discount than have a room go vacant. If price is a consideration, ask for weekend specials, senior discounts, AAA membership rates, whatever; just ask until you find something.

The following recommendations are places Catherine and I would choose for a romantic getaway in the city.

Large Hotels

HOTEL MONACO

201 Rooms. This is the splashiest new hotel in San Francisco. Located in the theater district, this is an ideal place to stay when you are planning to see a

play and do some shopping in nearby Union Square. The Monaco made boutique hotelier Bill Kimpton the owner of the most hotel rooms in the city. The hotel features a stunning entrance, several comfortable seating areas, and a lavish dining room. Like most Kimco hotels, this one offers tastefully decorated, smallish rooms and moderate rates.

501 Geary Boulevard. 292–0100.

MANDARIN ORIENTAL

158 rooms. Hotel rooms occupy the top eleven floors of an office complex in the financial district. The location is quiet on weekend nights. Most rooms offer great views of the city and the bay, luxurious furnishings, and spacious marble bathrooms. The ground floor lobby is sedate and quiet. Expensive.

222 Sansome Street. 885–0999.

SHERATON PALACE

550 rooms. The public rooms such as the Garden Court are the most sumptuous, although the bedrooms in the remodeled hotel are more than adequate. This is a busy hotel, within walking distance of shops and theaters. Moderate to expensive.

2 Montgomery Street. 392–8600.

RADISSON MIYAKO

218 rooms. Featuring many rooms with Japanese baths, the Miyako, in Japantown, offers a quieter alternative to the downtown hotels yet is convenient to shopping on Fillmore Street and is near the Civic Center theaters. Moderate.

1625 Post. 922–3200.

TRITON

140 rooms. This is Kimpton's hotel for the extremely hip. Here the clerks and bellmen all wear black slipover shirts and slacks, no jackets. The lobby is all pastels and geometric angles, and the bedrooms are done with stylish humor, the result of turning loose several designers and artists to do their own thing. It is located at the entrance to Chinatown yet on the fringe of Union Square. As a special nineties feature, there are twenty-four eco-rooms, with all-natural cotton linens, biodegradable soaps, special water-filtration systems, and even energy-efficient lighting. Inexpensive to moderate.

342 Grant Avenue. 394–0500.

HARBOR COURT

130 rooms. The hotel that benefited most from the removal of the Embarcadero Freeway, the Harbor Court offers many rooms with unobstructed views of the bay. It also offers use of the Y's ample athletic facilities. Rooms are small but comfortable and tastefully decorated with beds on platforms to take advantage of the views. The windows are soundproofed to mask out the noise of construction on the Embarcadero. In addition to a warm, welcoming lobby, the hotel also features the lively restaurant and night spot, Harry Denton's. Moderate.

165 Stewart Street. 882–1300.

MAJESTIC

59 rooms. This is a very tasteful small hotel away from the clutter of downtown. Limousine service is available to the downtown area. The Majestic is the kind of intimate hotel you might find in England: overstuffed chairs,

soothing quiet, and understated refinement. There's also a fine restaurant on the premises. Moderate to expensive.

1500 Sutter Street. 441–1100.

QUEEN ANNE

49 rooms. A girl's school converted into an inn, the lobby has an austere quality, but the rooms are spacious and lovely and extremely quiet. Moderate to expensive.

1590 Sutter Street. 441–2828.

SHERMAN HOUSE

14 rooms. This converted mansion in Cow Hollow is San Francisco's most luxurious hotel. If you are splurging and want to stay where the folks in the next room may just be Hollywood stars, this is the place. Many of the rooms and all the suites have stunning bay views and balconies. There's a first-class dining room, too. Expensive.

2160 Green Street. 563–3600.

Bed and Breakfast Inns

THE ARCHBISHOP'S MANSION

15 rooms and suites. In 1904 the home of the archbishop of San Francisco on picturesque Alamo Square, this is now a Victorian jewel of an inn. Inside the rather austere gray fortress of a building, it feels as though you're entering a museum filled with antiques, crystal chandeliers, a grand staircase, and a stained-glass skylight.

Rooms and suites are named for operas, and each is individually decorated in full Victoriana. In addition to continental breakfast, afternoon wine is served in the parlor while music is performed on a piano once owned by Noel Coward.

There is a two-night minimum on weekends. This would be a great spot for a midweek getaway, as it is not typically a business hotel. Moderate to expensive.

1000 Fulton Street. 563–7872.

WASHINGTON SQUARE INN

15 rooms. A charming bed and breakfast inn at the northeast corner of North Beach's "town" park. A perfect location for those who love walking around the city, day and night. Continental breakfast and afternoon wine are served. Also, evening tea. Inexpensive to moderate.

1660 Stockton Street. 981–4220.

JACKSON COURT INN

10 rooms. If you plan ahead, you can stay in the heart of Pacific Heights. This is both an inn and a time-share, so reservations must be made at least two months in advance. The incentive is the opportunity to stay in a converted mansion in one of San Francisco's most exclusive neighborhoods. The rooms are spacious and tastefully decorated, with a mix of antiques and contemporary furnishing. Staying here feels more like a visit to a home than an inn. Continental breakfast included. Moderate.

2198 Jackson Street. 929–7670.

Motels

PHOENIX INN

44 rooms. Here's where the low-budget rock bands stay, the ones who can't afford the Triton. Two floors of well-decorated and affordable motel rooms

overlook a courtyard filled with a decorative swimming pool, several modern sculptures, and diners from the adjoining Miss Pearl's Jam House. Inexpensive.

601 Eddy Street. 776–1380.

SEAL ROCK INN

Really just a plain motel, but what a location. This is for those who want to hear the roar of the ocean when they go to bed. Inexpensive.

545 Point Lobos Avenue. 752–8000.

CHAPTER 18

Rendezvous Spots

When you are meeting a friend or mate in the city, it's important to find a spot where you can be comfortable and warm in case one party is late, which is usually a pretty good bet. Instead of picking an outdoor spot or a well-located store, why not rendezvous at one of the city's many hotel lobbies? Hotel lobbies are a great resource that locals rarely take advantage of. For many visitors the lobby of one of San Francisco's fine hotels will be their first impression of the city. For the rest of us, it's a place where we can lounge in style, use well-maintained rest rooms or the telephone, and watch the passing parade of international visitors. And if he or she happens to be late, so what?

FAIRMONT HOTEL

The setting for the TV series *Hotel*, the Fairmont is the city's busiest hotel and an ideal place to meet if you are in the Nob Hill area. See page 54.

HOTEL MONACO

In the former run-down Bellevue Hotel on Geary, the city's largest hotel operator, Bill Kimpton, has created his biggest venture yet. Unlike the Kimpton boutique hotels such as the Triton and the Harbor Court, the Monaco is competing with the big boys, such as its neighbor across the street, the Clift. The Monaco has more than two hundred rooms, a large and ornate restaurant, the Grand Café, and several public areas.

The result is a beautifully and elegantly designed new hotel mixing style and humor to provide a congenial spot for waiting for your spouse, date, or friend. The location makes it a perfect meeting place for a rendezvous before the theater. The designer, Cheryl Rowley of Los Angeles, said she wanted to create the feeling of an ocean journey, and her end result is certainly a trip, down to the reception desk, which is patterned after a 1920s steamer trunk.

After you take in the spectacle of the grand marble staircase, the two-story fireplace, and the painted clouds, balloons, and airplanes that greet you on entrance, make your way to one of the four seating areas that provide cushy club chairs, burning fireplaces, and reading materials. Everything is done in earth tones and pastels with surprising mixes of colors and designs. Rest rooms are open to the public and are easily accessible. People-watching is not as active as a busy hotel such as the Fairmont, but you can watch and listen unobtrusively.

501 Geary Street. 392–0100.

HYATT REGENCY

If you are a Mel Brooks fan, you will instantly recognize the lobby of the Hyatt Regency. This was the setting for much of the film *High Anxiety*, the comedian's lampoon of Hitchcock. The lobby's floor-to-ceiling atrium and vertigo-inducing open elevators that look down on the open space were perfect for the story of a shrink who was afraid of heights. You can ride up to the top and back and also get out and see how almost every hotel room door opens up to the atrium, making the simple act of checking in or out or going down to breakfast something of an adventure for those of us who don't like looking down.

The lobby is spacious, with many seating areas and a fountain that never fails to delight kids. It features the smoothest, most imperceptible flow of water imaginable so you don't really believe it's a fountain until you touch the water.

This is a very busy place where you can find your own space and get lost in the crowd without feeling conspicuous. Rest rooms and telephones are easily accessible. If you are cooling your heels while your partner shops in the Embarcadero stores, you can rest in comfort here.

5 Embarcadero Center. 788–1234.

SHERATON PALACE

The oldest hotel in the city and in many ways the grandest is the place locals still call the Palace. Originally the brainchild of the financier William Ralston, the Palace was designed to be the most spectacular hotel in the world. After a few earthquakes and years of benign neglect, in the early 1990s Sheraton spent many millions to restore the hotel to its original splendor.

There is not much of a central lobby area to the Palace. The best seating is alongside a long corridor that runs the length of the hotel and is near easily accessible public rest rooms. Off this hallway are two of the major attractions of the Palace: the Garden Court and the bar called Maxfield's. The latter is worth peeking in to see Maxfield Parrish's huge mural *The Pied Piper of Hamelin.*

The Garden Court is one of the great rooms in the city. Originally built as a large open space to accommodate the vehicles of the carriage trade, the Garden Court is a large, open dining room filled with plants and brightened by a domed glass skylight. The effect is like eating in an elegant greenhouse. The food never quite matches up to the visual splendor, but if you have never seen this room, you should schedule at least a peak.

There are many historical photos along the corridor of the Sheraton Palace. If you want a bit of privacy, there is a small sitting area at the south end. Just turn right at the end of the hall, toward the Grand Ballroom. There are also many surprising nooks and crannies, best seen by joining one of the City Guides free tours of the hotel. Ask to see the private mezzanine room with windows that open above the Garden Court and the Presidential Suite. They can be shown if vacant. For a schedule and information, call 558–3981.

The Sheraton Palace is a convenient hotel meeting spot for the financial district and the downtown shopping area. It's also located at the Montgomery BART station. For the best visual effect, enter on New Montgomery.

633 Market Street at New Montgomery. 392–8600.

WESTIN ST. FRANCIS

Its prime Union Square location makes the St. Francis (as locals will always call it) ideal for meetings around shopping or theater dates. The hotel lobby is as busy as that of the Fairmont but with a smaller seating area, which is unfortunately a bit smoky. The best place to meet your friend or mate is, in the local tradition, "under the clock." In the far right corner of the large open lobby at the main entrance to the hotel, you will find an impressive grandfather clock that has been a hotel institution since 1907. This Viennese Magenta clock was installed exactly one year after the great earthquake and fire as a symbol of the hotel's recovery and has remained in its place ever since. With its elaborate wood carving, it's a work of art and a mechanical marvel that reveals its inner workings of chains and pulleys.

Although there are only a few benches in the grand entry lobby, it is good place for hanging out and watching the passing scene. The rooms is enormous, with marble columns topped with gold leaf, an ornate ceiling, and, at this writing, a hole where until recently a sizable crystal chandelier hung. Without warning, in December of 1995, it crashed to the ground à la *Phantom of the Opera*. Fortunately, no one was nearby at the time. Presumably, there is a new chandelier in its place by now.

While lobby seating is not a plus here, there are two large public rest room areas off the lobby, one featuring a shoeshine parlor. We should also add that a $50-million, five-year renovation project is under way, so many areas will be upgraded.

Like the Fairmont, the St. Francis has outside elevators as part of a newer addition. These offer only a view to the east, showing the financial district and the Bay Bridge, but not the Golden Gate. It's still a nice or scary ride, depending on how you feel about heights.

There are several free tours offered at the hotel, including an hour-long historical tour, a behind-the-scenes tour, and a suite tour, which includes the MacArthur suite and the infamous location of the Fatty Arbuckle scandal. These tours are offered at irregular times. For information call the public relations office at 774–0118. A self-guided walking tour is also available. Pick up a map at the concierge desk.

Powell Street from Geary to Stockton at Union Square. 397–7000.

HOLIDAY INN—CHINATOWN

This skyscraper hotel actually borders Chinatown and the financial district. It's a convenient spot to meet when you are planning a foray into either area or to North Beach, which is only a few blocks away. Inside, there is a quiet, dark lobby with comfortable chairs and couches and many well-placed tables for those who want to write on a portable computer or on old-fashioned pencil and paper.

Rest rooms and telephones are readily available, and the Portsmouth Square municipal parking garage is across the street, all factors that make this a good meeting place.

Corner Kearney and Sacramento. 433–6600.

CHAPTER 19

Art Where You Might Not Expect It

There are countless art galleries and museums showing changing collections. Check current listings to find shows that appeal to you. There are also places where art displays are incidental to other business but offer a visual treat where you might least expect it.

ESPRIT COLLECTION

In the Esprit Corporate headquarters, art adorns the walls in the form of a wonderful collection of antique American quilts. At any given time forty or fifty quilts out of the collection of hundreds are on display throughout the work spaces. Pick up a self-guided description at the front desk, and then wander through the open and congenial work environment to see the quilts. One quilt might be outside a design studio where artists are busy creating new fashions, another could be inside a conference room. The office space alone is worth a visit to see a successful modern working arrangement that is a far cry from the old-style individual cubicle look. The quilts are clearly works of art and are shown with care.

900 Minnesota Street, east of Potrero Hill toward the bay. Open Monday through Friday 9 A.M. to 5 P.M.; by appointment for groups of six or fewer; large groups may schedule a tour by curator Julie Silber for a fee. 648–6900.

LEFTY O'DOUL'S

Even though I have lived here for more than twenty years, I never stepped inside this Union Square area establishment until I began researching this book. I always assumed it was just another tourist joint. Well, better late than never.

The attraction for me isn't the food, although it's solid cafeteria fare with roast beef, turkey, spaghetti and meatballs, fresh salads, and the like. This is a surprising photographic gallery of sports history. The walls are covered with rare and stunning pictures that will evoke a response in anyone who has ever watched a baseball game. How about young Willie Mays standing in front of Seals Stadium in 1958 for the first game between the San Francisco Giants and the Los Angeles Dodgers? Or the two most famous Joes of their time, Louis and DiMaggio, grinning at each other in their best suits and ties? There are many photos of Lefty himself, who was one of the few players ever to be on all three New York teams of his era: the Yankees, Giants, and Dodgers; his lifetime batting average was an unbelievable .349. Lefty died in 1969.

The restaurant itself is imposing. There's a bar in front, then a long-beamed rathskeller-type room, which opens up to another dining area. The clientele ranges from workmen to tourists to a charming gent in his eighties who was dressed to the teeth in a three-piece blue suit with a straw boater and a pince-nez. Although he could probably afford to eat anywhere in town, this is his regular spot. "I think I'll forego the spaghetti and meatballs today and try the spare rib special," he told the counterman properly.

333 Geary near Powell, one door in from Union Square. Open daily 7 A.M. to 2 A.M. Inexpensive. No credit cards. 982–8900.

JOSEPH SCHMIDT CONFECTIONERS

Joseph Schmidt is a chocolate artist. His truffles and other candies are carried by fine stores around the city, but his showroom/shop between the Mission and the Castro district is where to see his art in full flower. Here you will see chocolate as sculpture in many forms. Schmidt makes tulips, bowls, vases, and whatever else sparks his very active imagination. Expect to find creations to match every season and holiday. Everything is edible, and everything is beautiful. Be sure to try at least one truffle.

3489 Sixteenth Street. Open Monday through Saturday 10 A.M. to 6:30 P.M. 861–8682.

Circle Gallery

Certainly you expect to find art in a gallery, but you don't expect to find great architecture on tiny Maiden Lane, a half block east of Union Square. The Circle Gallery is such a place. This is the only building in the city of San Francisco designed by Frank Lloyd Wright.

In a fairly small space Wright designed what turned out to be the forerunner of his Guggenheim Museum in New York. Built in 1948 as the V. C. Morris gift shop, the building is distinguished by its sand-colored brick wall and its circular, cavelike entrance. Whether or not you like the art on display, it's worth a few minutes of your time to walk up the circular ramp and to take in the views and the sounds from various vantage points. There's no other building like it in town.

140 Maiden Lane. Monday through Saturday 10 A.M. to 6 P.M.; Sunday noon to 5 P.M. 969–2100.

Corporate Lobbies

Art is displayed prominently in the lobbies and galleries of many of the city's corporate headquarters, most notably Bank of America and Transamerica. B of A is at California and Montgomery. Take the escalator up to the mezzanine floor, and enjoy the various exhibits. The changing art shows at the Transamerica Pyramid are on the ground floor, with entrances on Washington and Clay Streets, and Montgomery.

When You Just Need Some Peace and Quiet

CHAPTER *20*

San Francisco has one unusual feature that is often overlooked and underappreciated. It is a city that offers an escape from the noise and general urban energy that is often equated with big city life. If you find yourself stuck in a traffic jam or surrounded by construction, peace and quiet are usually minutes away.

The obvious refuges are places like Golden Gate Park, but even then you need to know where to go to find something resembling solitude. Here are a few places that always work for me.

SHAKESPEARE GARDEN/ GOLDEN GATE PARK

This park within a park is one of the quietest places in San Francisco, offering a perfect refuge for reading the Bard or the local newspaper. See page 149.

AIDS MEMORIAL GROVE/GOLDEN GATE PARK

A work in progress, this large grove is being transformed into a living memorial for those who died of AIDS. See page 149.

COLUMBARIUM

I have always been surprised by the appeal I find in cemeteries. Seeing how loved ones are remembered as they are returned to the earth can be a very touching experience and can teach a lot about a community.

At the Neptune Society's Columbarium, that fascination takes on a different dimension as the ashes of loved ones are stored in an unusual, four-story, domed building that is tucked away behind busy Geary Street, near the Coronet Theater. The building is a gem, a perfect circle with four stories of nooks and crannies filled with urns. You'll recognize many of the names memorialized as you wander through on your own. Whereas the size of tombstones is often an indication of the affluence of the departed, here it's the size of the urn and the elaborateness of the display case.

The building itself is worth seeing and the grounds, although small, are quiet and restful as a cemetery.

Columbarium, 1 Lorraine Court (off Anza between Stanyan and Arguello Streets). Open daily 10 A.M. to 1 P.M. Free. 221–1838.

GRACE CATHEDRAL

San Francisco's most impressive cathedral welcomes people of all faiths. See page 55.

Open 7 A.M. to 6 P.M. Guided tours are available Monday through Friday from 1 P.M. to 3 P.M.; Saturday from 11:30 A.M. to 12:30 P.M.; and Sunday from 12:45 P.M. to 2 P.M. A particularly moving experience is the singing of vespers every Thursday at 5:15 P.M. A schedule of services and special events is available at the door. Admission to the cathedral is free, although donations are gratefully accepted.

SWEDENBORGIAN CHURCH

If you are exploring the streets of Pacific and Presidio Heights, take a few minutes to acquaint yourself with one of San Francisco's most unusual churches, the Swedenborgian Church. This is a quiet and beautiful corner of the city that few know about, and the story of this esoteric Christian sect is fascinating.

Even though this 1895 building is barely noticeable from the street, the church is one of the more popular wedding spots in the city, and you'll see why as soon as you enter the wooded garden. There is even a specially designated private bride's room opposite the entrance to the chapel. Inside the small church the sensation is that of stepping onto the set of an Ingmar Bergman movie set in Berkeley. Giant timbers support the vaulted ceiling of the building, which is spare and dark. Individual craftsmen chairs are set in rows instead of traditional church pews. You can see the hand of one of the three architects, Bernard Maybeck.

At the entrance to the church, several pamphlets are displayed for sale, which you can buy on the honor system. For 50 cents you can learn all about the Swedenborgians, followers of Emmanuel Swedenborg, an eighteenth-century scientist and mystic. He has been called by some the smartest man who ever lived. Among his admirers were Ralph Waldo Emerson, Helen Keller, William Blake, Samuel Coleridge, William Yeats, Elizabeth Browning, Jorge Luis Borges, and Henry James. Perhaps today he would be most identified with the New Age movement. There are only a handful of Swedenborgian churches in the United States, also called the Church of the New Jerusalem.

2107 Lyon Street. Sunday services are held at 11 A.M., but the doors are open daily from 9 A.M. to 5 P.M., except when there is a private wedding. 346–6466.

WAVE ORGAN

This is one of the quirky attractions that help give San Francisco its special flavor. Listen to the sounds of the bay as you enjoy spectacular views. See page 141.

To get to the Wave Organ, enter the driveway to the San Francisco Yacht Club, which is just before you get to the Golden Gate Bridge entrance off Bay Street. Continue past the Yacht Club until you can drive no farther. Park your car and walk to the end of the spit to the Wave Organ.

PART 6

Food, Glorious Food

CHAPTER 21

Celebrity Restaurants

As travelers continue to rate San Francisco as their favorite American city, one of the top reasons mentioned is its great restaurants. This is an eating-out town, blessed with some of the best chefs and some of the best natural resources of any place in the world. The list of top-notch restaurants grows each year. For the record, some of the finest and most expensive are the following:

MASA'S

Where business travelers on expense accounts mingle with folks celebrating special occasions. Chef Julian Serrano runs the best French restaurant in town, and maybe the country. 684 Bush Street. 989–7154.

THE DINING ROOM OF THE RITZ CARLTON HOTEL

California/French cuisine in the best hotel restaurant in San Francisco. 600 Stockton Street. 296–7465.

ALAIN RONDELLI

Imaginative French cuisine served out on the Richmond District. A favorite of food critics. 126 Clement Street. 387–0408.

POSTRIO

Wolfgang Puck's splash of L.A., with an open kitchen and a dining room designed to be seen in. California cuisine with a touch of show biz. 545 Post Street. 776–7825.

Hawthorne Lane

The former chefs at Postrio, Annie and David Gingrass, took the plunge with their own place and had an immediate hit. 22 Hawthorne Street. 777–9779.

Rubicon

This is the first San Francisco venture for the New York restaurateur Drew Nierporent, along with investors like Robert De Niro and Frances Ford Coppola. 558 Sacramento Street. 434–4100.

Vertigo

An extremely attractive and popular restaurant in the Transamerica Pyramid. The kitchen specializes in artfully presented seafood. 600 Washington Street. 433–7250.

Cypress Club

Perhaps the most stunning decor of any restaurant in town. Fortunately, the California-style food keeps pace with the surroundings. 500 Jackson Street. 296–8555.

Stars

Jeremiah Tower's restaurant and bar turns up in the society columns almost daily. This is where the city's elite meets to eat, and the California/Continental menu appears to have something for every taste. 150 Redwood Alley. 861–7827.

La Folie

This restaurant, owned and run by the French chef Roland Passot and his family, combines the cooking techniques of France with the style and ingredients of California. Every plate of food is artfully decorated. 2316 Polk Street. 776–5577.

BOULEVARD

One of the most spectacular creations of the restaurant designer Pat Kuleto, Boulevard offers American food by Nancy Oakes, who first wowed them at Pat O'Shea's sports bar. Now the price has gone up, but the plates are still packed with interesting and plentiful combinations. 1 Mission Street. 543–6084.

CHAPTER 22

Backroads Favorites (in Alphabetical Order)

Although the well-publicized, crowded celebrity restaurants certainly earn their laurels, there are other, usually less expensive, options that we would like to recommend. Many of the restaurants listed also appear in other sections of the book.

ANANDA FUARA

If you happen to be catching a show at the Orpheum Theater, consider Ananda Fuara. You can park for free on the street before the theater rush and eat in the peaceful surroundings of a vegetarian restaurant whose name means "fountain of bliss." Despite the rather seedy atmosphere of Market Street, this place is indeed a quiet and comforting place to have well-prepared vegetarian dishes like the delicious neat loaf with mashed potatoes or one of their spicy curries. With all the healthful veggie food, they also bake sinfully rich desserts, including something for any chocoholic.

1298 market at 9th. 621–1994. Open Monday through Saturday for breakfast, lunch, and dinner. Inexpensive. Cash only.

ANGKOR BOREI

There was great excitement surrounding the opening of this Cambodian restaurant in the Mission several years ago. Friends in the area insisted that we have dinner there as soon as possible, and we're glad they did. To palates accustomed to Chinese cooking, this Asian cuisine is filled with new taste combinations and new discoveries. The mixtures of hot and cold, spicy and sweet, crunchy and chewy add up to a multitextured dining experience. In other words, whatever you get, it will be swell.

3471 Mission Street, near Cortland. 550–8417. Lunch and dinner daily. Inexpensive. Credit cards.

APERTO

The choices are easy at this small neighborhood trattoria with an open kitchen. They don't try to overwhelm you with menu selections. At lunch you could have pasta or panini (sandwiches such as roast chicken with red peppers and aioli on foccacia) or one of the daily specials. At dinner they bring on the arrosti (roast chicken, veal, and the like) as well as specials. The emphasis is on fresh ingredients, prepared without fuss.

1434 Eighteenth Street. Moderate. Lunch and dinner daily. Credit Cards. 252–1625.

APPAM

A very attractive Indian restaurant specializing in clay pot cooking. This is the only Indian place in town that serves "Yiddish" naan, which is a flat bread stuffed with beets. Go figure.

1261 Folsom. 626–2798. Lunch and dinner daily. Credit cards.

ASIMAKOPOULOUS

This café and deli has been a fixture on Potrero Hill for years. It's one of the few Greek restaurants in a city that seems to have scores of places in every ethnic dining category. Asimakopoulous is very informal, serving such specialties as chicken-lemon soup and moussaka as well as skewered lamb and chicken dishes.

288 Connecticut Street at Eighteenth. 552–8789. Lunch Monday through Friday; dinner nightly. Credit cards.

BACCO

Noe Valley's stylish northern Italian restaurant specializes in a variety of interesting pasta dishes that are a long way from the old spaghetti-and-meatball, tomato-sauce fare of the Italian places I grew up with. The emphasis is on fresh, tasty ingredients,

737 Diamond Street, at Twenty-fourth. Dinner nightly. Moderate. Credit cards. 282–4969.

BARNEY'S

Part of a group of hamburger joints that started in Oakland. Every variety of burger imaginable—and some you never thought of—is offered along with bountiful salads and side dishes. These are juicy, three-or-four napkin burgers. Also, try their curly spicy french fries, but be prepared for a huge portion. For those who don't want to eat beef, they have chicken and turkey burgers, too.

4138 Twenty-fourth Street, west of Castro. 282–7770. Lunch and dinner daily. No credit cards.

BELL TOWER

If size is a consideration, you might want to try the half-pound burger at this neighborhood bar and café in the Russian Hill section of town. The burger, cooked as you order it, is served with lettuce, tomato, onion, pickle, and a heaping serving of french fries. Sometimes the little things make you feel good about a place. For example, I asked the waitress to hold the onions, and she wanted me to know that there were some onions mixed into the burger in case I wanted to change my order.

This is a cozy corner bar with daily specials such as meat loaf, fried chicken, and lamb stew.

1900 Polk Street at Jackson. 567–9586. Lunch and dinner daily. Moderate (the burger was $6.50). Credit cards.

BETELNUT

You won't find Bloody Mary chewing betel nuts here, but you will find the foods from Asia blending together for an adventure in Pacific Rim cuisine. You'll also find alcohol-laced Bloody Marys plus lots of tropical drinks that seem to pick up where Trader Vic left off. This is a stylish popular spot where you're likely to taste dishes you've never had before. You can enjoy a wide range of tastes by having a series of "small plates."

2030 Union Street. 929–8855. Lunch and dinner daily. Moderate. Credit cards.

BUCA GIOVANNI

Surprisingly, for an Italian neighborhood, North Beach doesn't have that many great Italian restaurants. Buca Giovanni is one of the exceptions to the rule. In his intimate cellar Giovanni offers the kind of food you might get in a traditional restaurant in Tuscany. Nothing trendy or "lite" here. The food is substantial and hearty. Let the waiters help guide you through your selection of homemade pastas and roasted meats and fowl.

800 Greenwich Street. Tuesday through Saturday for dinner. Moderate. Credit cards. 776–7766.

CAFÉ JACQUELINE

This restaurant is the cholesterol fairy's nightmare. There is one thing that you get at Café Jacqueline: soufflés. Oh, you can have a salad to go with it, and some French bread, but the entrees and the desserts are all soufflés. They also happen to be the best soufflés you've ever had. When you are ready to forget about cholesterol and fat for a night, this quiet, romantic spot is a treat.

1454 Grant Avenue. 981–5565. Open Wednesday through Sunday for dinner. Moderate. Credit cards.

CAFÉ MARIMBA

The chef, Reed Hearon, brought the Marina district this brightly colored, splashy restaurant that might first look like a folk art gallery, but in fact Marimba offers Mexican food that goes far beyond the taco and burrito. Food from many regions of Mexico is featured, as are colorful drinks. Experiment. Go for a series of the small dishes for a variety of delicious—and often spicy—tastes.

2317 Chestnut Street. 776–1506. Lunch Tuesday through Sunday; dinner nightly. Moderate. Credit cards.

CARTA

So what do you feel like eating tonight? Spanish, Brazilian, Russian, Turkish, Indian, Caribbean? You'll find it all at Carta and more. This unusual restaurant features the food of a specific country or region each month, and somehow they manage to pull it off very well. It's a good idea to call and make sure you are interested in the food from the cuisine of the month. Since the menu is small, feel free to inquire about specific dishes.

1772 Market Street, near Gough. 863–3516. Lunch and dinner Tuesday through Sunday. Moderate. Credit cards.

CHINA HOUSE BISTRO

The word "bistro" gives you the first clue. This is not your typical neighborhood Chinese restaurant. China House is a stylish, continental dining room serving specialties from Shanghai. You will be served dishes that may be new to you in a more sedate setting. This is a restaurant for a romantic and adventurous evening rather than a place to take the whole family and let the kids be kids.

The best way to order is to let your waiter or the hostess/owner, Cecelia Chung, help you choose.

501 Balboa Street. 752–2802. Dinner nightly. Moderate. Credit cards.

Cinderella Bakery and Cafe

Long before the latest wave of Russian immigrants to the city, there was the Cinderella Bakery and Café. Since the 1940s regulars have been coming in for hearty soups with dark Russian rye bread, piroshki, beef stroganoff, and especially pelmeni, meat-filled dumplings served in soup or with sour cream. Waitresses speak Russian and some English and hug the folks who come in every day and don't even have to announce their order. I confess I couldn't take my eyes off an eightyish woman who looked like the lost Princess Anastasia.

The bakery is in front and the café in back.

436 Balboa Street. 751–9690. Breakfast, lunch, and dinner daily. Inexpensive. No credit cards.

Dame

If your name was Dame, what would you call your restaurant? (There is nothing like a . . . ?) The owner/chef, Kelly Dame, took the most direct route for her California-style Italian restaurant on the eastern edge of the Castro district. The Italian influence is evident in the antipasti and pasta courses; the California touches come in with items like Gorgonzola french fries and the sumptuous desserts. Decor is not a strong point here; all the money goes into the food.

1815 Market Street. 255–8818. Lunch Tuesday through Friday; dinner Tuesday through Sunday; brunch Sunday. Moderate. Credit cards.

DPD

This tiny restaurant shares the best "hole in the wall" award with its neighbor, House of Nanking. When you can't get into one, try the other. You'll get huge plates of delicious food at ridiculously cheap prices. The specialty here is Shanghai noodle dishes, but everything is good. There are daily lunch specials for $3.95, but get there early if you want a seat.

901 Kearny. 982–0471. Lunch and dinner daily and open late at night. No credit cards.

E'ANGELO'S

According to a Herb Caen column in the *San Francisco Chronicle*, a fan recognized Robin Williams on the street one evening and expressed his admiration. Williams responded by suggesting that the fan have dinner where he and his family were heading, E'Angelo's. This is a neighborhood institution in the Marina, where families pile in for pasta, pizza, and other traditional Italian-American dishes. Robin won't always be there, but do expect crowds and a joint that is always jumping.

2234 Chestnut Street. 567–6164. Dinner Tuesday through Sunday. Moderate. No credit cards.

ELIZA

The Potrero Hill Chinese restaurant always gets raves form the food critics. Although the big splashy neon sign on top of Eliza's advertises Hunan and Mandarin food, the menu seems to appeal to a mostly Caucasian crowd interested in familiar items such as pot stickers, sesame chicken, mu-shu pork, and Mongolian beef. Whatever you call it, the food is very good and plentiful, and no MSG is used. The kitchen is glad to make your dishes as spicy or mild as you like. Special lunch plates are mostly under $5.00.

1457 Eighteenth Street. 648–9999. Lunch and dinner daily. Credit cards.

ELLA'S

This restaurant bills itself as serving neoclassic American cuisine. What that means is you can find items like macaroni and cheese and chicken pot pie and terrific hamburgers. Each burger is hand shaped into a roundish mound, grilled, and served on a perfect homemade bun. It tastes best if you sit at the counter and watch the process. Breakfast is a specialty of the house, as are the baked goods.

500 Presidio at California. 441–5669. Breakfast and lunch daily. Inexpensive. Credit cards.

El Toro

When you are in the mood for a bulging burrito or a taco filled with flavorful and fresh ingredients, get in the cafeteria line at El Toro. There are so many good taquerias in the Mission that choosing one is basically a matter of personal taste. I've never been disappointed at El Toro, and it's generally easier to find a place to park nearby than at some of the Mission Street places.

598 Valencia. 431–3351. Lunch and dinner daily. Inexpensive. No credit cards.

Enrico's

The center of the recent revival of Broadway, Enrico's sidewalk café is a place to see and be seen. Once the domain of Enrico Banducci, who brought the likes of Mort Sahl and Bill Cosby to his Hungry I nightclub in the 1950s, the café fell on hard times and finally closed in the 1990s. Enter chef Rick Hackett and his partners. They remodeled the place, put in a contemporary Italian menu, and made it an institution again. There's one menu for lunch and dinner and late into the night, and all the food, which includes hearty pasta dishes, pizza, and seasonal specials, is terrific.

The design of the indoors at Enrico's is also worth special mention. One of my pet peeves is being seated at a table for two when all I can see beyond my dining partner is a wall. Enrico's solves that problem for me by placing mirrors behind all the booths and tables so that no matter where you sit, you see the entire room.

504 Broadway. 982–6223. Lunch and dinner daily; open late at night. Moderate. Credit cards.

FIREFLY

A whimsical Noe Valley restaurant serving food with an international flavor. I hope they named this eclectic and sometimes humorous Noe Valley restaurant after the Groucho Marx character Rufus T. Firefly. There is nothing too outrageous for the chef to try, from seafood pot sticker to "swamp stompin' bayou gumbo." The menu changes weekly and offers food from around the world, all served with a California sensibility.

4288 Twenty-fourth Street. 821–7652. Dinner Tuesday through Sunday. Moderate. Credit cards.

FLOOGIE'S SWAMP CAFE

This may be as close to Louisiana as you are going to get in the Bay Area. The Cajun and New Orleans music greets you when you enter the long, narrow dining room, which is decorated with a touch of Southern whimsy. The menu offers such standbys as jumbalaya, red beans and rice, catfish, cornbread, greens, and fried oysters, and the portions are enormous. It's not Paul Prudhomme caliber, but it's fun, and they promise that they made every effort to leave the fat in Louisiana.

1686 Market Street at Gough. 864–3700. Lunch Tuesday through Friday; dinner Tuesday through Saturday. Credit cards.

FLYING SAUCER

This is one of San Francisco's most popular and unusual restaurants, where each plate is a work of art. An evening at the Flying Saucer may be the most unusual dining experience you've ever had. Certainly you will eat creations that don't appear in cookbooks but spring only from the imagination of the chef/owner, Albert Tordjman. On a recent visit, I had duck confit in a dark rich brown sauce, served with a potato-pecan pie, a hunk of artichoke, sliced zucchini, beets and other vegetables, leaves and herbs, all artfully arranged on a huge plate. This was preceded by an appetizer of an unusual squid salad with shredded vegetables and squid cooked two different ways. Every plate is a spectacular work of art, piled high with food. You will be stuffed.

All this is in a Mission district setting that resembles what I would describe as artsy-thrift shop. The joint is jumpin', but the waiters and the cooks seem to handle it all with humor and grace.

1000 Guerrero Street at Twenty-second (there's no sign for the restaurant, just a neon flying saucer in the window). 641–9955.Dinner Tuesday through Saturday. Moderate. Credit cards.

42 DEGREES

Aside from the food, there are two compelling reasons to have dinner at 42 Degrees: there's plenty of free parking right in front of the restaurant, and there is live jazz most evenings beginning around 8:30 P.M. The decor is also lively, in an ultramodern industrial way, and the food is fine. The title of the restaurant indicates cuisine from Italy, Spain, Greece, and California, all of which share 42 degrees latitude. There is a spacious outdoor patio, which is nice and warm on sunny days.

235 Sixteenth Street, in the parking lot behind the Espirit outlet store. 777–5558. Lunch and dinner daily; open late at night Wednesday through Saturday. Moderate. Credit cards.

FRINGALE

Although Gerald Hirogoyen's French bistro is extremely popular and he is always ranked among the city's top chefs, he has managed to retain the bustling charm of his small restaurant and keep the prices down as well. This is one of those places that is just plain fun. Chances are you will have to wait for your table even though you have a reservation, but that gives you the opportunity to see what everyone else is eating and to chat with others. Tables are so close together you feel like trading tastes with your neighbor. But the food is great, and you'll feel like you've had a quick trip to France.

570 Fourth Street. 543–0573. Lunch Monday through Friday; dinner Monday through Saturday. Moderate. Credit cards.

GEVA'S CARRIBBEAN CUISINE

This cozy spot used to be directly under the freeway extension to Franklin Street. When the quake-damaged structure came down, Geva's had a lovely garden seating area to add to their small dining room. The food hasn't changed, though. It's wonderfully spicy fare from the islands, mainly Jamaica. If you've never had jerk chicken before, this is the place to try it. Or try the gumbo or curries, but let them know if you don't like your food hot and spicy.

482A Hayes Street. 863–1220. Lunch Monday through Friday; dinner nightly. Credit cards.

GOLD MOUNTAIN

Every visit to Chinatown should include at least one dim sum lunch. If you've never enjoyed the experience, all you have to do is sit down at a table and then choose as carts or trays of little dishes are brought by for your selection. Try a series of dumplings, soups, noodles, rice dishes, meats, and even desserts until you have had your fill.

It can be a rather frantic process, so you might want to go to a parlor like this one, where you can get an explanation of the various dishes. Gold Mountain manages to satisfy local Chinese and non-Chinese customers with grace, despite the crowds.

644 Broadway. 296–7733. Open daily for breakfast, lunch, and dinner. Inexpensive. Credit cards.

HAYES STREET GRILL

When people ask where to go for good fresh fish, I invariably advise avoiding Fisherman's Wharf and heading for the Hayes Street Grill. Modeled after San

Francisco institutions like the Tadich Grill, the owner and restaurant critic Patricia Unterman offers only the freshest grilled or sautéed fish, served with interesting seasonal vegetables. Their french fries are probably the best in town. *Simplicity* is the key word here, so you can be assured that sauces or seasonings will never get in the way of the featured food. Because of their location near the Symphony and Opera, they are usually crowded before 8 P.M.

320 Hayes Street. 863–5545. Lunch Monday through Friday; dinner nightly. Moderate. Credit cards.

HAZEL'S KITCHEN

Fast food, Potrero Hill style. Let's say you want to grab a bite on the run but wouldn't be caught dead in a fast-food franchise joint. If you happen to be on Portrero Hill, you're in luck. Get in line at Hazel's, which is sort of a closet that opens out onto Eighteenth Street. Every day there's a freshly made soup, a daily special such as lasagna, several salads, and a choice of sand-wiches using top ingredients. Take your meal with you or sit with the locals on the benches and planters on the street.

1331 Eighteenth Street. 647–7941. Inexpensive. No credit cards.

HELMAND

In the North Beach area known for Italian food, the city's first Afghan restau-rant serves wonderful dinners. You've probably never had Afghan cooking before. I certainly hadn't before I had the pleasure of dining at Helmand. The food is best described as a cross between Middle Eastern and Indian. Lamb dishes are a specialty, as are the variations on pasta. It's the seasonings that make the food so exotic and delicious. Although the dining room and the ser-vice are elegant, the prices are surprisingly low.

430 Broadway. 362–0641. Dinner nightly. Inexpensive. Credit cards.

HOUSE OF NANKING

Plan to wait in line outside for this extremely popular and inexpensive Chinese café. One of two jammed "hole in the wall" restaurants that occupy the block on Kearny between Jackson and Columbus, the House of Nanking is the Chinatown equivalent of "grunge hip." The few tables at the House of Nanking are filled with the young and trendy. They are drawn not only by the unusual and tasty food but also by the dirt-cheap prices. It's a scene to eat here, banging elbows with the person at the next table.

The food is chef Peter Yang's Americanized version of Shanghai cuisine, heavy on noodles and dumplings, with lots of sautéed dishes. Everything is cooked right in front of the twelve-seat counter.

919 Kearny Street. 421–1429. Lunch and dinner Monday through Saturday; dinner Sunday. Inexpensive. No credit cards.

HUNGARIAN SAUSAGE FACTORY

This cozy little Bernal Heights café and deli doesn't look much like a factory. They do make sausages in back, but out front there's a charming little dining room where you can have a sandwich or a salad and sample their Hungarian specialities such as stuffed cabbage and, of course, sausages. Outside there are a few tables for sunning while you enjoy some of their pastries and a coffee or tea.

419 Cortland Avenue. 648–2847. Lunch and dinner daily; takeout all day. Inexpensive. No credit cards.

HYDE STREET BISTRO

This is a charming and popular Russian Hill neighborhood spot. The cuisine crosses the border between Austria and Italy. You might start with a vegetable strudel salad then move on to a risotto or pasta, and then have a grilled fish served with spaetzle. The dessert specialty of the house is the warm apple strudel. This is a friendly, spare restaurant where the money goes into the food, not the decor. The chef will accommodate special dietary requests.

1521 Hyde Street. 441–7778. Dinner nightly. Credit cards.

ICON CAFE

Icon is a funky café that was formerly the Billboard, a haven for artists. Now it's decorated in computer art, with futuristic cybervision creations on the wall, TV monitors and video installations all around, and world music on the box. The menu is filled with current hip choices such as polenta with garlic, Hunan pot stickers, crispy calamari, and zuppa d' dayo. The food is OK. I had a Caesar salad with grilled chicken, but while I was eating, I got to sit at their computer and get my introduction to browsing the internet. For a $5.00 minimum food or drink order, you can use the computer as long as you want if no one else is waiting in line. Cyberspace being what it is, the entire operation could be changed dramatically by the time you read this. Check for the current incarnation of this café.

ICON, 299 Ninth Street at Folsom. 415–861-BYTE (2983); e-mail: ICON@BYTE-BAR.COM. Credit cards.

IDEALE

This is one of the newer Italian restaurants in North Beach, a part of the Upper Grant Street renewal. Billed as a Roman-style ristorante, Ideale specializes in subtly seasoned pasta dishes and grilled and roasted meats. Eating here as opposed to one of the older, larger neighborhood restaurants with their mushy pasta and heavy tomato sauce is like having a quick trip to Italy.

1315 Grant Avenue. 391–4129. Dinner nightly. Moderate. Credit cards.

IROHA

Noodle dishes are a staple of many Asian cultures. For Japanese diners this usually means a choice of either ramen, soba, or udon noodles, often served with tempura, roast pork, or even pot sticker–like dumplings. You can enjoy all of the above at this low-key restaurant in Japantown.

1728 Buchanan Street. 922–1321. Inexpensive. Credit cards.

ISUZU

This popular restaurant for local Japanese families specializes in seafood of all kinds, from sushi and sashimi to fish cooked in a variety of styles. Check with your waiter to see what is fresh, and order accordingly. Your entree will be accompanied by several dishes of vegetables and salads.

1581 Webster Street. 922–2290. Lunch and dinner daily. Moderate. Credit cards.

JUDY'S CAFE

There is nothing trendy about Judy's. This Chestnut institution has been serving huge portions of omelettes and other breakfast treats, plus soups and sandwiches. This is not low-fat diet food. Their promise is that you'll feel like you're dining at Grandma's house. They've even bucked the trend and don't have an espresso machine. The food is good and wholesome and the decor would please Grandma, too.

Judy's Café. 2268 Chestnut Street. 922–4588. Open every day for breakfast and lunch. No credit cards.

KATIA'S

One block down the street from the venerable Cinderella Bakery and Café is a prettier, more Americanized version of the Russian café. Katia serves all the Russian favorites: borscht, pelmeni, and the like, but the treatment is more delicate and the atmosphere is more contemporary.

600 Fifth Avenue. 688–9292. Lunch and dinner Wednesday through Sunday. Inexpensive to moderate. Credit cards.

LIBERTY CAFE

Some restaurants can be intimidating when you walk in alone without a reservation. At this attractive but unpretentious neighborhood spot, you are made to feel at home right away and if you get there before or after the lunch or dinner rush, you should have no trouble finding a table.

The food is straightforward American, with the emphasis on fresh and organic ingredients. The menu changes monthly but usually features such items as pizza and chicken pot pie. A wonderful eggplant, mozzarella, and sun-dried tomato sauce sandwich on focaccia with salad cost me $6.50. Save room for dessert. They make wonderful pies and cakes here, plus the only chocolate creme brulée I have ever tasted.

410 Cortland Avenue. 695–8777. Breakfast, lunch, and dinner Tuesday through Sunday. Inexpensive to moderate. Credit cards.

L'OSTERIA DEL FORNO

This is a tiny storefront restaurant on Columbus Avenue that you will probably recognize by the line waiting outside. The key word here is "forno," which is Italian for "baked." Everything is cooked in a brick-lined oven, and the result is comfort food at its homiest. There's a daily pasta, pizza, and my favorite, the roast pork in milk.

519 Columbus Avenue. 982–1124. Lunch and dinner daily, except Tuesday. Inexpensive. No credit cards.

MAHARANI

If you order off the menu and skip the inevitable lunch buffet, you will get a fine meal at the Maharani. All the essentials of a successful Indian restaurant in America are there: the Tandoori Grill for tasty meats, fish, and bread; hot and spicy curries; and fresh, interesting chutneys and condiments. The added bonus, if you are looking for privacy and romance, is the separate rooms behind curtains, where you dine on cushions and buzz for your waiter.

1122 Post Street. 775–1988. Lunch and dinner daily. Moderate. Credit cards.

MARIO'S BOHEMIAN CIGAR STORE

You won't really experience North Beach until you eat at least once in Mario's. The tiny café, which overlooks Washington Square Park, packs them in at lunchtime for their huge sandwiches on focaccia. The favorites are the meatball and the grilled chicken, but there are several other choices. Try for a table by an open window, and enjoy a cappuccino or a glass of wine with your sandwich; you won't want to leave.

566 Columbus Avenue. 362–1536. Lunch and dinner daily; open late. Inexpensive. No credit cards.

MANGIAFUOCO

Across the street from the popular Flying Saucer and practically next door from Le Trou, this Italian restaurant would look and feel right at home in Firenze. Roasted and grilled meats and fowl and pasta are the specialties, and the food is delicious.

1001 Guerrero Street. 206–9881. Moderate. Dinner Tuesday through Saturday. No credit cards.

MISS MILLIE'S

This is a whimsically decorated café in the former Meat Market Coffeehouse, which was a former meat market. The big draw here is breakfast, with such regulars as omelettes and french toast, plus specials like souffléed lemon pancakes and roasted root veggies as an alternative to home-fried potatoes. Unfortunately, breakfast stops at 11:15 A.M., and the lunch menu is limited.

4123 Twenty-fourth Street, west of Castro. 285–5598. Breakfast Tuesday through Friday; brunch Saturday and Sunday. Moderate. Credit cards.

MISS PEARL'S JAM HOUSE

On a sunny day Sunday brunch or an early dinner by the pool at Miss Pearl's can be a great treat. The "Jam" in the title stands for Jamaica, and the food is based on the cuisine of the islands. Although there are many tempting selections, including an unusual pasta of the day, I always gravitate to the spicy jerk chicken. Everything thing is good here, but it seems to taste better outside overlooking the pool of the Phoenix Inn. At night the bar, which is the focal point of the restaurant, can get to be quite a scene.

601 Eddy. 775–5267. Dinner Tuesday through Saturday; Sunday brunch. Moderate. Credit cards.

Mo's Gourmet Hamburgers

This is my pick for the best burger in town. From the outside window you can watch the counterman grill 7-ounce hand-shaped burgers in this North Beach café. It looks like an old-fashioned soda shop with a white tile floor and black and chrome dinette tables and chairs. You will dine under the goofy gaze of Three Stooges posters (inspiration for the name Mo). Choose from a no-frills burger served on regular roll, or customize your own with seven choices of cheeses, mushrooms, grilled onions, and the like. These are at least three-napkin burgers.

They also serve vegetarian specials such as grilled eggplant on focaccia. There's a long counter, as well as plenty of tables and booths. If you're not counting calories, you can wash down that burger with a classic milk shake.

1322 Grant Avenue. 788–3779. Open daily for late breakfast, lunch, and dinner. Burgers start at $4.95. Credit cards.

Nob Hill Grille

The name might appear a bit "fawncy" considering the neighborhood and the *e* at the end of *grille*, but this is a very informal coffee shop/diner where you can sit at the counter or hope to get a table. What you get is American food of the grilled-cheese and beef-stew variety, and it's all plentiful and good. Soups of the day are hearty, the sandwiches and salads are bountiful, and the desserts are far from low-cal. You might have lunch surrounded by women in business suits on one side with guys in overalls on the other.

969 Hyde Street. 474–5985. Breakfast and lunch daily; early dinner Wednesday through Friday. Inexpensive. No credit cards.

ORIENTAL PEARL

The number of restaurants in Chinatown can be overwhelming, especially since so many of them are geared for either tourists who (1) want bargain basement prices or (2) want lavish decorations fit for an emperor. Oriental Pearl fills the gap nicely. It's a pleasantly decorated dining room with well-dressed and very helpful waiters, and it's a medium-priced restaurant. Best of all, the food is very good. Here you will eat interesting but accessible Chinese creations using all the finest ingredients. Dishes that you have had in many neighborhood Chinese restaurants somehow rise to a new level here. Your waiter will be glad to guide you through the menu.

760 Clay Street. 433–1817. Lunch and dinner daily. Moderate. Credit cards.

PANE E VINO

The name means "bread and wine," which is a subtle way of describing what you get at this popular neighborhood trattoria in Cow Hollow. This is delicious basic food, celebrating the simplicity of fine Italian cuisine. The menu items may look like those in countless other restaurants, but here they taste special because of the care taken in choosing the finest ingredients, which are not overwhelmed by the sauces and seasonings. Whether you have one of the many pasta dishes, meat, fish, or chicken, you will be in for a treat.

3011 Steiner Street. 346–2111. Lunch Monday through Saturday. Dinner nightly. Moderate. Credit cards.

PAT O'SHEA'S

Famous as a sports bar with TV's blaring three or four events at a time and a sign that proclaims WE CHEAT DRUNKS AND TOURISTS, Pat O'Shea's Mad Hatter is a surprise food mecca. This is where Nancy Oakes started putting out sumptuous dishes before she opened the wildly popular Boulevard restaurant. You can still get wonderful gourmet meals here, and it's also one of the better places in town for a big juicy burger, which seems to fit the general atmosphere more.

3848 Geary Boulevard. 752–3148. Lunch and dinner daily. Weekends during football season tend to be very crowded. Credit cards. Inexpensive.

PAZZIA CAFE AND PIZZERIA

I just happened into Pazzia one day, after I couldn't get in to a neighboring restaurant. What a nice find! First, they greeted me with a wonderful house-baked bread and some olive oil to dip it in; then the waiter led me through the choice of daily grilled specials, such as chicken breast and rabbit (tastes like chicken). There are four or five pastas and many thin crust pizzas available, too. Pazzia is a small spot with the feeling of a neighborhood café in Italy.

337 Third Street. 512–1693. Lunch and dinner daily. Moderate. Credit cards.

PIER 23

For a city with such a favorable climate, San Francisco does not have as many places with outdoor dining areas as one might expect. One of the surprising spots is a little joint right on the Embarcadero near Broadway called Pier 23. As you first enter, you see a rather funky bar with several tables and some unusual art works. But in back there is a sizable deck that juts out onto the bay and is protected from the wind. Here, surrounded by potted plants and trees and serenaded by hip music from the sound system, you can enjoy lunch in the sun.

The food is plain and good if not spectacular. You'll receive a generous hunk of sourdough bread and then choose from several fish dishes, burgers, salads, or their house special, homemade Cajun meat loaf with mashed potatoes.

If you take the kids, be forewarned that the bathrooms are X-rated, featuring vending machines with items your youngsters, or certainly you, might find embarrassing. This is a swinging scene at night, with music and wall-to-wall singles.

Pier 23, Embarcadero west of Broadway. 362–5125. Lunch and dinner daily. Credit cards.

PLUTO'S

Certainly Pluto's is destined to be a chain operation. The initial café on Scott Street was designed to be duplicated, and it's an idea that should catch on. You order cafeteria-style from a selection of roasted poultry and grilled meats, salads, vegetables, and beverages and get to pick from a variety of fixings and condiments. The food is fresh and tasty, and there's nothing on the menu above $5.75.

3255 Scott Street off Chestnut. 775–8867. Lunch and dinner daily; breakfast Saturday and Sunday. Credit cards.

R AND G LOUNGE

Like many of its neighboring restaurants on Kearny, R and G Lounge offers lunch specials for under $4.00 that are terrific and filling. The main reason for the restaurant's popularity, however, is the seafood, much of it pulled fresh from the tank and served in the original space downstairs and in the newer upstairs dining room. If you are feeling experimental, urge your waiter to suggest some dishes that may not be on the menu.

631 Kearny (entrance to the upstairs dining room is on Commercial Street). 982–7877. Lunch and dinner daily. Inexpensive to moderate. Credit cards.

REAL FOOD DELI

A spinoff from the Real Foods Market up the street, this corner café has become a Russian Hill hangout. Take your choice of specials displayed in the huge deli case: tortas, pasta salads, quiche, sandwiches, soups, and desserts. The emphasis is on natural and vegan foods. Place your order, and it will be delivered to you at your inside or streetside table. There is pleasant classical music playing on the stereo, and the atmosphere is conducive to eating alone.

2164 Polk. 775–2805. Open daily 8 A.M. to 8 P.M. Inexpensive. Credit cards.

RISTORANTE ECCO

South Park's touch of high style is represented by this sleek Northern Italian restaurant. This is where the suit and tie and classy dress crowd has lunch and dinner in this center of activity for the multimedia crowd. The dining room looks out onto the park, while the larger barroom has the feeling of a clubby meeting place. In back of the restaurant, there's a to-go counter where lunchers can pick up their food to take to the park or back to the office.

101 South Park. 495–3291. Lunch Monday through Friday. Dinner nightly. Moderate. Credit cards.

ROSMARINO

An intimate neighborhood restaurant set back in a courtyard behind the upscale Sacramento Street shopping area, serving modern Italian cuisine. This is the kind of food that will satisfy you without leaving you feeling stuffed. An excellent place for a quiet lunch outdoors in their small patio.

3665 Sacramento Street. 931–7710. Lunch and dinner Tuesday through Saturday; brunch Sunday. Moderate. Credit cards accepted.

SAN FRANCISCO BBQ

The look of the Potrero Hill café might lead you to expect a scene out of Memphis or Austin, but this is Thai barbecue. There's a grill with marinated chicken, ribs, sausages, fish, and whatever else is available, served best over noodles with chopped peanuts, lime, and cilantro. You can also get sticky rice and carrot salad, as well as occasional dessert specials.

1328 Eighteenth Street. 431–8956. Lunch Tuesday through Friday; dinner Tuesday through Sunday. Inexpensive. Credit cards.

SOUTH PARK CAFE

Even if you've never been to Paris, you will immediately recognize the feeling of the South Park Café. The narrow dining room, the decor, the small park outside, and the specialties that are delivered to the tables are all what you would expect to find in a classic French café.

108 South Park (between Second and Third Streets). 495–7275. Breakfast and lunch weekdays; dinner Monday through Saturday; open late. Moderate. Credit cards.

STARS

Jeremiah Tower's bustling restaurant is about as close to New York as San Francisco gets. Everyone who is anyone eats there, and the place has the aura of importance. The most fun, and the best deal, is to find a seat at the bar and have a burger or, believe it or not, a hot dog. You'll be rubbing elbows with the movers and shakers, and it won't cost you as much as the folks at the tables.

150 Redwood Alley. 861–7827. Lunch Monday through Friday. Dinner nightly. Credit cards.

SUPERKUCHE

For those of us whose experience of German food meant heavy portions of meat and starch, welcome to German "lite." The food at Superkuche is delicious without leaving you with that about-to-explode feeling. I had a great sauerbraten with spaetzle. Catherine had goose that was somehow cooked with the grease removed.

The crowd is young with many people gathered around the huge bar, sampling the many German beers. Unfortunately for nonsmokers, the smoke from the bar wafts over the rest of the place. You share long tables with other diners, and the feeling is often that you have walked into an ongoing party. Superkuche plays a major role in the Hayes Valley Renaissance.

601 Hayes Street at Laguna. 252–9289. Lunch and dinner Tuesday through Saturday. Inexpensive to moderate. Credit cards.

Ti-Couz

This is San Francisco's answer to the International House of Pancakes. Actually, this comfortable and informal Mission café serves French crepes in a mind-numbing assortment of choices. This is a great place to eat alone, sitting at the counter watching the crepe maker at work on the round steel pans. Salads and a few other items are also available, but it would be a crime to come here and not have at least one of these luscious crepes.

3108 Sixteenth Street. 252–7373. Lunch and dinner daily; open late. Inexpensive. Credit cards.

Tisane

In a hip neighborhood of artists, musicians, and writers going under the acronym NEMIZ for Northeastern Mission Industrial Zone, you'll find Tisane. The decor is industrial modern, which some might find a bit cold with its sharp edges and stainless steel finish. The chef calls herself a food conceptualist and offers a variety of contemporary faves, including pizza and big salads. One of the more popular items is a new treatment of fish and chips.

As the name implies, teas are a specialty here. This is a good place to stop in for dessert on a weekend night and enjoy live music.

2170 Bryant Street (at Twentieth Street). 641–8458. Lunch Monday through Friday. Dinner Tuesday through Saturday. Credit cards.

Town's End Restaurant and Bakery

The owners of this South Beach restaurant used to have a great breakfast place called Home Plate on Lombard Street that was filled with baseball memorabilia. It must have come as a surprise to them to see that the Giants' new stadium is scheduled to become their neighbor. Breakfast is still served at Town's End, but the menu has been expanded for excellent lunches and dinners. The food is California/Italian, with pastas, salads, and daily specials. Save room for dessert. The baked goods are special.

2 Townsend Street. 512–0749. Breakfast daily; lunch and dinner Tuesday through Saturday. Credit cards.

2223 MARKET

The Castro district was waiting for this place, a stylish, semi-upscale restaurant that serves contemporary California cuisine. Although the clientele is predominately gay, this is a place where a straight person feels completely welcome. The menu somehow touches all the bases, with offerings of pasta, pizza, salads, grilled and roasted meats and fish, and daily specials. There is also a bar menu featuring killer cocktails for $6.00 a piece.

2223 Market Street. 431–0692. Lunch and dinner daily. Credit cards.

UNIVERSAL CAFE

A predecessor to its neighbor, Tisane, the Universal opened in industrial surroundings where no one expected to find a restaurant and became an immediate hit. Maybe it was the giant coffee roaster that sits near the counter and is used to prepare some of the best coffee in town. Certainly the food is a draw. There's a limited menu featuring wonderful combinations such as a baked chicken breast stuffed with risotto or a pan-seared filet mignon with Gorgonzola mashed potatoes and string beans. At lunch pizza and focaccia sandwiches are the main draw.

One day I found myself eavesdropping on the conversation at the table next to me and finally joined in. I was welcomed by Dennis McNally, the publicist for the Grateful Dead, the writer Burr Snyder, and R. Crumb's publisher, Baba Ron Turner, all neighbors who consider themselves regulars of the café.

2814 Nineteenth Street between Bryant and Florida. 821–4608. Breakfast, lunch, and dinner Tuesday through Sunday. Credit cards. Moderate.

Vicolo Pizzeria

This is another establishment run by the folks who bring you the Hayes Street Grill. In a funky shed in an alley behind Hayes Street, pizza unlike any other you have tasted is served. It's so rich, thanks to the cornmeal crust and the plentiful toppings, that it's difficult to eat more than one slice. That, along with one of their three or four terrific salads, can make a good quick lunch or dinner. By franchise pizza standards, the $3.50 or $4.00 per slice seems expensive, but you will be full and satisfied on less here.

201 Ivy Street. 863–2382. Lunch and dinner daily; open late. Inexpensive. Credit cards.

Woodward Gardens

You could drive past this restaurant a million times without even realizing it's there. Under the freeway overpass at Mission and Duboce Streets is about as unlikely place to put a restaurant as I can imagine, but folks certainly find it and keep coming back. There is something about the location and the tiny dining room and the view of the miniscule kitchen that makes this an appealing adventure. What makes it pay off, though, is the wonderful food, which is based on whatever's fresh and seasonal. The cooking style is California/Mediterranean, with special attention to vegetables and fruits.

1700 Mission Street. 621–7122. Dinner Wednesday through Sunday. Moderate. No credit cards.

Yank Sing

Of all the dim sum parlors in the city, this is my favorite. Yank Sing used to be on Broadway in Chinatown, but moved to more spacious quarters in the financial district many years ago. Eating there is a simple process. You take your table and wait. Then tray after tray of dim sum, or tiny tastes of food, are offered. They could be dumplings or tiny spare ribs or meatballs or shrimp toast or whatever has been created that day. Eat until you've had your fill, and the waiter will figure out your bill by counting your empty plates. At Yank Sing you know you are getting the best ingredients and that serving dim sum at lunch is their only business.

427 Battery Street. 362–1640. Lunch daily. Moderate. Credit cards.

YA YA CUISINE

Most of us are creatures of habit when it comes to eating. For example, despite the fact that at home we have grilled or roasted chicken more than any other dish, I have to fight to resist ordering the same thing at a restaurant. This is never a problem at Ya Ya. You will not have to worry about having something you can make just as well at home.

The food here is Middle Eastern with California modern art presentation. Lamb, beef, and chicken are flavored with coriander, cumin, cinnamon, cardamom, tamarind, pomegranate, and the like but come out in forms you have not seen before. It's beautiful and delicious. Trust me. In addition, the restaurant is exotically attractive and the prices are quite reasonable.

1220 Ninth Avenue, near Lincoln, across from Golden Gate Park. 566–6966. Lunch Tuesday through Saturday; dinner Tuesday through Sunday. Moderate. Credit cards.

CHAPTER 23

Lunch in the Tenderloin

The Tenderloin, which runs from just west of Union Square to Van Ness Avenue, has a reputation as one of the roughest sections of town. To be sure, there are plenty of prostitutes working the streets at night and plenty of drug deals going down at all times, but it's also a neighborhood that has been reinvented by the immigration of families from Vietnam, Laos, and Cambodia.

While we still wouldn't recommend wandering along Ellis or O'Farrell Streets at night, the daytime offers an opportunity to eat wonderful Asian food at dirt-cheap prices. What's more, if you are patient, you can usually find metered parking within walking distance of the major intersection for restaurants, Ellis and Larkin. The area is also well served by public transportation with the Geary and Van Ness bus lines and a BART station not far away.

Three restaurants are on my "A" list, all of them serving hearty meals for under $5.00. At the corner of Ellis and Larkin is Vietnam II, which specializes in crab and fish dishes. At lunch, however, nearly everyone is having noodle soup, which is served in a giant bowl with either beef, chicken, or pork and with a side plate of cilantro, sprouts, and hot peppers for you to add as you wish. The soups are delicious, but you might want to make sure you know which meat you are ordering. Those who do not go for tongue or organ meats should stick to the well-done brisket, chicken, fish, or vegetable offerings. As though the price were not low enough, they also throw in a complimentary filtered coffee or soda with your lunch.

Across the street at 707 Ellis, is Hai Ky Mi Gia, which offers Vietnamese and Chinese food. Again, the specialty at lunch is noodles and soup. There are three pages of choices, the most popular being the seafood soups. Our favorite is the satay soup, which has a delicate peanut-sauce flavor. They also serve filtered coffee, which is the Asian version of a cappuccino: rich filtered coffee topped by a thick sweetened milk instead of foam.

Down the street at 611 Larkin, try the First Restaurant. Here the food is billed as Chinese. Try the sautéed vegetable of the day (usually asparagus or green beans) with chicken. The veggies are always cooked perfectly, so they have a nice crunch, and the garlic and soy seasoning is just right.

All of these restaurants are open for lunch daily, and none takes reservations. Be prepared for waiters and waitresses who speak little or no English. The English translations on the menus might also either baffle or amuse you.

Vietnam II, Corner Ellis and Larkin
Hai Ky Mi Gia, 707 Ellis
First Restaurant, 611 Larkin

All open for lunch daily.

Index